THE STORY OF HARRY

WILLIAM MCGEHEE

Order this book online at www.trafford.comor email orders@trafford.com

Most Trafford titles are also available at major online book retailers.

Printed in Victoria, BC, Canada.

ISBN: 978-1-4269-2904-5 (sc)

ISBN: 978-1-4269-2905-2 (hc)

Library of Congress Control Number: 2010903295

Our mission is to efficiently provide the world's finest, most comprehensive book publishing service, enabling every author to experience success. To find out how to publish your book, your way, and have it available worldwide, visit us online at www.trafford.com

Trafford rev. 6/7/2010

 www.trafford.com

North America & international
toll-free: 1 888 232 4444 (USA & Canada)
phone: 250 383 6864 ♦ fax: 812 355 4082

The Story Of Harry

Bill rested his arms over the parapet and looked down onto a large, lavishly decorated open air patio.

The flooring was all tiles and highly polished, Persian carpets were strewn around the floor. A large round coffee table with wooden bowls of fruit decorated the table. There was a man wearing an expensive looking silk robe reclining on what looked like some kind of massive lounge covered with colorful cloth and he was reading what looked like a newspaper under an ornate lamp and was puffing on a water pipe, the hose of which was long and also decorated in bright colors.

Suddenly there was a banging on the door. The man stayed motionless and didn't act as if he even heard the noise. Out of a door in the back of the huge patio room, a servant came who was wearing the typical dress of the Iranian houseman, just a full length gown of sorts, white but nice and clean. He wore *geevas* on his feet, a slip-on shoe with woven cloth tops. The soles are multiple layers of cloth folded like an accordion and bound together to make about a three-quarter-inch sole. A piece of horn from a cow is built into the toe and heel; an inexpensive slipper, worn by most of the people at least at home. He made almost no noise running to open the door, but before opening it he looked through a small peephole to see who was there.

When he opened the door, there was a soldier standing there in his uniform that looked like it was a hand-me-down. It fitted him all right but was rumpled and although it looked clean it just didn't look like it belonged to him. He was holding a man by the arm that looked very frightened but wasn't trying to pull away. The soldier didn't step into the house, but pointed, calling for the man in the robe. Bill couldn't make out what they were saying; he didn't speak Farsi well enough at that time. The man hesitated for a little but then rose from the lounge and went to the door. The soldier said something, first as if repeating a schooled explanation of some kind, then the man whom the soldier had by the arm argued with the man in the robe. Their words quickly became heated. The man reached into his robe, pulled out a pistol and shot him, point blank killing him. The shot tore the man out of the grasp of the soldier holding him and he fell backwards into the dust of the street. The man must have been a colonel or higher in rank He waved his arm to the soldier as in an order for the soldier to take him away. He went back to his lounge put his feet up on a stool and continued reading again as if nothing had happened. It was 1947.

Bill was on the roof of a bordello where he had been taken by a little *felfeli.* A *felfeli* is a small boy, called so because *felfel* means, "pepper" in Farsi and is often used to refer to young boys. This small street urchin, who seemed to be the night watchman of the streets, took Bill there to spend the night on the roof. He said it would be OK, no one ever comes up here and even if they did they wouldn't bother you. Of course that was said with lots of gesticulations and some words that bill understood. Because of a 12-o'clock curfew imposed in the country, if you were caught on the street after that hour it was very possible that you could be shot or arrested unless you were quite lucky. So the *felfeli* really did Bill a great favor. Oddly enough the boy didn't even ask bill for any money and before he knew it the boy was gone.

Death and killing was no stranger to the people of Iran in those days. However, other than restrictions such as the curfew, everything was quite easygoing with freedom of movement to move about the country as you wished. There weren't guards and/or inspectors asking for identification everywhere one went. The general population was very polite and hospitable. The country was interesting, and many places were quite beautiful, but lacking in infrastructure such as sewers and a telephone system. Bill had been there as an invited businessman to conduct an import/export section of an Iranian business, based in Isfahan.

Bill's friend, Bob, had been a major in the American army during the Second World War and was based in Isfahan, where he became acquainted with the owners of the company. They wrote to Bob in the States often asking him to come there to engage in their business.

Bob and Bill were sharing a small apartment in west Los Angeles while going to school on the GI bill after the war when Bill noticed those letters Bob kept getting from Iran. Bill had been an entertainer nearly all of his life and had even worked in a Marine Musical Comedy called "All fouled up" in Hawaii produced by Tyron Power; on his way home from his tour of duty in the South Pacific. The school he and Bob were going to was a school of acting called "The Ben Bards School of Drama". He had planned to continue his theatrical career.

Bob explained about his experience as a major in the US Army during the war and told Bill what those people wanted of him. He hadn't enjoyed being there during the war. He didn't speak the language and didn't particularly like the country. Even though he didn't have any quarrels with the people there he just didn't think he wanted to go back but Bill had itchy feet all his life and after a lot of talking convinced Bob to write to them to see if they would accept both of them for the venture. After nearly two months they received an answer back extending their offer for both of them to come. In their letter of approval they also outlined the provisions they offered: namely food and board and spending money until the business got going, then 20% of gross profits, etc. etc. That was how Bill happened to be in Iran there in the first place.

It wasn't easy trying to put together enough money for the two of them to travel all the way to Iran but the thought of impossibility wasn't in Bills vocabulary. They scraped up enough money to buy a bus ticket to Florida where Bob's family lived. Food on the trip was highly rationed and both of them confessed that they had been in such positions on the trip that neither of them had ever been in before. It was such a long trip from California to Florida. It was like torture.

They stopped in Louisiana to see Bill's cousin who lived there and whom he had never met. He took them on a tour of the city of New Orleans which was a lot of fun and interesting.

In Florida they were wracking their brains out on how to get enough money to go on to Washington DC and from there to Iran. It almost seemed like a hopeless task but they had an offer of a business and adventure and they were going to do it no matter what. Bill tried to get a job at a pharmacy in the small town from a pharmacist that Bob knew but the man just didn't need anyone. Then Bob remembered that he had a nice gold ring that might bring enough money to get them to Washington and it did. They had a ticket and $1.50 leftover.

On their arrival they rented a locker at the bus depot for ten cents to have a place to store their baggage, what little there was. Bill put on a suit he had with him and said he was going to go and try to find a job.

He had taught ballroom dancing at Arthur Murray's in West Los Angeles so he went to the Don Martini Dance School and asked them to let him teach. After talking to the manager and showing him that he really did know how to dance and how to teach, they gave him a job and told him to come to work the next day.

Bill went back to the bus depot where Bob was and told him to come with him that they were going to go have dinner. Bob was excited and thought that bill had been paid. The dance studio was on the third floor of the building on a corner and on the ground floor was a nice restaurant.

They went in and Bill told Bob to order whatever he wanted. When they were almost finished Bill told Bob to get up and go on out and walk down the street and if necessary to indicate to the cashier that Bill would pay. Bob was immediately upset and asked: "You mean you haven't any money?" Bill just told him to do as he said and not to worry. Bob left and when Bill went to the cashier to pay but feigned that he had left his wallet at home and said that he worked up stairs at the studio and would pay them tomorrow. They said that was OK and that was that.

At the studio Bill met a girl who was Egyptian. She was a handsome girl, tall but a little heavy. She took a liking to Bill right away. They danced together when they weren't busy and talked a lot. Bill told her about his and Bob's plan and that they were trying to get enough money to get to Iran. She became excited and eventually said that if they would do her a favor she would finance their trip. All she wanted was for them to write to her about the opportunity to do business as an importer of goods from Egypt. She had always wanted to open up a store there in Washington of Egyptian goods, knowing that there was a stop in Cairo on the way to Iran, Bill thought that would be no problem and agreed. So teaching dancing at the studio was short lived.

Bill had a birthday coming up on the June 11, and the girl insisted on throwing a dinner party at a nice restaurant. It was a very pleasant gesture, which Bill appreciated. She had the house photographer take a photo and Bill kept a copy.

The flight from Washington to London was exciting. They flew on Pan Am Airways. It was the first airplane that flew over the Atlantic with a pressurized cabin. They landed in Pool and were whisked to the train station in a taxi. Bill took a photo out the rear window of the taxi of Big Ben, the famous tower clock.

The train took them to Bournemouth and within two days boarded a Flying Boat called a "Duck" - an amphibious plane - for the trip to Basra in Iraq stopping in Egypt for two and one half days.. For some reason they were never told there would be other passengers boarding there. Bill remembered that seeing from the plane at a high altitude the Nile looked like a small pencil line and surely not big enough for this plane to land on. Arriving at Basra on the Tigris was even worse.

They found the information their sponsor was seeking in Egypt but didn't send her a letter until they got to Iran. They never heard back from her about it. The arrival at Basra was a little strange; they had to disembark to a small craft and were rowed to a big square-shaped steel pontoon dock. They saw six big Nubian porters standing on this dock waiting to take luggage for the passengers. They were barefoot and that steel dock was surely hot enough to cook an egg in about three minutes. They were lifting up one foot at a time, slowly, and you could see that there was a callus about the thickness of a big fat steak at the bottom of their sole. How they could stand on that steel dock was a mystery.

Bill and Bob were ushered into an old automobile, a taxi which had to take them some distance to a spot where they could take a launch across the Tigris to make the trip across the Island of Khorramshahr to Abadan, Iran. It was an all-night trip and a fellow who was supposed to meet them, Ali, had to be summoned by messenger. After a short wait Ali came and took them to his villa. Ali was a fairly tall fellow, rather handsome, with dark complexion and very short haircut and looked quite energetic. His movements were quick as was his speech and he spoke English quite well. He wore western clothes instead of a robe. It was noticeable that most of the men in Abadan and even in Isfahan wore western clothes.

On the way to the Villa they got a look at a very primitive place, Abadan however, was interesting. The next day they went to the open air food Bazaar where they saw almost every kind of fruit imaginable - and millions of flies. Three days later they took out in Ali's car for Isfahan, where they were to meet the owners of the company they were to work for. Ali's car was an old American car but it was in pretty good condition and there were no breakdowns on the way. It was evening when they arrived in Isfahan and they met one of the owners briefly, received a warm greeting and were taken to hotel Ferdosi.

The next night - after one good night's sleep - the owners invited them to a typical Iranian dinner that was a treat! They served Vodka in a small cruet at each plate. It was Russian potato vodka, quite delicious and very strong. The meat they served was called Shaslik, ground beef mixed with parsley, finely chopped onions and garlic, formed on a skewer and cooked over natural wood charcoal. The bread called Noon came in long flat pieces about nine inches wide and the meat was placed on the bread then folded over where more skewers of meat were placed and another fold and so on until you have a stack of meat folded up in the Noon. When you were served or you helped yourself you would just tear off a fold with the meat in it. Several other treats of vegetables are always served as well.

We were set up in an office that was being painted with a water based paint that looked like or actually was "Calcimine" but it was a light pastel blue and quite beautiful. Bill started writing letters to companies in the States in an effort to try to get something going.

After only about three months, Bob became very restless and disenchanted with everything about the country, the food and the isolation and it being so difficult to get the import- export business going.

In 1947 it was nearly impossible to buy any kind of machinery, including automobiles because in the States the factories were just converting their companies back into peacetime manufacturing. In most cases one couldn't even get on a waiting list to buy any kinds of equipment. The company there was only interested in American machinery of most any type.

So Bill and Bob scraped up some money, and Bob went off to Bombay to catch a ship as a work-away back to the States. Bill only heard from him once when he wrote to say that he made it back to the States and home. Bill stayed on to try to make something out of the business. He spent much time organizing a group of businessmen from Abadan to Tehran to collectively form and export-import shipping cooperative for the exports of their goods and the imports they were looking for.

His goal was to try to accumulate enough goods to make a big enough load to entice one or more of the big shipping companies to sail into Khorramshahr or Bandar Shahpur (now Bandar Imam Khomeini), instead of transhipping cargo by Dhow to or from Bombay, a system which was restricted in size and weight of cargo and took a very long time in transit. It was a difficult task. He had to get permission from the banks to use their Teletype machine and Morse code since there were no telephones to communicate with the different businesses. It was also necessary to make some personal trips to talk to some of the companies.

The people he was working for thought Bill's idea was a good one and they were all in agreement with the organization and what he was trying to accomplish. After all the work and when everything was ready to be put into action, the people he was working for kept saying "*fardah*" (tomorrow), but *fardah* was a long way off. There was one delay after another. It seemed hopeless and Bill wondered if it would ever happen. So, Bill was just biding his time even though he was still writing letters to as many companies in the USA as he could.

The hotel Ferdosi where Bill was set up in was nice enough and the food was good. In the States it would most likely he called a "flop house" but at least it was clean. The owner was a very nice man, a Greek actually. He and Bill became good friends. The days passed by without much accomplishment and aside from his efforts to get the import business going he would pass any idle time in the business section where he could watch the Silver artisans: and wood workers or at the *mokless* (warehouse) where the company had Persian Carpets stacked up higher than Bill's head, many stacks of the finest carpets ever made. He learned to distinguish some of the carpets by feel and colours as from where they were made.

An international theatrical troupe was coming to Isfahan to do a couple of shows in the local theatre. Actually it was a small opera house with a small stage but it was ample size for the show and they made do. The show went off very well and was enthusiastically received with a full house each night. There were few shows, especially of this type that ever came to town. The only other theatre was an open-air cinema that showed films made in other parts of the world.

The owner of the hotel where Bill was staying told him that the owner of this theatrical troupe was a black American. The Greek owner of the hotel, Philip, knew that Bill had been an entertainer most of his life as a dancer mainly so he was sure that he would want to see the show and meet his fellow American. Philip got tickets for himself, his wife and Bill.

He and Bill had become good friends, especially after Bill had taken on two men who tried to accost his wife in the dining room of the hotel. She had been sitting alone eating. These two men decided they wanted a closer contact with her and sat down at her table, saying something lewd to her. She was repulsed and stood up when one of them tried to take her by the arm... Bill happened to be close by and noticed these two mashers. It had been necessary to engage in a short round of hand to hand with them after throwing them out of the hotel dining room. It wasn't much of a fight as far as Bill was concerned. The gendarmes were close at hand and stopped the fight quickly, taking both the men and Bill off to jail.

By that time Bill was speaking Farsi quite well, and when he was taken to the commander's office to have him tell what the fight was all about, the commander was delighted that Bill spoke Farsi and the two of them soon became friends. The commander listened with great interest and anger, when he learned how the two men had mistreated Philip's wife, who happened to also be his friend.

The two men stayed in jail and the commander escorted Bill back to the hotel where they had some vodka with Philip. The vodka they served in Iran was the same powerful drink but it was extremely tasty. At dinnertime they would serve a small decanter at each plate. The officer enjoyed talking to Bill and listening to him speaking his language. He kept asking him questions about the USA, as well as many other things. Bill found him to be a very pleasant and interesting man, very well kept with a big, but well-trimmed moustache, and a well-fitted and clean uniform. He was about 40 to 45 years old.

The theatre was packed but Philip had arranged for seating and the show was a thrilling extravaganza with entertainers from eight different countries, all speaking their different languages. Harry, the black American owner of the troupe was able to converse with all of them in their own language since he spoke so many languages. There were jugglers, acrobats, dancers, and a singer from Lebanon who sang with a beautiful vibrant voice with movements typical of the Lebanese, seductive yet subtle. The songs she sang had so much life and rhythm. Harry played the Dumbek- a drum held under the arm- along side of her as she sang. Her songs were thrilling and it made Bill want to get up and dance. He could hardly sit still.

Philip and his friend, the producer of the shows there in Isfahan, took Bill to met Harry backstage after the show. This producer was also from Greece, and from the same town as Philip. Meeting Harry was something Bill will never forget. Harry had a personality that was electrifying and captivating, a genuinely friendly smile and an air of grace about him that was to be exemplified to Bill even more as the days rolled on. He noticed that Harry was wearing white gloves and spats. It seemed a little strange to see him in this attire, but Bill found out later that Harry was a very meticulous dresser. This was the style of the times and Harry seemed very comfortable with it. After all he was an entertainer. Harry introduced Bill to Nadia, the singer. She was tall, with long jet-black hair, pulled into a bun at the back of her head. She had black eyes, a lovely dark olive complexion, and a large but beautiful mouth that was lovely when she smiled. Her native language was Arabic of course, but she also spoke French. Harry translated the English for her. The two men and Nadia went to the hotel to have a fine Greek dinner with Philip. They became a friendly group.

CHAPTER I

Fortune-Misfortune

The story of Harry begins here. Harry is a living history of hardship, sorrow and success wrapped up in many facets of life, which we will explore.

He was born in the United States, a baby boy of a loving mother and father. His father wasn't rich but did have a good education having attended a collage In Chicago. He made good money as an accountant for a big corporation. He had worked very hard over the years, saved his money, and bought a house. It wasn't a very large house, but a nice one, in a good neighborhood in Chicago.

Harry was born in 1906. His mother had a very difficult time the last few days of her pregnancy and ultimately died of complications at his birth. It just about broke his father's heart. After grieving for almost five years and trying to overcome the loss of the lady he loved so much he decided to take his employer up on their offer to go with the company who was moving to Germany and setting up a large facility there and they wanted him to go with them because he was such an asset to the company. He figured that with the move he could better deal with the hurt and get his life together. It was 1911, his company owners were German and they were setting up operations in Berlin.

Harry's father put his house up for sale, sold his car, and literally got rid of all of their possessions. They had no other relatives. Harry's father was an only son and both his mother and father were deceased. He didn't get married until he was 34 years old. So when Harry was only 5 years old, and with only a few personal possessions and a treasured picture of his wife, he and Harry took off for Germany.

On arrival, suffice to say it was a very different life style and they weren't sure that they were going to like it however; it took him only a few days to see that except for the language there was really little difference than living in Chicago. Through the company he secured a permanent resident visa for himself and Harry, and became an American citizen living in Berlin. Harry's father had put him in a private school and in just a short time he was becoming proficient in the German language.

Harry was just nine when his father suddenly died of a heart attack. He had been working at his desk when his heart gave out, his head went down on his desk and his co-workers thought he had fallen asleep but then they couldn't imagine him doing such a thing and cautiously came to see if it was true but they found out that he had died right there. There had been no warning of trouble with his heart and his death was sudden and devastating to Harry. What was he going to do? He had no relative's back in America, and only friends of his father's company there in Berlin.

They had been friends and quite close with one of his father's co-workers, Marvin. He and his wife liked Harry a lot and she told her husband to bring Harry to their house, at least until they all decided what to do for him. It took them a while to figure out what they should do. In the meantime, they tried to make his life as pleasant as possible.

At first Harry didn't have much to say and didn't particularly want to do anything. He missed his father and turned into himself. Marvin and his wife was patient with him realizing what a terrible blow it must be to a small boy, all alone and especially in a strange country. It was several days before they could get him to go back to school. They felt very sorry for him. Finally Harry agreed to let them take him places after having turned into himself and trying to work out his own solution to his misfortune.

As most children do, Harry loved the circus. He loved to watch all the acts, but especially the man who was the boxer. He was big, trim, and moved smoothly about the ring. While Harry was staying with these nice friends, they took him different places trying to occupy his time from thinking about his misfortune and the pain of losing his father.

Since Harry liked to go to the circus most of all, they went quite often. After several visits there, he started getting friendly with the boxer, whose name was Gunter. He indicated to Gunter that he thought he would like to be a boxer some day. Black people in Germany in 1915 were rather a rarity. So when Harry kept showing up at the circus, he was a bit of an oddity and noticeable. He enjoyed talking to Gunter mostly, but he visited with everyone.

The people there started to know him as a very friendly and enthusiastic boy with a good personality and they all took a great liking to him. He was bright, spoke well and was polite.

Gunter was interested to know about Harry and where he came from. In their conversations, Harry, trying to hold back a tear, told him about his father and that he was now orphaned and didn't really know just what he was going to do. If the Company sent him back to America, he would be put into an orphanage. But these nice people who brought him to the circus were trying to find some family or close friends in the United States to send him back to. They had written many letters but no one offered to take the child and it seemed as if he was destined to be put in an orphanage. They were very hesitant to do this. They had reluctantly considered taking him in themselves. It wasn't that they didn't like Harry. They thought he was a very fine boy, but they were young and planned to have their own children and didn't make all that much money. It was a big problem to try to solve. They didn't want to go to the German authorities for fear that they would be put him in a German orphanage.

Gunter and his wife Hilda discussed the matter with Harry's friends and said that they wished they could take Harry to live with them as their own. They couldn't adopt him legally since they didn't want to go to the authorities but the legal part of it wasn't important.

When Gunter asked Marvin and his wife if they could have a talk in this regard, he made sure that Harry was to be there also. It had to be Harry's decision more than anyone else's. Sitting in their comfortable trailer at the circus with every one there he spoke directly to Harry and he said:

"Harry, Hilda and I would like for you to come and live with us..." Although he was big and tough, he spoke in a soft and gentle voice and started out saying: "We think you are a fine boy. We would like to take care of you and keep you safe, and perhaps we can learn to love one another, like a family."

He spoke softly and sincerely. Harry couldn't find any words for a long minute or two.

Finally he asked Gunter:

"You, want me to come and live with you in the circus?" Gunter grinned at the question, but said:

"Yes, with Hilda and me. But you will be a part of the circus also. We will be your family."

Gunter took his hand and said:

"You see Harry, Hilda and I could never have any children. Maybe you can fill the empty place in our hearts."

Harry looked in his eyes for a long moment then said to him:

"You mean I could be like your son?" Hilda was sitting beside Harry all this time not speaking, but when Harry said "your son" her heart skipped a beat and she put her arm around him and hugged him to her and said, "You will be our son if you want to".

It was settled then. All of Harry's things were gathered together, brought to the circus and Harry started a new life, with a new family but now he had a mother as well as a father. He would never forget his father though, who had been good to him, he had loved him, and he would always miss him.

Harry liked these people. They were warm, gentle, and sincerer with him and showed him love and affection. They kept him busy teaching him things about the circus. Soon the loneliness and hurt of losing his father were eased by their kindness. Besides, he was very busy learning all the tricks of the circus. They taught him tumbling, dancing, music, juggling, and literally all the different trades in the circus life. But he was mostly interested in learning to box..

Gunter's part in the circus was to take on any one of the customers who attended thecircus. He was a very big and tough man but also a gentle person and came to love Harrylike the son he had always wanted. Of course, Harry had long since learned to speakGerman like a native, which is not rare for young children, but he never forgot his Englishand he was still an American citizen, with an American passport.

For the next three years, most of Harry's education was about the circus. The wife ofthe juggler, who had been a school teacher, was educating him properly. He was a goodstudent, exceptionally smart, but his concentration was mainly on becoming one with thecircus and mostly on becoming a good boxer.

The year was 1915. During those years in Germany there was much unrest. They had already been at war with Belgium, France, England and Russia, and that wasn't all. The fact that Harry was an American, black, and highly noticeable wherever he went, made Gunter and his friends worried for his safety.

For the next three years they kept Harry hidden as much as possible. They arranged for him to take his studies at night when the circus was on so the few people who did come to the shows wouldn't see him but also so he wouldn't be left alone. The army and police were often stopping people and asking for identification, a normal activity during war, and Harry was vulnerable.

In 1917 the Americans entered the war with the Allies. They were in France and it began to look bad for the Germans. The army had already taken several of the men from the circus and put them on active duty. Times were hard. People didn't have money to go to the circus, and it would soon have to be closed down. It became more and more dangerous for Harry and beside everything else his Visa had expired.

They stuck it out until February 1918. For his safety, Gunter decided that Harry must leave Germany. But how to get him out of the country was another thing. Gunter started to ask around quietly about sympathizers with the Allies. He also knew that there were many Frenchmen in Germany when the war broke out and that there was talk of some resistance activity. Over the years he made friends with many of the French people there. In fact he was quite sympathetic with the French. He hated the aggression that Germany was inflicting on her neighbors. He had let it be known with his French friends for some time how he felt. He decided it would be best for Harry to get out of Germany, perhaps into France, if for no other reason than that the Americans were there and he thought he would be safer. He had no idea how that would help, except that it might be the best way to keep him alive. Regardless, it was with the French that he had the contacts to get anything done.

It took Gunter a while to find the right people but eventually he found out about someone who was engaged in some resistance activity. When he finally got to confront those people with his problem of getting Harry out of the country, they were convinced that he wasn't just trying to spy on them. Gunter explained all about Harry and the things that he had already gone through. He told them he loved him like his own son. It was for this reason he wanted to get him to safety, although he hated the thought of losing him. They worked on a plan to get Harry out of the country but because of his color it wasn't going to be easy. They couldn't chance taking him through any checkpoints. They might not think him to be an American but he was obviously not a German, and that alone could cause insurmountable problems.

It was decided to take the child through the woods in trucks or anything to keep him out of sight of the German Army or police. He would go undercover but it was a long way to go from Berlin to the French border.

Those French people were very kind and would continually risk their own lives for the benefit of others. They were willing to do anything to get this lovely, handsome, intelligent, twelve year old boy to safety.

Generally, they could only move at night unless Harry was under the cover of some kind of car, truck, or anything that would keep them out of sight. Otherwise, during the day he had to be secured in a house. This all had to be set up before they left Berlin: where to stop along the route and the exact route, who to contact and the different types of transportation. Getting across the border into France through the countryside was not thought to be an insurmountable problem. Even when they had to travel on foot, except when it was raining, the weather made it quite nice since it was in March, which was a plus for their journey.

There were always troops that scoured the countryside however, looking for any underground operations and the possibility of being shot could not be discounted. In the three years that Gunter had been like a father to Harry. He had taught him boxing continually. They worked out nearly every day. Gunter wasn't just a street fighter either, he had also been taught by some professionals and had been a contender in some pretty big fights and won. But he got married at an early age, and Hilda was so afraid of him getting hurt if he continued to fight professionally. She convinced him to stop and go into the circus. Of course there was still the possibility that someone might come long some day and hurt him, but it wasn't likely. The rounds he fought were never over three minutes. By the same token, Gunter had never hurt anyone either. He had knocked a few men out, but he was never brutal.

Gunter came to love Harry like a son, and it was only because of his fear for his safety that he wanted to arrange for his escape from Germany. He wanted to go along with them to the border of France but the people who had agreed to take him said it would just be added danger. So they all had to say their good-byes there in Berlin. Hilda made a big dinner of the famous sauerkraut and knockwurst with all the trimmings one night. After the circus closed they invited all the people who were left in the circus to come and say good-bye to Harry. It was a very sad affair for him. Each one of these artists had taught him their own art under the tent. He could fly on the trapeze. The catcher said that he had an uncanny sense of timing. He learned how to juggle and was quite good at it. He could work with 5 balls after only a short while. He excelled at dancing. One good reason he took a liking to the dance was that Gunter said it would be good for his agility in boxing. He could tap dance with the best of them. Harry was a fast learner at most anything he studied. He was intensely devoted to learning all that anyone wanted to teach him.

It had taken some time for Gunter to make all the arrangements, but finally the time camefor Harry to leave. The Frenchmen came to the circus as was pre-arranged. It was a sadgood-bye. He kissed all the friends who had been like a family to him for the past threeyears, but when it came to Gunter and Hilda, he broke down as Gunter picked him up andhugged him and kissed him for the last time and said: "Maybe we will meet again someday my son, maybe not, but I know that you will make a fine man. I love you and wish you luck."

The trip with the many stops along the way was not all that bad except for having to be very careful all the time. The French were good at their jobs and had a well-planned schedule There was only one time it got a little scary when they were in the forest just before crossing over into Belgium. They had to hide in a thicket because of a scouting party that came up on them. Harry and his various custodians were numbered 15 in all by the time they finally got to Mons Belgium. It took nearly three weeks to make the trip. Once just outside of Hanover in a little town of Boarding-house, they had to hole-up for three days waiting for safe passage by way of a meat truck packed with ice, which took them to Innsbruck where they had to wait for two days more before going on. Sometimes they could only go a few miles before they would have to hole-up because of some troop movements, or when they were on foot in the daytime.

CHAPTER II

The General and Jeanne

The Germans had invaded Belgium in 1914, just four days after the war was declared. At this time there were just as many Germans to be worried about seeing them there as there were in Germany, but they decided to go through Belgium just the same, because of a more direct route to Paris. They also wanted to travel through the northern part of the Ardennes, whose mountainous and wooded territory offered more cover than city streets. A woman headed up nearly all of what resistance there was. This tall, handsome, tough woman was well known to anyone who was active in any resistance activity and was referred to as "the general". Her perception of the war and the movements of the German Army were uncanny. Her name was Kathleen.

Kathleen had been born to farm people just outside of Brussels. Her parents were quite old when she was born in 1883. Her mother died of a brain tumor. Her father succumbed to a heart attack just nine months later. Kathleen was just turning 31 years old in June, just a little over two months before the Germans invaded Belgium in

August, 1914. Her uncle, Perot who had been working in Germany at the time in a logging camp that produced wood for the army's use, was not too far from Berlin. He had been quite close and loved his brother. Perot came to pay his last respects. Kathleen went back to Germany with him since they had no other relatives. She was a grown woman and capable of taking care of herself but she had no training for any kind of professional work. She and her uncle thought it would be easier for her to get some kind of work there in Germany.

After about one year helping her aunt in the home, and perfecting her German language, Kathleen got a job at the army camp in one of the canteens. She was beautiful with long black hair and blue eyes and skin so soft and touchable. Often she had to struggle to keep the men off her, especially after any of them had a few drinks, and that was frequent. She was speaking German like a native by this time quite easily. Living so close to Germany in Belgium many people spoke two and even three languages and she was no exception.

The new colonel in charge of the officer's canteen took a keen liking to Katy, as she was called. Most everyone knew her. She had been working there for nearly two years and was well liked. She and the colonel spent a lot of time together. His name was Rolf and he was the epitome of the starched German soldier. He was dedicated to the German movement and the Kaiser. He was a strapping man and quite handsome, typically blond and blue eyed and meticulous. It wasn't hard to accept his attentions but to her he was still the enemy and she was determined to do her part in the struggle against these aggressors. She learned all she could about the German army and some of the movements of the troops in the areas where they were going to make from him and from overhearing conversations or when some soldiers with too much to drink started to talk about things they shouldn't have.

Passing this kind of information along to the Allies is how she got started in a resistance movement. If she had to go to bed with some officer whom she thought she could get some vital information from, she would figure it was little sacrifice compared to the lost lives of those thousands of men of Belgium and the other allies who were fighting against the central powers of Germany, Austria, and Hungary, as well as the Ottoman Empire.

But now, in 1918, when Harry arrived Kathleen was back in Belgium. She would mingle in the streets and in the shops as well as the cafes where very often she could hear bits of information the soldiers were talking about; always with her ear tuned to any kind of information she could come across.

Most of the Belgian army was fighting on French soil after Germany overran them in 1914. They were only able to hold on to a thin strip of land on the west of Belgium. The Americans, entering into the war with the Allies in 1917 were engaged in a heavy battle in Chateau Thierry in June of that year. Together with the other forces they were able to stop the offensive of the German war machine.

Germany had been sending many troops to the Marne and creating some tough battles for the Allies since 1916. Kathleen thought she could be more valuable in this area, closer to where the battles were being fought, so she changed her point of operation.

When Harry showed up the first week of April after spending over three weeks in nearly every conceivable moving vehicle there was, including once in a truck loaded with horse manure, he was a very tired boy. Kathleen found it hard to believe that her people had been able to bring him all the way from Berlin without incident. She decided to take over his final journey on into France. He stayed there with her while they tried to map-out a routing and connections for his passing over into France.

They would have to arrange to go a northern route since there was too much heavy fighting in the area of Chateau Thierry and the Marne. They were in Mons Belgium where several battles had already been fought. In fact, many battles had been fought there before the First World War, the Spaniards in the 16th century, the Dutch in the 17th, and the French in the 18th.

Mons was a coal mining town and a shipping center at the junction of two major canals, the canal Du Centre, and the Conte-Mons. Kathleen thought that they should try to utilize the river for their crossing into France. It was no more dangerous than trying to go overland and probably would prove to be much faster.

They only had a few miles to go before entering into France. However, they found that the river flowed in the wrong direction: east. They couldn't afford to try to use any kind of motor-driven craft because of the noise so that plan had to be abandoned. They had to wait and find out which route would be the safest to travel. Kathleen asked her best men to find out where the Germans were the most concentrated and where the fighting was in preparation to laying a plan of travel. So they waited some more. Whenever Kathleen wasn't busy, she was working with Harry, teaching him French, and learning about his past. The more she heard the more interested she became in his future. He was a very interesting young boy. Whenever they could she made him speak in French for the practice. She wanted him to be as fluent as possible whenever he did arrive in France.

Harry told her about his father and how they came to Germany, and about learning so many interesting things from the circus people. When he danced for her she fell in love with his ability and his presentation. He was a true entertainer who appeared to be much at ease when performing. He juggled for her and tumbled, walked around on his hands, did front flips and somersaults but it was the coupe-de-grace that prompted her to enlist one of the men who was about a head taller but otherwise close to his size and weight to go three rounds with him. This fellow also had been an amateur boxer.

They got hold of a pair of boxing gloves and the fight was on. They went three three-minute rounds and the older man couldn't lay a hand on Harry. He was quicker than greased lightning. The fellows watching and the man he fought were ecstatic that Harry was so well trained. Harry was quick to tell them about Gunter, his patience, and attention to technique. They could all see how much he loved Gunter, it was in his voice whenever he spoke of him, and for that matter all of the other people he had lived with for over three years. He would get a look on his face of longing and a sadness that was evident he missed them a lot. Kathleen thought to herself, how terrible a war like this was, since she knew that not all the people of

Germany agreed with the Kaiser. So many of them were good people like Harry's friends back at the circus.

With all his achievements, Harry was still a soft spoken, polite and warm personality, and anyone could see he was a very alert young man, older than his years. Kathleen promised herself that she was going to ensure that he was well cared for when he got to France.

Since General Hindenburg had launched an all out offensive against the Allies that took them almost to Paris, there had been swarms of German soldiers flocking to the front. Most of the fighting had stopped in the East due to the signing of the treaty with Russia so Hindenburg was concentrating all his force against the Allies. With all these troops passing through Mons and Charleroi, just to the south of them, Kathleen was afraid for Harry to even go outside the barn, much less into the streets.

They were holed up in a huge barn. They had chosen a particularly run down farm just off the beaten path of the town. The old farmhouse was some distance back from the road and there were many trees around. It was quite obscure. Around the back part of the farmhouse was a huge barn. In the loft they had stacked up the hay high enough to hide a wall they erected, closing off the back part of the loft, which ran to the end of the barn. The size of the great room wasn't noticeable because of cow and horse stalls, which ran all the way to the back of the barn on the ground floor. If anything it looked like it might be an attic.

Within this huge room they had made smaller rooms, for the men and women and sometimes children who came looking for shelter, on their way to France or other safe havens. They could always make more room, whenever others would come. All the cooking was done in the main house since they had a good big kitchen. They just had to be careful that someone wouldn't suspect that it looked like it was being used for more people than just the two old people and Kathleen who posed as their daughter. All of the foodstuff they could get hold of - and it wasn't plentiful - was stored in a small room behind the cabinet next to the stove. What had been the door was made into a cabinet to hide the room.

Kathleen made a nice spot for Harry in the barn in a room they had used for storage of the many tools they used for some of their operations. She and Harry cleaned it up and put a makeshift bed in one corner. The people who stayed in the barn had plugged all the air holes in the barn to keep the wind from blowing in. The roof was good. Other than that it got cold in the winter. But now the weather wasn't bad except for getting a little cold at night. Kathleen would have had Harry stay with her in the house, but she thought it would be too dangerous. On more than one occasion some of the German soldiers would stop by to get something to eat. She had to be especially careful at times like these. She always tried to make herself as ugly as possible, and wore loose, old raggedy outer garments to keep the men from getting any ideas about using her.

She spent a lot of time with Harry in the barn and in the back of the barn, which butted up to one of the coal processing plants. It was idle now because of the war but there were great mounds of slag in rows between the building and the barn. They could go outside there and no one could see them from any direction. It was nice to be able to spend some time outside without worrying about the enemy but they had to be quiet. It was just too dangerous for them to try to make a crossing over into France and into Paris from where they were at this time. Kathleen decided to wait for some kind of a break. Since the Americans had joined in the struggle along with Romania, Portugal, and Greece to follow, she hoped that just maybe the war was near an end. From where she was she could see that the German army was in pitiful shape.

Kathleen had a friend who had worked with her in Berlin. Together they had gained some valuable information that they passed on to the Allies. Jeanne had been the carrier of the information that Kathleen had overheard from a drunken colonel late one night when he had asked her to take him to his apartment. He hadn't really drank as much as he let on, hoping that she would take a little pity on him and help him home. When they arrived at his apartment he began to get amorous right away. She decided that since he was involved with troop movements, and there was a chance she could learn something, she would play him along and stall him off as long as she could. Just when it looked like she was going to have to succumb to his insistence, the phone rang. He was irritated to have to answer. In his state of drunkenness, though not actually drunk, he proceeded to talk to the person on the phone who obviously was a superior giving him orders about moving some artillery up to the front during the battle of the Marne, along with the routing.

After Kathleen allowed him to have his way with her, he fell soundly asleep. She left with this information and passed it on to Jeanne and she took it to where it would be passed on to the Allies. The Allies were able to intercept and destroy the artillery squadron. Both she and Jeanne felt very good about it and opened a bottle of wine for a small celebration. It was then that they became the closest of friends.

Jeanne was a French girl who had lived in Germany for many years just as Kathleen had. They were nearly the same age. She had been an orphan and was adopted by a Belgian couple. Later, her adopting father became a restaurant owner in Hamburg. It was a fairly small restaurant but it made a nice living for them. Jeanne went to school there but she was never able to get along with the German children very well. There were a few friends along the way but-never close friends. Somehow she preferred older people. She helped her parents in the restaurant and the older people treated her better and made nice compliments.

She fell heavily in love with a fellow several years older than she was when she was only 16. They were quite discreet around her parents and in public but Jeanne was a very sensuous girl and quite beautiful with an excellent figure, with breasts that pointed up to the sky. She had hazel eyes and natural blond hair that she wore just to below her shoulders. Mik, who was a Hungarian, was a handsome fellow and well built. When he made love to her she felt as if she were in a dream. She loved Mik, but that wasn't the only reason for the way she felt when making love. It was because she liked the loving and the feeling. She didn't even think about the man making love to her as Mik. It could have been anyone she imagined. But of course, it made a difference before and after, when she was happy it was Mik.

Mik however, wasn't a real nice guy. He didn't have a good job and didn't make much money, not because he wasn't talented or smart, but because he was lazy and didn't like the idea of having to get up in the morning everyday to go to a job, especially one that he wasn't interested in. So he never kept a job for very long. He was, however, a good talker and made friends easily. People liked him right away and with his gift of gab he could get people to do almost anything.

Mik met an influential man in a club one day just after Jeanne's seventeenth birthday. The man was in his forties, a successful businessman. He was married and had a couple of children, but he could never get enough loving from his wife, and was on the lookout all the time for new-talent. He confided in Mik that he would like to meet some nice young girl and would be willing to pay handsomely for the pleasure. Mik decided that Jeanne would be that girl

He made an appointment to meet the gentleman at the same club a couple of days later. Beforehand he took Jeanne to the club and sat her into a booth where she could see the man he would be talking to. He cut the conversation short, but told the man that he thought he had found the girl he was looking for and would meet him the next evening at the same place.

Mik hadn't told Jeanne exactly what he was up to until after she saw this man. Then he asked her what she thought about him. Was he nice looking, not too old, nicely dressed, and did she think she would be willing to go to bed with him? She was a little shocked at the question. She looked at Mik for a long time, thinking that perhaps he was kidding but she was not necessarily repulsed when she realized that he wasn't. Mik told her what the man had said: that he was willing to pay quite a lot of money for the pleasure. She told Mik that she would think about it. She did think about it and the next day she told Mik that if he wouldn't be jealous, she would be willing to do it one time. That was the start of her career as a prostitute.

She was choosy with whom she went with and Mik was always there to help her make the right contacts. Soon though he was forced to either leave Germany or take the chance of being forced to serve in the German army and he surely didn't want to do that so went back to Hungary.

Jeanne decided that she could be of use to the Allies. No one knew that she was originally from France, and by this time she had made some friends in the army, some pretty high ranking officers, and if she worked it right, she just might do some good. She did, and it did do some good, and that is when she met Kathleen. Kathleen told her that she was going to Mons, and for the same reasons Jeanne also decided to go. She told Kathleen that she would follow as soon as she could make arrangements. She was happy that they would be working together again, but she didn't know anything about Mons.

Jeanne arrived about three weeks after Harry did. Kathleen introduced him to her, and she and Kathleen talked about some of the things they had been able to do for the war effort. They never actually told Harry about the sex part of their activities but they also didn't try to hide the fact that they would do nearly anything to carry out their chosen missions. Harry was no dummy, and it was obvious to him that these two ladies who were so wonderful to him and who he depended on were ruthless in their desire to help in any way possible to defeat the Germans.

Chapter III

War Ends

June passed and it was into July. It looked like the war was turning in favor of the Allies. They had stopped the Germans at the Second Battle of the Marne and were preparing further attacks. Kathleen and her charges could see that there was already some of the German army retreating.

The General made up her mind to stay where they were and wait out the end of the war, which came soon enough in November. Everyone was very happy about the final end of the war, but at the same time they were truly sad for the millions of people, mostly young men, who had given their lives for it. By this time Harry was speaking French very well. Jeanne had a more difficult time with her French, because she was taken to Germany when she was just a little girl and never had the chance to learn it well. Her parents never tried to teach her to speak their language wanting her to learn the German language for her own good. However, they did speak French in the home fairly often. She did remember some of it so now, being with Harry and Kathleen, it was coming back to her.

New Years Eve in Paris, Nineteen Eighteen, was a roaring time for those who could afford it. There were still many people hurting from the war. Famine and epidemics added to the estimated ten million dead and twenty million wounded in the war. It was a devastating figure, but still, it was over and the people who died were fighting for the freedom of those who were left, and it was worth celebrating and remembering their sacrifice.

Jeanne and Kathleen went to work right away. They both had a little money saved and they rented a nice apartment on rue Faubourg Montmartre, just one block from L' Opera and one block from the Follies Berger. They could ply their trade in either direction and find gentlemen of culture and money. For Jeanne and Kathleen such men weren't hard to attract.

They didn't dress like most of the other ladies of the night. They wore fashionable clothes and were always clean. They had been with many upper-class German officers, and although they would have killed them if they had to, they were nevertheless intelligent men and many of them were quite elegant. No one would be ashamed to be seen with either one of these two beautiful women. In fact, many of the men they tricked were very happy to be seen with them. Of course, they charged accordingly.

Harry had his own room in their apartment and his room led into a hallway, which led to a back stairway in one direction and into the main part of the apartment in the other. At night, if he had a reason to go out, he would always use the back stairs in case the girls had company.

He knew of course, how the girls made their money, but they never flaunted it or talked about it, or allowed their clients to know or talk to Harry. They were also never heavy drinkers. When Champagne or wine was part of the evening's entertainment they always faked drinking a lot. They didn't like to make themselves vulnerable by drinking. They always liked to keep a clear head.

The tutor Kathleen found for Harry was a very learned man of about 40. He was a writer and a poet. Kathleen noticed him one day on Blvd. Des Italians in one of the department stores where he had a table set up displaying his latest book of poetry and signing autographs. He was a rather handsome man with a Vandyke and casual clothes of tweeds which made him quite attractive but the most impressing thing was his voice, deep and mellow, and the lyrical manner in which he spoke made her want to know more about him.

In their conversation, she found out that he had students whom he would train to become writers. He confessed to teaching anyone because his writing and poetry weren't really all that lucrative, and he needed the money.

Kathleen made an appointment to meet Lousier with Harry at his place, which was only a few blocks from where they lived, in the direction of the Bastille. Lousier showed her his teaching credentials, and she was convinced that he should begin tutoring Harry right away. She told him that she wanted Harry to have a good education and to concentrate on French and Latin. She wanted him to study Latin because she knew that by learning Latin it would give him a grammatical base for learning other languages. Also, she was insistent that he have a good knowledge of mathematics. Lousier assured Kathleen that he felt confident that he could comply with her wishes, and promised that he would make every effort to not only teach Harry but to make him enjoy the studying as well.

An agreement was made regarding the payment for his services, which weren't cheap. However, both Kathleen and Jeanne felt that Lousier was a perfect model for Harry. Aside from the fact that Harry needed a male figure in his life, it was evident that Lousier was a gentleman. And Harry was going to spend a lot of time with him.

They got off to a good start. Lousier told Harry that he was an enthusiastic supporter of the fight game, and could list all the names of the boxers of any renown for the last ten years. He even knew the name of Gunter and remembered one fight he had with a fellow Frenchman in Germany when the Frenchman lost but he hadn't heard anything of him since then. Harry told him that it was probably because of Gunter's retirement from the ring.

CHAPTER IV

Lousier

They just sat around and told one another stories about their past for the first three hour day of the schooling. Lousier thought it would be a good way for Harry to learn to relax with him and to gain his confidence; it worked. As always, Harry was a fast learner. He almost seemed to have a photographic memory. Few things he was taught had to be repeated. It took him no time at all to perfect his French. Naturally, it was much easier because of speaking it every day. The German language didn't do him any good in France in those days at all. About the only thing he had to work on was to keep the German accent out of his French. Lousier would give him elocution exercises to work on and sometimes would put a clothespin on his nose to help with the French accent.

To make studies more interesting they would take "field trips" to the Louvre, or walks along the Seine and to the Pond at the formal gardens of Tuilleries and watch the boys sail their miniature boats. Walking along the Champs Elyse one day, they saw a fellow tap dancing. It was a familiar sight to see jugglers, acrobats, and various other types of entertainers performing on the streets, hoping that people would throw money. Often there were small string quartets as well as other musicians, and many of them were very good at what they did. Watching the tap dancer one day, Harry said, I can do that.

When they returned to Lousier's studio, Lousier just a little sceptical, asked Harry to demonstrate his ability at tap dancing. Starting with a soft-toe and ending with a buck and wing Lousier was delighted and surprised at the same time. He was roaring with laughter and clapping his hands before Harry finished. He thought it was fabulous and it was evident that he was much better than the man on the street. Harry told him he could also juggle. He picked up three of Lousier's glasses and started to demonstrate for him. It made Lousier nervous, because the glasses were part of a set that was rather expensive. Harry, however, was very confident that he wouldn't break any and assured Lousier of it. Nevertheless, he was happy when Harry stopped.

Their school sessions were set up to start at nine o'clock in the morning and run till noon but they often ran over that time if Lousier didn't have another pupil, and especially if they were out on a field trip.

Each morning Harry would run, as he was taught to do by Gunter. He liked to run because it made him feel good. He wasn't getting any boxing practice and he missed that but he liked to keep up his physical training. One morning, as he was rounding a corner of a building about a quarter to eight, he almost ran into Lousier. He excused himself but kept on running, yelling to Lousier that he would see him at nine. Later, Lousier asked him how long he had been doing that. Harry told him that he always did it, even in Germany and Belgium when he couldn't go outside and ran in the streets he would exercise and run around in circles inside the compound or the barn, like he had to do in Mons. He told him also that he really missed boxing.

Since he was a devotee of boxing, Lousier knew where there was a good gym and where many of the amateur boxers trained and worked out. He used to go there and watch and he knew a couple of the trainers as well as the manager of the gym. He promised Harry that he would take him there to see the place as soon as they could arrange the time.

The gym was a big place. There were young boys working out, punching the bags that were lined up along the wall and fellows sparring in the rings. There were four rings and it was very noisy. Harry was thrilled to see all the activity. He couldn't wait to get into some trunks and start working out but he had to wait and watch, at least for a while. He told Lousier that Gunter had been teaching him boxing and that he liked it but Lousier didn't take him very seriously. They watched for a while and at Harry's urging Lousier asked the manager how much it would cost to belong to the gym so he could go there and work out with the other fellows. Jerome, the owner, wrote out all the charges for getting set up in the gym. It wasn't too expensive but a boxer had to furnish his own gloves and there was a small fee for the towels they used. But for just working out on the equipment the gym dues were enough, and they could also take showers.

Kathleen and Jeanne were both very concerned about Harry going to the gym alone. After all he was only 13 years old and even though he was bigger for his age than most boys and could probably take care of himself, they were a little worried about this environment. Jeanne insisted that one of them go to check out this gym before allowing Harry to join.

When Kathleen walked in with Harry, the activity in the gym began to slow down andsoon the whole place was quiet and everyone was focusing his attention on Kathleen. Shewas accustomed to having men look at her wherever she went. They were supposed to.That's why she dressed well and kept herself in good shape but this attention the whole gym was paying her made her very self-conscious and she asked Jerome if they couldgo into his office. She felt a little more at ease now and they got down to business.Jerome called to Hero to come with them. He introduced him to Kathleen and explainedthat Hero would be Harry's trainer and would spend a lot of his time with him. Shecouldn't help taking a liking to Hero right away. He was a big man, with a soft voice. Heexplained a little about how they would get started and how the training would progress.She felt very confident of this man. She was a good judge of character. She paid for one full year's membership and had Jerome explain all the rules andregulations as well as schedules of opening and closing. She wanted to know how theywould handle it if anyone got hurt.

Jerome, (they called him "Jerry") told her of his experience in the fight game and that he had attended to many scrapes and bruises and knew how to tend to the eyes. But for one thing they had very few accidents. All the boxers wore headgear when sparing and none of the equipment was dangerous. Sure there were a lot of pulled muscles and bruises but no one considered this a big problem.

Jeanne insisted on taking Harry shopping to buy the things he needed like boxing gloves shoes and good socks, trunks, sweats with tops, three of everything. He also had to supply his own headgear. She spent several hundred francs but it really made her happy to do it and it wasn't as if she didn't have the money. Nearly all her clientele were rich, and paid plenty for her attention and no one complained. She was blond with hazel eyes, a little on the greenish side, a little shorter than Kathleen but every bit as beautiful, only a much lighter complexion than Kathleen. She dressed elegantly, and for all their experiences during the war, neither of them looked to be aging. It seemed that they would be good for several more years yet.

Jerry introduced him around to some of the fellows in the gym. Hero was the head trainer. His real name was Herodotus. With a name like that, it was obvious why everyone called him Hero. His mother was a romantic and was influenced by Greek Mythology. He had a pug nose and a receding forehead, long arms, and looked like he had been a pretty tough man to fool with when he was younger. He shook hands with Harry and welcomed him. When he took his hand you couldn't even see Harry's hand in his, it was so big. Harry liked him right off. Not everyone was as pleasant as Hero but most of them were OK. A couple of them seemed a little cold and Harry wondered if it was just their way or maybe they didn't like strangers. Harry was rarely made aware of his color difference, except when he was with his beautiful foster mothers, then people would look and you could see the wondering on their faces but no one ever made any remarks, so Harry never thought much about it

Harry or his mothers were never much about religion or going to church but Harry accepted anyone as a friend regardless of their age, color, race or their religion. To him they were all people he wanted to know and make friends with and he did that easily and with a winning smile and a sincerity that you couldn't dismiss.

The gym was in the Pigalle area fairly close to Le Sacre Coeur. It was up hill from where he lived and about six blocks to the gym. He decided that it would be good to start out his exercise by running to the gym, doing his work-outs, then run back home and take a shower before going to school. The gym didn't open until seven o'clock in the morning but since he would already have half of his leg of running in before he got there, and an hour of work-out would be plenty, then he could run back home, shower and be at Lousier's in plenty of time. Of course, he didn't do that every day but at least three times a week.

To Lousier, Harry seemed to be even brighter and better equipped to learn the lessons he gave him than he was before he started his workouts, if that were possible. He was also obviously very happy.

One morning before Harry finished his exercises Jerry asked him if he would like to go a few rounds sparing with another lad about his same age and build. The boy wanted to become a boxer and needed someone to work with him. He jumped at the chance and asked if he could set it up for the afternoon and not in the mornings because of his school. Jerry said that the other boy also had to go to school and that the afternoon would be the only time he could make it. Harry didn't know the boy because he always worked out in the afternoons and Harry did his in the mornings. Harry warmed up, took some stretching exercises and took about five minutes on the bag. Gunter had told him to never go into the ring cold. Harry had just turned fourteen and this boy Thomas was nearly 15 but he was about the same size and he had been training with Hero also. They squared off and danced around a little and Thomas threw a punch at Harry and he ducked it easily and counter-punched with a left jab to the head. It wasn't a very hard punch but it threw Thomas's head back enough to see that Harry had contacted.

Thomas was a weaver. He liked to keep both his hands up in front of him and throw his left out with jabs when he thought he had a chance of scoring, but Harry was one thing if nothing else, and that was fast. Thomas had a hard time making contact with Harry with his left or his right but managed to land a few. Harry took stock of Thomas's actions and learned quickly that when he would weave to the right and then back he would be prepared to throw a left jab on the way back. Harry's timing was primed to counter his punch or beat him to it and often he could get a good right straight to the head just after sidestepping his jab. He looked to Hero like a thinking fighter. One who could think fast enough to move in on a critical bad move by his opponent. Hero was very surprised with Harry's ability. He could see right away that he would have to work on his power, but his speed and technique were superb for such a young boy.

Thomas was a good sport and took his shortcomings with a grin. Harry and he became quite good friends and worked out many times together. Whenever they did, Hero would watch and give both of them pointers. He taught Thomas to stand up straighter and to stop telegraphing his moves. Harry worked on his punch with the body bag. Hero didn't even want him to use the punching bag at all for awhile. It was good for speed but Harry had that. He needed to beef up his wrists and get the feeling of powering into the bag. Hero also had him work out with some heavy weights during his workouts to put some weight on his muscles. He taught him how to follow through with his weight behind the punch.

Harry actually looked more like a swimmer than a boxer. He was about five foot one and weighed around 60 kilos which wasn't bad for a boy of his age, but he was a little taller than most at fourteen so he looked slender. He was very well proportioned and he was nearly all muscle, and the muscle was sinewy and long like a swimmer's. His build and the exercise he was accustomed to doing must be attributed to the build and the speed. But the mind must tell the body what to do and Harry had the mind to do it.

His days were completely taken up with his studies and his infatuation with becoming a boxer. His -Mothers- wanted to be sure that Harry also knew how to act, dress and behave like a gentleman. Even before he started school they were starting him on a course that any royal prince would have to go through, especially if he was expected to take the throne some day. First was cleanliness: body, nails, hair, teeth and everything that it implied was not only taught and demanded of him but was explained why it was important, not only for the social reasons but for his health. When Jeanne or Kathleen couldn't explain adequately they would employ someone who could.

An old Chinese apothecary and herbalist, Mr. Sing, looked like he was old as the hills. His hair and long chin whiskers were white and his beady eyes seemed to be closed all the time but you better believe that he could see well enough. He didn't even wear glasses. He was short and wore his traditional Chinese robe, sash and little round cap with no bill but a little tassel on top. It was all very colorful but when he moved he was as graceful as a twenty-year-old.

The first day that Jeanne took Harry to see Mr. Sing she and Kathleen wanted him to explain about how germs could be introduced into the body through unclean hands as well as other foreign objects. But more important how the body could react to these various germs and how some of them manifested themselves in the body. That is, how to detect they were there.

Sing told Jeanne to leave Harry there with him and he assured her that when Harry left he would know all that he needed to know to protect himself. So she left with confidence. Sing was a little curious about Harry and his two guardians, both of whom Harry insisted on calling Mother. He was very careful not to anger or embarrass him so he skirted the actual question by asking Harry about how he came to be in France.

It took Harry a good while to tell Sing the story of his life but that is pretty much what he did. Sing was in a trance by the time he got through. He was beginning to hope that the story wouldn't end. For a boy of 14 he had seen an awful lot, but seemed to be none the worse for it. On the contrary, Harry was in every way a level-headed, pleasant and very well mannered young man and Sing liked him more and more.

Sing did tell Harry about how dirt and germs were carried under the fingernails and on the hands, even when they looked clean but surely when they were dirty. But one couldn't go around washing their hands all during the day. He simply told Harry to get in the habit of not getting his hands into his mouth and to be sure to always wash well before eating and to pay attention to keeping his nails clean and cut. He also showed him some pictures of Ameba and Intestinal worms in their beginning state and when they had grown to be the size of snakes. To say the least, it scared Harry and made him wonder just how he survived all this time, especially when he was escaping from Germany. He asked Sing about this and he told him that one thing you had to give the body credit for was that it could build up a certain immunity to some infections and luck for others. Dirt alone wouldn't make you sick. There had to be the right kind of germs also but if they were present, it wasn't hard to get sick. And since it could happen to anyone, Sing also described how to detect the symptoms of the Ameba, and said never wait to do something about it if they showed up.

Sing began to speak in English. He told Harry before he left that first day that the next time he came in he would tell him about his life, about how he left China to go to the United States and work on the railroad, then to get an education as an apothecary and to come to France during the war, thinking to return to the United States after the war. Harry couldn't wait until he could return.

For his education in regard to dress, both Jeanne and Kathleen would buy the latest fashion magazines. They would go to fashion shows, and when they did they would see to it that Harry was most likely the best-dressed young man there. Suffice it to say that Harry knew how to act in high or for that matter in any society. He had seen it all. The days rolled by quite pleasantly for this family of three. Harry was doing very well with his studies. He had mastered his French, had continued his German and English and was now studying Italian with another tutor

Lousier recommended this professor of languages who was Italian. He was a linguist who spoke seven languages fluently and taught all of them in the Paris University (the Sorbonne). He told Harry that he enjoyed teaching there for the usual reasons a teacher likes to teach but at the Sorbonne, especially because of its ancient history. Robert de Sorbonne founded the University of Paris in the year 1201. In those days and up to 1885 when the University of Paris faculty took it over, it was dedicated almost totally to studies in theology.

Faggio Del Borromeo was a descendant of an earlier Cardinal of Italy. Education had been a cornerstone of the family down through the years. Languages were a specialty of Faggio's because he liked people and liked to travel and he couldn't stand it if he couldn't talk to people he would meet on his journeys while travelling with his father who was an ambassador. So at an early age he began to study every language he could.

When Faggio was old enough he went to a university in Genoa. Genoa wasn't his hometown, but he had travelled most of his life. So anywhere in Italy was home. He wanted to go to Genoa because here there were multitudes of foreign people, tourists, shippers, tradesmen, and it gave him an opportunity to find people he could converse with in the different languages he was studying. Besides, Genoa was a beautiful place rivalling Marseilles as the leading sea port on the Mediterranean. He had the chance to see Paris during the war when the Italians broke with the Germans and became one with the Allies. He had been sent to Paris with a small contingent of army diplomats if for no other reason than that he spoke French and English fluently. He liked France and decided to return after the war. He submitted his credentials to the university and was accepted. Since the war he had been in Paris teaching and was very happy there.

Both Faggio and Lousier were bachelors, their passion for education, writing and teaching seemed to take up so much of their time. Except for recently, teaching really didn't create the kind of an income they felt they could be comfortable with for supporting a wife. Also, they knew that they might be rather difficult to live with, at least until they could find someone who had the same interests as they and so far that hadn't happened. It was, however, a fact that Faggio was a very amorous fellow and liked women of all nationalities. He didn't like much to go out to the various nightclubs to meet someone. He would rather try to meet a lady through some of his activities or friends. There had been a few that he really liked when he did make dates. He would enjoy taking these dates to one of the clubs that offered some entertainment such as the Follies Berger, or L'opera. But these dates didn't always turn out to be conquest, and a hot-blooded Italian needs an outlet, which is how he came to know Jeanne.

It was a little odd that Lousier happened to be a friend of Faggio's and he in turn was also a friend and a customer of Jeanne's. Jeanne and Faggio were both very surprised to see one another when an arrangement was made for all of them to get together to decide if they wanted Faggio to be Harry's language tutor. Lousier had done a beautiful job with his French and Latin as well as helping him keep up with his English and German but he didn't have the command of any other languages, such as Italian or Spanish or any others, so he recommended Faggio. And now it was just a little embarrassing to both of them. Neither of them let on that they even knew one another when they met at Lousier's apartment. Actually it was rather a come-on for Faggio because Jeanne was a beautiful woman and Faggio would have taken her more often if he could have afforded it. However, he was happy that he could have her once in a while. The fact that he didn't throw away his money on bars and bistros made it possible for him to have her at all. Nothing was ever mentioned about them knowing one another, not even to Lousier. The first chance that Jeanne had to talk to Faggio in private one night, she told him that if he was going to teach Harry, their relationship would be no different than it was before. In other words, it would be just as if he was teaching someone that Jeanne didn't even know. There would be no swapping lessons for her favors. He was still a customer to her but that she would appreciate if he never mentioned or discussed it with Harry. After all, Harry was a young boy, and although he may not be dumb about life, they never let him be any part of their activities and she wanted to keep it that way.

Faggio assured her that he had no intention of divulging anything to Harry, and in fact he would prefer that he didn't know, presumably for the same reasons as Jeanne's. One would think that Harry was rather a protected child but that was not the case. Both Jeanne and Kathleen were explicit and open with Harry as to any of his questions about life as he witnessed it in his growing up. Although the two women made their fortunes in an illicit manner, both of them had a good education and realized that they had to maintain a family type of relationship and make sure that Harry was not isolated from society. They were only very careful about whom he selected as friends, and when he told them about someone that he had just met, they always acted as if they were very interested and allowed him to tell them all that he knew about the one in question. Then at the very first opportunity, one of them would arrange it so they could meet that person.

All of this intervention in his social development they kept very discrete. They didn't want Harry to think that he didn't know good from bad in the people he came in contact with. They felt it was a delicate matter that could have repercussions if he thought he was being watched over too much or being too protected. After all, he had gone through an awful lot already and felt of himself as a man rather than a boy, and rightfully so, but that didn't stop them from wanting to help guide him in the right direction.

With all of Harry's experiences he still was rather shy about some things, girls for example. It wasn't often that he had an opportunity to come in contact with girls because of his private schooling and being so busy with his training and the boxing. Attending boxing matches with Lousier, and later with Faggio who also enjoyed going, he was quite satisfied with is life. He was doing what he liked with the people he liked and respected. One couldn't ask for much more.

Lousier heard about a Sorbonne student activity held outside of the school involving the theatre and performing arts. Before he told Harry anything about it he went to the group and asked the person in charge if they would allow Harry to come and participate. After all, he was a student even if he wasn't going to a public school. He was nearly sixteen now but acted older. The fellow in charge told Lousier that the theatre group accepted all ages. Those who wanted to participate would have to audition for a character or a part, whatever it might be.

Lousier knew that they were planning on producing a musical comedy, almost a variety show as it was decided, with a story line running through it. So Lousier told Harry about it. Harry asked Lousier if he thought he would be welcome, not going to the same school and being black. Lousier said that he told the person about Harry's color, but it didn't seem to make any difference. When he told them also that he was an American, they were very anxious to meet him.

On a Saturday morning when the group usually got together, Harry was due to meet with them. Adrian was the fellow who was the organizer of this group and the one in charge as he was the most knowledgeable about the theatre. He was a major in the theatre arts at Sorbonne. He wanted to be a writer, producer and director but he was also a musician. Adrian played the piano, and he played it very well. His education had been classical, but he played all the popular music and also enjoyed the American blues. When Harry walked in and Lousier introduced him to Adrian, who in turn called all the people in the group over and introduced Harry to them. They were a group of warm and personable people. Harry took a liking to them right away. With the entire group still around, Adrian asked Harry what he did in the way of the performing arts. Harry never was one to brag but he told them how circus people had trained him. He didn't think it was a good idea to tell them that it was in Germany. When they started asking a lot of questions, Harry said that if Adrian would play the piano he would perform a dance for them and maybe they could see if they thought he was good enough to be in the show with them.

CHAPTER V

New Friends

Adrian anxiously agreed and asked him what kind of piece he wanted. Harry tapped out a rhythm with his foot and Adrian fell right in with it and they took off together. About half way through his dance they all started to clap in time with the music. When Harry called Adrian to go out, it would give him eight more bars of music. He caught it and they finished together and they all clapped and roared for his performance. Harry thanked Adrian for his excellent accompaniment and he became a part of the group without reservation.

Adrian wrote in a part for Harry by the next Saturday. Each week on Saturday morning and some Sundays and occasionally a night during the week, they would rehearse the show.

The production was scheduled for a Friday and a Saturday and it just happened to come on the Saturday, which was Harry's birthday. He was to be sixteen, but no one in the show knew it. Harry wouldn't tell them because he wasn't sure they even knew how old he was and he perceived that they thought him to be older. That was better as far as he was concerned but Lousier knew and he told Adrian. He just casually mentioned it when Adrian was telling him about how well Harry danced and how much everyone thought of him, especially that he was such a gentleman, still very down-to-earth. It was then that Lousier asked Adrian if Harry had ever told him about his other talents. Adrian said no; he hadn't mentioned anything else. Lousier told him about all of his other accomplishments and what a good boxer he was. Adrian made up his mind that he was going to arrange a surprise party for Harry on the Saturday night after the show.

He got the gang together and they made the plans, but they needed some way of getting Harry to a certain restaurant after the show without him suspecting anything. Yvette had an idea about that. She was a girl of seventeen, a singer in the show, and she really liked Harry. She had tried to let him know about her interest in him, but he was a little naive and shy and didn't realize what she was up to. She said she thought she could get him to the restaurant without him suspecting anything. So they left it up to her. On the Friday night of the show, Yvette asked Harry to button up the back of her dress for her backstage. She asked him if he had any girl friends. He thought for an instant that he should lie and say yes, afraid that she would think maybe he didn't like girls much or that he was too young to have a girl friend but he couldn't do it and so he said no. She said, "Oh" And that was all, but she stayed rather close to him all through the show. The next night, she waited until they were alone backstage and asked him if he would like to take her to a small restaurant for a snack after the show to discuss the pleasure of working in the show together. It was rather a lame excuse but the whole idea was that she wanted him to know that she wanted him to be with her and it worked. Harry, a little confused but elated over the invitation, looked into her beautiful eyes and thinking to himself, is this really happening to me and said: "I would love to, thanks."

The audience went wild both nights, over the show. They especially liked Harry and made him come back for an encore both nights. Of course, there were many relatives there of the young people in the show but there were also many others, strangers, who had bought tickets that no one knew, who also thought the show was wonderful and let it be known with their applause. Adrian had said that they weren't going to have any kind of celebration after the show because all the relatives wanted to have each of their young people to themselves but that they would get together the next Saturday afternoon to celebrate and think about their next show. So they all agreed to meet then. Of course, it was a cover for the surprise for Harry.

Yvette asked Harry about half way through the show if he had changed his mind about going with her after the show. Harry not only hadn't changed his mind, he couldn't keep his mind off the thought that this beautiful girl was asking him to go with her any place and he could hardly wait. He told her he was looking forward to it.

After his spot was done, he rushed to the bathroom, took off his shirt and washed up as much as he could. He had brought a towel with him and some baking soda to powder under his arms to keep dry and guard against any offensive odors. Kathleen had taught him this little trick that she used all the time to smell fresh. In her business it was important, to say the least.

He put on a clean shirt he brought, a starched white one, and he left the second button open to let some of his chest show through. He put on a beautiful jacket that Jeanne had bought for him for his birthday. Kathleen and Jeanne had wanted to give him a party or take him out somewhere, but he told them about the date with Yvette and they could see that he was so excited that they told him they could go somewhere on Sunday instead.

They didn't have time to find out anything about Yvette but for sure they would be checking to see what kind of a girl she was. They weren't too worried however, because being a part of the group, and a student just getting ready for graduation, they felt that she must be rather serious and told Harry that they hoped he would have a good time.

They had never imposed any restrictions on Harry being out late at night. For one reason, he never had much of a reason to be out late. He was usually ready for bed at an early hour since he was almost always rather tired from all his activities. Besides, from an early age, along with his training, Gunter had explained that an athlete had to get his rest. They just told him to be careful when he was out late at night for people who might have drunk too much since many people of this type get a little mean and like to cause trouble, and to stay away from dark streets. Of course, they knew that Harry could pretty well take care of himself as well as the girl, but as mothers, they were always concerned about his safety.

So the big time came. They all said goodnight after the show when all was cleaned up. They hadn't had much to do because they had stage crew, and that was their job, but they all helped just the same. The stage crew was just as excited about the show being a success as any of the others. Most of them were studying for this part of show business as well and that was their choice and they enjoyed it. Unknown to Harry, they were going to be at the party also. They had planned to come the next day Sunday and finish the rest of the work of striking the set.

On the way to the restaurant Harry was walking with his hands in his pockets and they were just ambling along taking their time. It wasn't very far from where they were but Harry especially wanted it to last as long as possible. Yvette did too. It wasn't her first date but she was just as excited as if it were. Harry wasn't only a very accomplished young man but he was very handsome, clean and confident and pleasant all of the time. She slipped her arm around his as they walked and Harry felt a tingle go up his spine at her touch. He acted nonchalant but he could have jumped ten feet in the air. He felt like he should do or say something. Finally he stopped and looked at her and told her: "Yvette, I'm really happy you asked me to be with you tonight. Thank you." She put her arms through his and hugged him around his middle and said: "Harry you're such a nice person. I'm so glad you came. *"Vous avez un bon Coeur."* She told him you have a good heart. She hugged him again and felt his muscular body and wondered about where this would lead. Then she stepped back and took his arm again as they continued on.

The proprietor, who was in on the surprise, met them as they entered. He led them to the back of the restaurant where there was an alcove and a room that was reserved for parties such as this. Of course, Harry didn't know. He had never been to this place so when Yvette walked through the alcove and he followed everyone shouted surprise and they sang Happy Birthday.

Harry was overwhelmed. He had made many friends in the past and many people had been very kind to him, like Kathleen, Jeanne, Gaunter, all the people of the circus and many others he really owed his life to, and he remembered them all and loved them but this was different. These people were not his protectors or his teachers or his trainers, these people were his friends. They like him just because he was Harry. He didn't think they even knew his last name.

He could hardly speak and a small tear of joy started to swell in his eyes. Adrian was standing near and he reached out for Harry's hand and shook it and kept on shaking it until Harry had control of himself. When they finished singing, they were all quiet and Harry looked at them all one by one and simply said: Thank you, "merci." But when he said it, they could all tell how much he meant it. Then they all crowded around and shook his hand and wished him "Bonne Chance," and told him how well he did in the show. Some said how happy they were that he had joined the group and all were very nice to him and they had a great time.

Adrian, remembering that Lousier told him Harry knew how to juggle, brought three balls from home. After they had finished the cake, he gave Harry the balls and asked him to show them how to juggle. He was very good at juggling but with just the three balls he couldn't do much but he did toss them over his back and under his leg and a few other tricks, which they all enjoyed.

They didn't stay too long. It was getting late so they all said their goodnights to one another and to Harry. Soon there was just Harry and Yvette. He told her he would take her home in a taxi and they had better leave.

It wasn't always the easiest thing to get a taxi at night on any of the side streets and they had to wait out front for a while before one came around. They could have walked up to the boulevard for one but Harry used the time to tell Yvette how overwhelmed he was about the surprise and how much he adored the cast, all of them. He explained to her that he had never had the experience of being together in a group of people of his own age having not gone to a public school. He said that he didn't know if he was missing anything not doing so but after tonight it made him wonder just a little bit.

In the taxi Yvette took Harry's hand in hers. He was still a little reluctant and wondered if he should be more aggressive. That wasn't his way, but when she took his hand he pulled it up to his lips and kissed it and told her that this was a night he would never forget. He had turned to her to say it and when he finished she reached up and kissed him. It was the first time a girl his own age had ever kissed him. She kissed him one the lips, beautifully and tenderly. He took his free hand and caressed her cheek then brought her chin back up to his lips and kissed her again, a long and tender kiss. She put her arm around his neck like she would never let go.

The taxi driver was telling them for the second time that they had arrived at her house before they realized he was even talking to them. They broke off and felt a little embarrassed. Harry paid the taxi and let him go. On the porch where Yvette lived and with a little privacy, he kissed her goodnight. She held him tightly and said: "I'll never forget tonight Harry, never."

It was a long walk back to his apartment in the center of town, but Harry was walking on air and he didn't even think about it.

He was still in a kind of a trance the next morning when Kathleen knocked on his door. She was anxious to tell him how much she and Jeanne had enjoyed the show, especially him. They wanted to know how the date went. She didn't ask just like that. She said: "did you have a good time last night after the show?" Harry's eyes filled, his throat got a little catch in it. He cleared it and looked at Kathleen with an expression that she had never seen on his face before. She couldn't tell right away if he was sad or swooning. She could tell that something had happened to affect Harry in a way that nothing ever did before.

CHAPTER VI

Yvette

He started telling her about the surprise at the restaurant. He went into great detail mentioning something about almost everyone who was there, explaining who they were and what part they played in the show, even to the stage crew. He became more animated as he kept going. Then Kathleen asked him if he came right home after the party? He hesitated a moment and then told her: "No, I took Yvette home. I was telling her how much I enjoyed being with her and what a great evening it was and she kissed me." Kathleen thought for a moment, then realizing that this might have been his first kiss, sat down on the bed beside him and put her hand on his shoulder and said: "Were you surprised?" "Yes!" That was his only reply.

"You shouldn't have been surprised. You are a beautiful boy, a wonderful young man in every way. There will most likely be many girls who will want to kiss you. Did you like it?"

"Yes!" he said, softly, a little shy. "Did you kiss her back?

"Yes!" in an even softer voice, almost a whisper.

Kathleen laughed, a knowing laugh, thinking of her first kiss. She pulled Harry to her and hugged him and said: "You deserve the very best my love. You are going to be a great success, but don't forget that a great success only means that you are happy with what you get out of life, to do the things you want to do, to take pride in the life you make for yourself."

She kissed him on the cheek and held him at arm's length and asked him when he was going to see Yvette again. He said that they didn't have any plans but that they were all going to meet again on the next Saturday to talk about the next show. He said: "I think I'll probably see her there."

"I'll tell you what I think we should do. Let's invite Yvette and we'll all go to a nice restaurant for dinner, perhaps the Etoile! What do you say? Then we can meet Yvette too." He gave a resounding, *"Oui"! Vraiment, quand?* He was excited and wanted to know how soon.

Harry worked out extra hard during that week and when he was running in the mornings all he could think of was Yvette. He had a hard time concentrating on his studies and both Lousier and Faggio asked him if he was feeling OK? He didn't admit what the trouble was. He just said yes, he was OK just dreaming a little.

Saturday morning didn't come fast enough. He wanted to run all the way to the theatre, but he didn't want to get all sweaty. So he forced himself to walk at a normal pace, but he was still early. No one was there yet and he had to wait almost ten minutes. It seemed like an hour.

First came Adrian. He shook Harry's hand and asked him how he was and if he survived the party last Saturday. He said he had a wonderful time, one that he will never forget and thanked Adrian again for making it happen. All the while he was watching for Yvette. Some of the others came, and they went inside. Harry didn't want to go inside preferring to stay and wait for Yvette but he felt that Adrian and the others would think it strange because they were all asking him questions. They were sitting in the front rows of seats in the theatre when Yvette came in. She saw Harry sitting there and sneaked down and put her hands over his eyes and said, "Guess who Mr. Birthday?"

Harry knew of course but he just sat there with a big grin on his face and didn't seem to be able to say anything. Finally he said hello with a kind of crackly voice. Yvette came around and extended her greetings to everyone and gave Adrian a peck on each cheek as was their custom.

Harry wished he could kiss her like he did in the taxi. He fantasized how he could just take her in his arms and tenderly kiss those beautiful lips. The fellow sitting next to him was asking him a question and he didn't even hear him until he nudged him. He came out of his trance and was a little embarrassed. The fellow was asking him what he got for his birthday.

He started to answer by saying that "His mothers bought him" and they all stopped him and asked him what he meant by "his mothers." They were rather confused. So Harry said that he thought he was one of the luckiest fellows to have two lovely ladies who had taken care of him since 1918 when he was only 12 years old. How they had kept him safe in Belgium until the war was over. He said he never knew his real mother, but he loved Jeanne and Kathleen as if they were his real mothers, so he just got in the habit of calling them "my mothers." When he finished the story, even though he left out an awful lot, his friends just seemed to be stunned. No one said anything right away, and Harry was beginning to think that he shouldn't have told them anything. Then Adrian and Yvette, almost in unison, and with wet eyes, said, "What a wonderful story."

They laughed because their two minds had the same thought. The question about the birthday gifts were forgotten and they all talked for a few minutes then Adrian called them all together to get started on trying to decide on what they wanted to do for the next show.

When they all were ready to leave Yvette hung behind with Harry as they all left the theatre. They said bye-bye to everyone and Harry took Yvette's hand and led her in the opposite direction. After they had walked a little way, he said: "How would you like to go to dinner with my mothers and me?"

"What brought this on" she asked, in a nice, anxious way; anxious to know if he had asked his mothers to invite her. He said he told them the whole story about what a wonderful time he had and what a fine and beautiful girl you are. So Kathleen suggested it. "They are anxious to meet you."

"Well after the story you told us back there, I really want to meet them too, and I would love to go with you," she said, taking his hand. He got a taxi and took her home, but in the daylight he was too shy to try to kiss her, though he wanted to. He would just have to wait until he got her alone. He thought that people who displayed themselves that way on the streets degraded the women and make them look cheap and he didn't want that to happen to this wonderful girl. When they reached her house he told the taxi to wait. He got out and opened the door and squeezed her hand to say good-by but she reached up and kissed him like she did Adrian, only much sweeter. She smelled so good it was intoxicating. He paid the taxi and told the driver he wouldn't need him anymore.

Harry walked down to the Seine and sat on the steps just looking at the water, not even noticing the activity on the river. He wasn't really thinking much of anything. It was like being in a daze. He felt like he wanted to do something. He felt anxious, like he wanted to run but he didn't want to run. He just sat there for a long while. Finally, he decided he was really in love, and what's more he knew that Yvette loved him too.

He got up and began to walk. He was feeling a little better now, more sure of himself. He looked at his watch. It was almost five. Kathleen and Jeanne usually slept until around six depending on how late they worked. He rarely knew when they went to bed since he was always sleeping. He was anxious to get home and talk to them about the dinner.

When he entered the apartment Jeanne was in the kitchen making coffee. She had her hair fixed and her makeup on but she was still in a dressing gown that looked to him like she could wear it out to the finest restaurant. She was beautiful and he told her so.

She kissed him and hugged him and said, "Oh, thank you my sweet boy."

He didn't mind her calling him a boy even though he was nearly a man. At sixteen, he was like a man of about 30 for all his experiences but he was such a loving character. One would never think he was a very accomplished boxer. Jeanne said:

"Why don't you go say hi to Kathleen? She should be out of the bath now." "That's a good idea."

He knocked on the dressing room door. Kathleen said:

"Who is that knocking at my door?" She had heard his voice through the door talking to Jeanne.

"Your son!"

She opened the door. They hugged and they both laughed. She held him at arm's distance and said: "Well let me look at you. You're getting to be that big beautiful man we've been looking for." Harry loved her so much. He just looked at her with a big grin on his face and then he took her in his arms again and hugged her some more and said: "What a lucky guy:"

"Now what are we going to do about this little girl you picked up on the street? What was her name? Yvette?" She tried to look serious but it didn't work. Harry told her what Yvette said when he asked her about going to diner and then explained about how he had slipped up and said "my mothers," and had to explain about how he got to Paris and why he thought of them both as his mother. Jeanne was listening by this time and asked, "Did anyone make any remarks?"

He told them what they said and that some of them got a little teary eyed, "*Ils ont bon coeur*" he said, they all have a good heart.

Kathleen remembered how she first met Harry. There was such danger. At any time the soldiers could have come and taken him away or just shot him right there. No one would have asked anything about it, at least no one of authority. But Harry never seemed afraid. He would do as he was told without question. It was evident that he trusted us, and the others who were trying to help.

"Harry, she said, you are such a fine boy, were so proud of you. How is your boxing coming along?"

"Hero wants to schedule a fight for me, amateur of course but he did say I would get paid."

"Well who would you have to fight?"

"I don't know yet but hero said it would be someone in my same class. He said he thought I was ready to start my competition."

"How do you feel about it?" she asked.

"I will never know how good I am until I try, will I?"

"No, I guess not. If that's what you want to do, we'll be at ringside to cheer you on all the way."

"I knew you would."

He pulled her to him and kissed her and then did the same to Jeanne. Now Jeanne said:

"How about this diner we're going to? Where do you want to go?"

He thought for about one second and said: "I don't care where, you two decide. As long as I take Yvette, it doesn't matter." *"Ooh-ooh-la-la!"* Both Kathleen and Jeanne cried. "Do we have a crush or do we have a crush?"

Harry blushed a little, and it showed in his eyes how much he cared for this girl. "Remember what I said." I want her to meet you both. You will like her I know." Kathleen took his hand in hers and said:

"I want to tell you something now that may never have crossed your mind, and perhaps it never should have, but the world is a funny place and there are many people who have a lot of different ideas about life. I feel that I, we, should tell you that you may come into some embarrassing moments one day when you're out with Yvette." Harry looked a little stunned.

"Why, he asked? We never do anything that we should be embarrassed about."

Yes we know how much of a gentleman you are and we have no worries about your actions at any time. That's not the situation. You may some day run into someone who may make a remark about you", a black-being with a white girl."

Harry was shocked. He just looked at Kathleen and then at Jeanne and was unable to say anything for a time. His mothers felt so hurt that this was a reality they had to prepare him for. They had talked it over and decided that they must tell him, that all people do not accept a mixed relationship. Although it is wrong and is in the worst taste, someone may make remarks about it and it has been known that some get violent. So they felt they needed to warn him of this situation.

"I can't wipe it off," He said, making a gesture of swiping over his face. What must I do?"

It seemed as if he might start to cry. But Harry wasn't thinking about himself. He was thinking about Yvette and how embarrassed she might be and he didn't know how to take it, how to understand why a person would do such a thing.

"What would you do if something like this happened when you were out with Yvette?" Jeanne asked him.

Harry thought it over for quite a long while.

"Seems like the only thing to do is to ignore it if at all possible. I think if I said anything back and got into an argument it would only be more embarrassing to Yvette."

Kathleen and Jeanne were astounded. They grabbed him and hugged him and kissed him and said that that was the most intelligent and honorable thing he could do and they were so proud that he would think like that. "What a wonderful man you will be, no! You are."

The amateur boxing was held on Friday nights. The matches were held fairly early in the evening. They went three rounds and there were only six events. So they decided that after the fight it would be a good time to go to dinner since Yvette would be there to watch along with them. Everyone was in agreement and when Harry told Yvette, she was thrilled.

Yvette told everyone in the theatre group about the fight. They all wanted to go to help cheer Harry on. They were sitting just behind Kathleen, Jeanne, and Yvette. They all wanted to meet Harry's mothers. Adrian asked them if they would tell about some of the things that happened during the war. Both of them said that they didn't like to talk about it much, but yes, one day they could get together and they would tell them a little about what it was like.

Harry's event was the third. He was unknown of course, this being his first fight, so when he came into the ring there wasn't much applause, except for his friends, who made up for it. They applauded and yelled and whooped, and laughed. It made Harry feel good but almost embarrassed. He took notice of them from the ring and waved. His opponent was a young man of Harry's same age, just a little taller, and about the same weight. Hero made sure that Harry wasn't going to be put in jeopardy with some one that wasn't equal in all accounts except for their own ability. That would have to be Harry's concern. Actually, this was the other boy's second fight. He won his first in the month preceding.

After the formalities the bell rang and the fighters came out with caution. They circled a little and the opponent -Jacques-threw a left jab. Harry noticed that when he did he would drop his right just a little. He let him do that a couple more times then on the third try Harry came in with a left hook when Jacques dropped his right and caught him a pretty good blow to the chin.

Again, Harry saw that when he contacted with his left, Jacques left guard went up and it looked like he would be able to get a right in under it He waited until Jacques threw another left jab and then came in with a left hook as before then followed through with a right. It knocked him into the ropes, and he seemed a little dazed. The bell rang and they went to their corners. Harry's friends were cheering and he glanced down at Yvette. She put her hands together as if in prayer and looked at Harry with a look which said keep it up.

Harry did keep it up, and although Jacques landed a few good blows, it was very evident that it was Harry's fight and it was, with a unanimous decision. Hero told him before the fight not to try for any knockouts. Just get in there and get experience learning what the other man is doing. That's just what he did.

The gang waited for Harry to get dressed. They all wanted to congratulate him on his first fight and wish him well. They really liked Harry. He was the kind of person one liked to be around.

Kathleen told all of them that they were going to go have some dinner and they were all invited if they would like to come. But they thanked her and begged off saying that they had planned to go up to" Le Cirque" and play around and that they hoped to see Harry the next day at the theatre.

They got a cab and went to a nice cozy restaurant close to the Arc de Triomphe. They didn't have reservations but the maitre-d' knew both Kathleen and Jeanne very well and had no trouble finding them a nice table.

Yvette sat close to Harry. She put out her hand for Harry and said to them: "How about this man?" She stressed the word man.

Kathleen said: "You really did very well tonight. You didn't look like you even got tired."

"I didn't. It was really quite an easy fight. I imagine that when I have to go 9 or 10 rounds it will be a little different. But that's what the training is for, endurance, that's why I run a lot."

They had a lovely meal. The waiter was an Italian so Harry ordered in Italian. He knew the language very well. ...

It looked as if Faggio had done a good job. Actually Harry was now studying Spanish and only reviewing the Italian, working on the accents and the precise grammar. Kathleen and Jeanne told Harry that he should take Yvette home in a taxi and they would be on their way. Harry knew that it was time for them to go to work but there was no argument about taking Yvette home. Yvette said how much she enjoyed meeting them and thanked them for taking such good care of Harry, all the time holding on to his arm. The mothers liked Yvette sincerely. She wasn't a giggler. She spoke intelligently and she was beautiful. They hoped that Harry didn't get into trouble with her. They asked themselves, had they ever said anything to Harry about - the birds and the bees? Jeanne laughed and said: "I don't think so and Kathleen said "Me too!" They laughed, but thought they had better think about it seriously.

CHAPTER VII

Mothers' Concern

The next day when they awoke Jeanne came into Kathleen's bedroom all excited. "I have it" she said. Let's get Faggio to do it!, "To do what?"

"You know" Jeanne told her. "Faggio is one of my customers and I can ask him to tell Harry about - err - *sauvegarde*," (protection). Kathleen laughed, but she said: "Do you think it would be better than us doing it? How about Lousier? I think Lousier is more of a friend. Faggio is more like just a teacher. Sure they're friends, but you know Harry confides in Lousier. Remember he was the one that got him started with that theatrical group in the first place:"

"Yes you-re right about that, will you ask him?" Jeanne said.

"Of course I will. I'm sure he will be happy to do it and I really do think it is better if a man tells him. You know how easily Harry gets embarrassed!" Kathleen sent a note to Lousier asking him to meet her for an early dinner at "Le Vieux Gaulois," on rue Faubourg Montmartre. It wasn't a fancy place at all, but the food was excellent.

They served a "Choucroute Jambon" (Pork and Sauerkraut), that was the best to be found anywhere in the world.

Kathleen hadn't told Lousier what she wanted to talk to him about. He was a little anxious to meet with her, and yet he was hoping that she wasn't going to tell him that she was going to send Harry to another tutor or something like it. But this was a beautiful woman he was going to have dinner with. And he wanted to look his best. He remembered that when he first met her he was wearing his casual suit of tweeds. He really looked like an outdoorsman, a hunter. It was his appearance he thought that actually resulted in their initial conversation. So he decided that he would wear something of the same, only of course, a new suit he had recently purchased. He made sure his shoes were shined and that he smelled good. A bath and bay rum took care of that as far as he was concerned.

Waiting for her in the cafe, he rose when she entered wearing a gorgeous long dress that was cut a little low at the bust line but discretely, high heel pumps and an embroidered vest that just fell open loosely. She made a striking picture. Lousier beckoned her to the table he had taken as far away from the door as possible. The cafe had tables that were long enough for six or even eight people to sit at comfortably, family style, and it was common for people to occupy the same table whether they knew anyone at the table or not. Lousier hoped that no one would try to do that this evening although it really wasn't actually evening, it was only five in the afternoon.

They sat across from one another. The restaurant always had "du pain" (bread cut pieces of the traditional "baguette noire). There was also a jar of delicious mustard and one could eat all they wanted of it. Lousier offered the basket to Kathleen and she took some of the bread and spread it with the mustard, and mentioned that this was one thing that she enjoyed coming here for, aside from the rest of the menu.

There was only one other couple in the cafe sitting across the room so Kathleen thought it would be best to get started with the reason for the rendezvous. "You know Yvette from the theatre group, don't you Lousier?" He said he did and that she was a very sweet girl.

"Yes we think so too. You know that Harry is madly in love with her?" And she grinned a little.

"Well I knew that they were seeing one another and I could see that Yvette cared a great deal for Harry. But they all like Harry very much".

"Yes, I know." she said. "Yvette is the reason I wanted to see you today."

"Oh!" He murmured and raised an eyebrow, a little puzzled.

"We don't want her to get into trouble. Harry, by every indication is a virgin and we don't think he knows much about sex. At their age their affection is for one another. We believe that anything (she stressed the word) could happen."

Lousier was beginning to feel strangely excited. This was a very sexy lady and her blue eyes looked at him when she spoke like she was talking about them. She was making him a little nervous when the waiter came to take their order.

Lousier was relieved for the break in the conversation. He didn't want Kathleen to see that he was getting "hot under the collar" She continued after they ordered.

"You and Harry are very close. He thinks the world of you, and for that matter we do also. We think it would be better if you, instead of Jeanne and I, would advise him of the dangers of sexual intercourse without the proper protection."

Lousier just about swallowed his tongue. He was really upset now and could hardly speak. He was starting to get an erection and he already felt embarrassed. He was just able to say "mmmmmuh."

Kathleen continued, not noticing how her conversation was affecting Lousier. With every word he would fantasize that the conversation was about him and this beautiful woman. She, on the other hand was quite matter of fact.

"You might find it a little hard to get into the conversation with him but I'm sure that if you can just be straightforward and brief, yet to the point, he will understand that you would only be advising him of something for his own good, but especially for Yvette. That is what you must stress, for the good of Yvette. For sure you wouldn't want her to get into trouble and ruin her reputation? You can tell him like that. He thinks so much of her; he will be appreciative to know how to avoid it."

The food came. Lousier still didn't speak. He couldn't, so he just started eating. Kathleen took a couple of bites and went on saying that she would give Lousier money to purchase some lamb skin and he could show or tell Harry how to use it. Lousier almost spit out his food. Kathleen finally realized what was happening to Lousier and said, "Oh! Lousier I am so sorry, I have embarrassed you. Please forgive me." She reached over and touched his hand and her eyes were so beautiful and her voice was so soft and "*sympathique.*"

He murmured, "*Ce la ne fait rien,* but he could hardly get it out.

She argued with him but he insisted on paying the bill. She had earlier put several franks in an envelope, much more than it would take to purchase the sheep skins, but she felt it was justified.

She told him that she knew it might not be easy to broach the subject and if he didn't want to do it she would understand. "However, it might be better and easier if you let him believe that you, as another man, were simply concerned with his well-being and safety. It's better than coming from his mothers, don't you think so?" Lousier thought that would definitely be the best way to go about it. Now he was beginning to compose himself. Slowly he continued. He told her that he didn't think it would be too hard to get around to it. He said that he had really come to love Harry. "How could anyone help it? He is a wonderful individual. These days it is really surprising that a boy or a man of 17 was still, err, a virgin. And as well, that this is his first romance incredible."

"Yes," she said, "that is why we think this is very important."

Walking home, Lousier was fantasizing about what it would be like to have Kathleen in his bed, with those soft features, beautiful lips, and her warm smile. He shook as if he had a sudden chill. He had to get her out of his mind he thought. He stopped at a club called the "*Nidi Vedette*" to have an aperitif. A little absinthe might soothe his nervousness but then he remembered that it was an accepted knowledge that absinthe was an aphrodisiac, so he decided he didn't need that now. He just had Pernod.

Thinking about how he was going to advise Harry about what he should do to protect Yvette. He slowly got Kathleen off his mind.

Their arrangement of Harry's schooling would be coming to an end in a little over a year. He had gone through everything but advanced math, calculus and trigonometry. But neither he nor his mothers thought he would need anything more than the advanced math since he had no preoccupation with any kind of engineering. He was an athlete, an entertainer and an actor and that was enough. His schooling that they had seen to was centered on these vocations in his life. He was just about as perfect in his grammar in every language he had studied as he could be. The effort to learn any other language now would be quite easy. He now knew Latin, English, French, German, Spanish and Italian. During one of their sessions in history, which Lousier had purposely designed to lead into the subject of health, they were recounting the terrible waste of human life for different reasons after war years such as there is now.

They discussed the famine, the pestilence and hunger, and then they got onto to the topic of sexually transmitted disease. Lousier pointed out that sexual disease was almost as bad as any other scourge that could be named. Many people didn't even know about the various diseases transmitted this way and more so, how they could be avoided. This subject gave Lousier a chance to discuss the use of the sheepskin and he did so with elaborate discourse. When he was sure that Harry understood exactly everything about it, why and when it should be used, he also explained that people who didn't want to have children could keep a girlfriend or a wife from getting pregnant by using this method. He went into the whole issue of how the eggs of the man made their way into the woman's womb and fertilized her eggs. And as well he said what a terrible thing it was that some young girls who had thought to have an abortion died because of infection that no one seemed to know how to avoid.

He also said that any young man with a girlfriend whom he cared for should always carry these sheep skins with him at all times, especially when he knows he is going to be with his girl. When loving a girl, kissing and touching, it can very easily lead into the sex act, especially if the girl loves the man too. He said a man aroused, has no conscience, so better be prepared.

This was the first time Harry had known about all of these things; about how a woman becomes pregnant and contacts disease. Sure he had heard about gonorrhoea. He read about it in some text at one time or another but it didn't mean much to him at the time. It was nothing that touched his life then, at least he didn't think so, and it just passed over him.

Lousier said to Harry in a quiet moment: "Perhaps you should have some of these sheep skins for yourself, just in case?"

It was the first time Harry had considered this conversation, the class, or study had anything to do with him. He was stunned and looked at Lousier and said quizzically, "What do you mean?"

"*Alors*! You have a beautiful girl that I think you love her very much, Yvette, is that not so?"

A little reluctantly he said: "*Oui, bien sur*," almost in a whisper. Lousier knew he was thinking about it very hard. He gave him time then said in a fatherly tone: "You wouldn't want anything bad to happen to her would you? -Still in a whisper.- Harry said: "*Non!*"

"You also have a great future ahead of you. The way you're going you could be the next middleweight champion of Europe, maybe the light heavyweight. And how about your acting career? One day you may be a famous name on the stage. If you aren't careful you could wind up married and a father long before you plan to and it could have big repercussions on any of your endeavors."

He said these things in a soft tone and with much compassion. Harry knew that he cared. Lousier Went on: "You are a man now. You're almost finished with your schooling, and you are very intelligent. You don't want anything to disrupt your future and I'm certain that you don't want anything to happen to Yvette."

Lousier put his hand on Harry's shoulder and said: "I'll tell you what I'll do. Let me get you a couple of these skins to carry with you just in case, how about it?"

Harry was a little embarrassed now and didn't look at Lousier, but he said: "Maybe it's a good idea." Lousier couldn't help himself. He grabbed Harry and hugged him and said: "I never had any qualms about the kind of a man you are. I knew you would understand." Finally, Harry said: "Well, was all this just for my benefit?"

Not angry, but wondering. "In the beginning, it was just another lesson, but as I got into the subject I thought it might be a good time to bring it up. After all, I introduced you to the Little Theatre group and practically to Yvette as well. I don't want anything bad to happen to either one of you, especially you, and really didn't know how much you knew. It's just because I have grown to love you like a son. If I ever do have one, I would want him to be just like

Harry was scheduled for another fight the next month, which was only two and one half weeks away. He was training a little harder now than he usually did, working on the bag and pumping some weights.

"Not too much" Hero said, "but enough to get some weight behind those punches."

Hero told him that he didn't want his muscles to get hard, like a weight lifter. He wanted them to stay long and supple. That was where his speed was. Reaction was most important, and the speed to carry it out was where Harry excelled.

Yvette said, of course she would be at the fight. She didn't intend to miss any of them. "My event isn't until the last one, so we will be eating a little late. I want you to go to dinner with me afterwards, if you can?"

"*Avec plaisir monsieur,*" she said with a laugh.

There was no knockout but Harry won easily on points. Hero said that was OK! Winning is what it was all about and the knockouts would come later.

Kathleen and Jeanne were also there and they sat with Yvette and cheered Harry on with abandonment. It was very exciting, especially because he was winning. Harry was on pins and needles over his date with Yvette. He hadn't seen her in over a week, and the sheepskins in his pocket that Lousier gave him made him bum with desire, yet confusion. He was actually afraid somehow and he couldn't put his finger on it but he thought it was because he was so afraid something bad might happen to Yvette or that she might get mad at him if he made the wrong advances to her. What to do?

They went back to the little restaurant by the Arc de Triomphe, where they went the last time with his mothers. The food was good and it was very cozy. Harry called before hand and asked the Maitre d' to reserve a table in a cozy corner for two. "*Certainement monsieur* Harry! Anything for you" he said.

Harry was well dressed, as usual, and Yvette looked like she had just stepped out of a billboard marquee. They had a lovely dinner with small talk sitting across from one another. Harry couldn't take his eyes off of her. He was attentive to every word she had to say, a lot of how well he looked in the ring, but it just went over his head. He was concentrating on her eyes, her lips and the sound of her voice, not much of what she was saying. A violinist was playing beautiful music, which added greatly to the ambiance. He asked the waiter for the check, who replied, "*Oui Monsieur, tout de suite*"

While they waited for it to come, Harry reached across the table and took Yvette's hand, took a deep breath and asked her: "Would you, I mean do you think you might like to come and see where I live?" He was immediately embarrassed, thinking he hadn't said it very well. "To your home?" She asked.

"It's an apartment we call home but part of it is separate and private and it's all mine."

"I think I would like that," she said in a soft voice that did exude a little excitement

He called the waiter and paid the bill. The waiter thanked him and said he hoped to see them again soon as he helped Yvette with her chair. Harry held her coat for her and they took a taxi to Montmartre and rue Bergere. They just lived a few steps from the corner, but since Harry always entered from the rear stairs, he had to explain to Yvette that his private living quarters only had the entrance and that was from the rear of the building. It was clean and there was light.

Kathleen had the concierge install two lights to illuminate the entrance at the side of the building and one over the stairs for Harry when he came in at night and made sure that he, the concierge, kept it clean. Harry wasn't embarrassed to take Yvette this way to his quarters. In fact, he was rather proud that he had his own place and he could come and go as he pleased. Jeanne and Kathleen never had any reason to restrict Harry from doing whatever he wanted when he wanted to. They felt he was too busy to get into any trouble and he didn't have any propensity to get into trouble anyway. He was explaining this to Yvette, about the kind of "confidence" they all had in each other, and how they respected one another's privacy, and in so many words, how much he loved them.

"You have come through a lot Harry and your mothers have taken very good care of you. I think I know how you must feel about them. We are much the same way in my family. My father is a diplomat with the government. He is a very busy man. I don't get to see him every day like you do your mothers. She had learned to say mothers rather easily, strange as it seemed. He has to travel quit often but when we are all together, with my mom, we have a good time, and I love them very much."

Harry helped Yvette off with her coat grabbing it by the shoulders as he was facing her. As it slid down over her arms they were very close and she reached up and kissed him. He was surprised but her lips were warm and tender as she put her arms around him. He let the coat drop onto the chair and held her close to him. With her arms around his neck, they kissed for a long, loving embrace. Harry was getting excited and she could feel him. He wasn't pressing into her. In fact it was more that she was holding herself close to him. When they broke, still holding herself close to him, she looked into his eyes and with a gentle smile said: "Aren't you going to show me your home like you promised?"

He looked at her as if he didn't hear her for a brief moment. Then, a little flustered, he relaxed his hold on her said: "But yes! *Mais oui*. I did say I wanted you to see my place."

It was a large room. Generally bedrooms as well as most other rooms in an apartment were rather small but this one was large. It was one of the reasons that his mothers had taken it and they had stayed here instead of moving. They could afford a home if they wanted, but for the convenience, both for them and for Harry, and the fact that he had this privacy, they had stayed.

It was neat and clean, everything in place. On one wall he had papered a map of Europe, taking in all the areas included in the war just passed. He had pinpointed those areas where he had grown up and the path that the resistance fighters took when they brought him out of Germany. It was a map made of enlarged pieces put together with great care to look as if it was all one piece.

On a table he had two pictures, one of his father and one of his real mother. She asked who they were, knowing very well that they must be his parents. He told her that he never knew his mother, and how she had died at his birth. How he loved his father, and what a great thing it was that he had brought him to Europe as a small boy. He showed her his American passport. As far as he knew, he was still an American. He had no idea however, what it meant be to be an American or what it would be like to live in America. He hoped one day to have the experience of going there and seeing what it was all about. He had read newspapers from New York since he always spoke English. America was a very foreign place to him and he figured that he was a very fortunate young man to have been where he had been and done what he had done and he owed most of it, especially his survival, to his mothers Jeanne, and Kathleen. Their pictures were hung on the wall in framed enlargements, one blow-up of their heads and one blow-up of the full body, each one separate. They were dressed in rich clothes and they looked like models, right out of a fashion magazine. Yvette looked at them for a long time. Finally she said, "They are so beautiful!" Harry turned her toward him. He cupped her chin in his hand and said: "Yes, I know, just like you" as he kissed her again.

Without taking his lips from hers, he reached down and picked her up gently and carried her to his bed. He stood there, before laying her down. He looked at her for some time and she looked at him, as if to say, "I'm yours."

He put her down on the bed ever so gently and sat down beside her. Looking at her, he took her hand in his and asked her in almost a whisper, "Do you think we should do this?"

She reached up and took him by the shirt and gently pulled him to her and said in a barely audible voice, "Yes." Then she kissed him.

He said: "Maybe you would like to make yourself more comfortable while I excuse myself for a moment?"

He went to his bathroom and took off his clothes. He cleaned himself on the bidet first. He fitted the sheepskin on himself as he was instructed and when he thought all was ready, he put his trunks back on. He glanced at himself in the full-length mirror not to see how handsome he was, or what a beautiful body he had. He wasn't over built like a weight lifter but his body was well proportioned and very firm. His skin was smooth, like satin. No, He only wanted to see if he looked presentable for Yvette. She had seen him in his boxing trunks, but now he was in his underwear and he was concerned that he was not in any way repulsive to her.

When he returned to his bedroom she had removed all her clothes, turned down the covers and climbed into bed. Harry was afraid he was going to be embarrassed because the sight of her in his bed obviously excited him so much.

He turned down the covers a little and sat down beside her again, reached down and kissed her, all the while removing the covers from her breasts and taking one of them tenderly in his hand. She began breathing hard and their kiss became intensive. He asked her,

"Do you mind if I look at you?"

She just shook her head. "No"! He rose up a little and began to pull the covers down little by little. When he reached her navel he stopped and kissed her breasts, first one and then the other, ever so tenderly caressing them with his mouth and his tongue. A more experienced woman would have thought that he had done this many times and perfected the art of lovemaking. Harry was naturally a very tender man and he loved this girl so much that his one ambition was to make their lovemaking the best he could for her although he felt like he was going to explode any minute.

He threw the rest of the covers completely off the bed. She looked like a young goddess laying there looking at him. She held out her hand to him and said: "Come, take off your underwear, and lie here beside me". She turned to him as he lay down, kissing him while running her hand over his cheek and down his stomach until she reached his manhood. She felt the sheep skin and asked him what it was. He explained that this was what he had been instructed to use to prevent her from becoming pregnant.

"How did you find out about it?"

He told her that he had read about it. He didn't want to say it was Lousier since they both knew him, and she might be embarrassed or even angry by it.

She took his hand and put it between her legs. He caressed her and she did the same to him. She was very wet and breathing heavily. She pulled him over onto her, raised her legs, and guided him into her. With the utmost care he entered her. He was afraid he might hurt her so he was very gentle, she, making most of the action.

Their loving was warm and fulfilling. She held him there for a long time after, not wanting to break their union. He couldn't say anything. He just kissed her and eventually rolled himself off of her and she followed tuning on her side, all the while caressing one another. They stayed there a long time, not saying anything. Yvette was the first to move.

Harry felt like a different person, more mature somehow although he was never like many other young people his age but rather acting more responsible and grown up. Now he seemed to have an inner confidence that he hadn't noticed before.

After he took Yvette home that night, he walked all the way home. It was good therapy because his heart was still pounding when he kissed her good night. But when he finally climbed into bed, he was asleep before his head hit the pillow.

It was good that it wasn't one of the days he went to the gym otherwise he would have been late. He didn't awaken until nine o'clock the next morning. He jumped out of bed and took a quick shower. He forgot that it was Saturday, and he didn't have anything to do, so he decided to go for a run. Just an easy jog that always made him feel alive. Of course, Yvette was on his mind. She just kept popping in and out. Pictures, lovely pictures.

By the end of his run he had more or less settled down. He took another good long shower. He had taken the sheep skin along on his run and dropped it into a trash can in an alley way along his path. He rather had mixed feelings about parting with it, thinking of its place in his life.

It was nearly noon after he dressed and was tidying up his room when Kathleen knocked on his door. When he opened the door and saw her standing there. He grabbed her and kissed her and said: "I love you". Good morning, good afternoon." She laughed and kissed him back.

They all went out and had a late breakfast. Harry was surprised how hungry he was and his mothers noticed it also. He was more talkative than usual, and seemed to be almost giddy. He hadn't mentioned anything about the fight the night before, but they finally said that they thought he was magnificent and they asked how Yvette enjoyed it. He stopped for an instant with his fork poised in mid air when they mentioned her name and a dreamy look came over him. He just sat there for a minute rather like he was in a daze, then finally he said, "Oh! She was thrilled."

They asked him where they went to eat and he told them and also said again how good the food was and what they ate. He remarked as to how nice it was to have the violinist playing all the while. Yvette liked it there. Then he stopped talking about last night and changed the subject. Jeanne and Kathleen looked at one another across the table. It was evident that they both had come to the same conclusion as to why Harry was acting the way he was. Jeanne put her hand on his and said: "So you had a nice time last night?" "Oh yes!" was all he said.

They figured they acted at just the right time. Harry was very precious to both of them. "So when is your next fight," Jeanne asked?

"Hero is negotiating a bout for me next month with a fellow from Nice. They say he is quite good and on his way for the contender of the title. He has seen this fellow fight and thinks that I shouldn't have any trouble staying with him but he is good and I have to work out a little harder especially on my punch. Hero says my punch is not powerful enough but he doesn't want to put any more weight on me. I'm almost classed as a light heavy weight now. He says if I grow any more, then I will be in the light heavy weight class and then I will have to put on more weight, only not too much. If 1 put on too much weight it might slow me down and the speed is where my advantage is."

Two nights later Harry was in his room. It was about ten thirty. He was reading an Italian magazine that Faggio had given him to read. Said it was better than studying out of school books because he would find language of different varieties that would help him to recognize patterns of conversation by normal people in normal circumstances, as opposed to the strict grammatical phrases found in the language books. It was difficult to concentrate because he wanted to see Yvette tonight but she was busy with her parents and couldn't make it. He hadn't met her parents yet and wondered what kind of people they were or if they would like him. He tried to imagine how they would look.

Suddenly he heard a loud bang against the door that led into his mother's part of the house. Curious, he went to the door and as he approached he heard a cry and another slam-bang against the door. Then he heard a man's voice. Normally he never went to their part of the house at night but he was afraid something terrible was wrong and one of his mothers might be in trouble. He opened the door and found Kathleen slumped against it, crying and holding her head. Her hair was all disarray and she looked frightened. She was dressed in her evening wear but it was torn. There was a man standing a few feet away. His coat was off and thrown on the floor and his tie was hanging loose but otherwise he was fully dressed and he had the look of rage. His face was flushed and he was panting.

Chapter VIII

Reality

As Harry bent down to help Kathleen she said: "Oh, Harry you shouldn't be here, I'm all right. It will be all right."

About that time the man, a little taller than Harry, started toward them. His fists were clenched and he was saying something but Harry couldn't quite make out what it was. It was more like just someone ranting, and not making any sense. Harry could see that he was going to try to hit Kathleen again, or perhaps him, he wasn't sure, but on instinct he rose up and caught the man a blow on the nose. The man fell and Harry was on top of him. He was dazed and his nose started to bleed. Harry caught him by the front of his shirt, and told him:

"I don't know what's going on here but you're going to leave and if you ever touch my mother again, you won't be able to walk, or talk."

Harry picked up the man's coat, threw it at him and pushed him toward the door. He never said a word after Harry hit him.

He went to Kathleen who was sitting on the couch now and sat beside her. He asked her if she was hurt.

"Aside from a probable black eye no. I am so sorry Harry. This man was a sadist. Do you know what that is?"

"Not exactly."

"It's someone who enjoys hurting people."

"Oh, yes I think I remember reading about it."

"Do you want me to get you something for your eye?"

"I'll just put a cold compress on it. If it's going to be black, there is nothing I can do to stop it, but the cold compress should keep the swelling down."

"I'll get it for you," he said.

He started to get up, she held on to him and kissed him on the cheek and said:

"My big wonderful protector, thank you."

"He'd better not try to hurt you again. You be careful, will you?"

She wanted to say something further to him, to tell him how much she appreciated the fact that he never questioned her or Jeanne about their work. They knew, and he knew, that it was dangerous. And even though the French government allowed it to exist with some reservations, it still didn't take much to be arrested, if some 'client' complained to the gendarmes.

So far, they had both been very fortunate not to have to discuss their business with Harry, or anyone else for that matter. They had always chosen their client's from classy people and they otherwise always acted like the finest ladies. They had made a lot of money. Most of their expenditures were on clothes and Harry's needs and they both felt that he deserved all that they gave him. In turn he made them know that he appreciated it. One day, not long after this incident, and before Harry's scheduled fight, Kathleen told Harry that they were all going to take a trip to Nice. Harry got excited and said that he had often wanted to go there and see what it was like and that he knew some friends at the gym from there.

Kathleen told him that they were going there to look at some farm property they heard about that they could get. Harry was a little taken aback. He immediately thought about Yvette. Would they be moving there? How soon? And many other thoughts popped into his mind. If we decide to purchase a farm, "a farm?" thinking to himself, what are we going to do on a farm? When he said it out loud Kathleen said, "Yes, it is a farm, but not a cow farm. It really is a vineyard, a grape vineyard, it's 10 hectares, about 25 acres. There is a home on it that is built like a castle, not as big they say, but very nice, and we can get it quite cheap. The owner is an old friend of mine. He is rather old and hasn't much of a family. Actually only a distant cousin who is in Hungary and has never been to France and they don't even know one another. We would take it from him but he will be allowed to live in it until he dies whether we move into it or not. That's the deal, and it sounds pretty good to me. What do you say my loves?" Jeanne already knew about the plan and thought it was great hut Harry became excited and didn't really know what to say except, "Maybe we should go have a look!"

"OK, then after your fight we'll get on the train and go see what it's all about."

Harry was training hard. He was doing the same running and workouts but he was working extra hard on his punch on the body bag and hero told him that he was doing much better and emphasized how important it was to have enough of a good punch to knock down his opponent. He might worry him to death, but that didn't always win fights, so he kept working harder and harder all the time.

One day about one week before the fight Yvette came to see him at the gym. She didn't go into the gym where Harry was working so as not to disturb him, rather she waited in the entryway down stairs. She didn't have to wait long because she knew about when he finished with his workouts and that's about the time she arrived. When he came down the stairs, tired, he saw her and it was as if he had had a shot of energy. He practically leaped down the rest of the stairs. She had on casual clothes, and carried some books in her hands but her hair was in that sort of disarray, not messy or undone, but like someone who had just come from the beauty parlor, and had walked into a gentle wind. She smiled and Harry's heart sank. He just looked at her for a moment, and then said:

"Gee, it's good to see you, come on let's walk."

They went out into the early evening twilight. He asked her if she had to get home any time soon.

"Not right away she said, I want to be with you as long as possible, but I won't be able to stay too long.

"Come on lets go up by the *Sacre Coeur*. It's beautiful this time of day and it's almost like being alone."

"I'd like that," she said.

"How did you happen to come over here today?" he asked.

"I haven't seen you in three weeks and I was thinking you might forget me, she teased."

He stopped walking and went over and leaned against one of the old iron hitching posts that were installed at various places along the rue de Faubourg Montmartre. They were used to tie up the horses of the horse-drawn delivery beer and milk wagons.

"Don't you know that all I have been able to think about is you? I eat, sleep, train, everything I do has your name on it."

Kiddingly he said, "You've put a spell on me!" "Come on" she said, and took his hand.

They went out on the platform in front of the cathedral and stood looking out over the city from the great wall surrounding the terrace. There were few people around. Harry leaned on the wall with his hands on each side of her and stood close. He put his head close to hers and kissed her lightly on the ear and said: "That view is almost as beautiful as you are!" Turning to him she said:

"I missed you so much. I had to see you, I couldn't wait any longer."

"Yvette, if you knew how I have missed you. I just couldn't get away. You know I have been training very hard for my upcoming bout. You're going to be there aren't you?"

"You know I wouldn't miss it but I'm always afraid you're going to get hurt."

"It's always a possibility of course, but you know I could get hurt just as easy walking down these streets or up a flight of stairs. At least in the ring I know what to expect. Hero says he thinks this fellow is a good match. I may not win but he doesn't think this guy can hurt me unless of course he gets in a very lucky punch."

The day before the fight Harry just did a light workout and rested mostly, but the night of the fight, about one hour before, he warmed up good, all alone, concentrating on his strategy. When they told him it was time, he was ready. Hero didn't talk to him any after that. He knew not to break his concentration with a lot of talk. They knew what the routine was so there was no need to go over it.

They were called to the center of the ring and given instructions but Harry didn't hear what the referee said. He already knew what he would say. Hero had told him the day before. He was just looking at his opponent, yet still not seeing him, just looking through him, seeing all of him, but none of him. It was like he was in a trance, yet he was sagacious, mentally acute, ready to spring, like a panther.

The bell rang and Harry was in the center of the ring before anyone knew it. His opponent danced to the left, threw a jab with his left and Harry hit him about three times with his left as the man left an opening, then Harry followed through with a hard right, and the man went down.

He wasn't knocked out, but he was so dazed he couldn't find his bearings and finally sat up, but was just gazing back and forth while the referee counted him out. They had to help him up and walked him out of the ring. He was still woozy when he got to his dressing room but he wasn't really hurt. Even if he had gotten up it would have been a TKO. Harry was a big winner and the crowd cheered him all the way to his dressing room.

His mothers and Yvette followed after just a few minutes. They went to the dressing room but waited outside until Harry told Hero to look and see if they were there. Hero let them in and went out into the hall for a few minutes to let them all be alone, but before he left he told them they could only stay a little, because Harry had to have a massage before he cooled down too much.

Harry told them he hoped that he hadn't hurt the fellow but he was happy to win. He said that he was really fighting someone else and not the fellow in the ring. He was looking straight at Kathleen when he said it, and she knew exactly what and who he was talking about. It was as if he was reliving that night in their apartment, and his anger came through with violence. Kathleen smiled at him and he knew that she got the message. Yvette was a little confused but didn't make a fuss about it. His mothers kissed him and said that they were going and they would see him tomorrow.

Jeanne said: "I guess you two will be going to dinner. I have another suggestion for you." She told them about another restaurant on the Rue du La Paix. It was just as cozy as the other one, and the food was superb.

They didn't talk much during the dinner but they couldn't stop looking at one another. There was a violinist serenading at the tables and Harry asked him to play for them while they were eating. The violinist asked him what he wanted to hear but Harry told him he didn't care, just something soft and melodious. Harry handed him a note that would be about what the musician would usually make in the whole night, so he was happy to stay and play beautiful music while Yvette and Harry enjoyed one another.

After Harry asked for the bill, Yvette put her hand on Harry's across the table and quietly said: "Do you think we can go to your place again?" Harry just squeezed her hand.

Their loving was just as good as the first time, perhaps even better. When Harry was holding her in his arms after enjoying one another Yvette said, "I have some terrible news to tell you and I don't want to, I never want to but I must." She began to sob.

Harry couldn't imagine what she was talking about, or why she was crying. He said: "Nothing could be too bad as long as we are together."

Chapter IX

Parting

"**That's just the problem. My** father is being sent to Algeria for the government for three years and I have to go with him and my mother."

"What? You can't go! Why are they taking you away? That's a dangerous country, you can stay here with me and we can get married!"

Harry was beside himself. He couldn't think straight. He held her tight as if not to ever let her go. She didn't say anything for some time, she was sobbing quietly and the tears were falling on Harry's chest.

"Don't cry my darling," he said, "we will have to think of something." They were still for a few moments. Harry finally asked:

"Do you think it's because of my color they are taking you away?" With total sincerity she said:

"No! I'm sure that they don't mind about your color. We have talked about it. I have told them about you. They saw you in the play we did, and they know about your boxing career. I'm sure that this is not happening because of our love. It is natural for a man in my father's position to have to go on assignment at one time or another. Actually we have been expecting it, but 1 was hoping that it wouldn't come so soon."

Harry held on to her and her to him. He reached for a towel and dried her tears. He kissed her. She kissed him back and they made love again. They didn't want it to end but last a long time.

For the next few days Harry was in a very sad mood. He used his workouts to vent his anger that such an event should take the thing he loved so much away from him. Finally when Kathleen said it was time that they should prepare to go to Nice, he told Kathleen he wanted to talk to her about something. She could see for the last few days that he wasn't himself. She was a little worried about what made him feel this way. She asked herself if maybe it could be something about either herself or Jeanne. She was a very attentive and sympathetic listener.

Somewhat relieved that it wasn't about them, she was very concerned about what Harry told her. She knew how much Harry loved Yvette and she was afraid of what he might do to keep from losing her. She assured him of her sympathy and told him that she would try to think of something. But for him not to forget that they were both young.

"Yvette wasn't going away forever. She might even come back before her father's work is finished there. You only have a few more months to finish your schooling then perhaps you can go and visit her." He looked at her for some time until what she had said sunk in.

"Yes! Of course, I could do that, couldn't I?" He felt better immediately. He got up and walked around talking. "I might even arrange to have Hero set up a boxing match there for me. Now wouldn't that be something?"

He was practically talking to himself and Kathleen was watching him. If he weren't so distraught it would be comical just to watch him. He would turn to her and pose a question but not wait for an answer, just keep on talking and walking.

In the gym the next day he told Hero that he thought he was ready for some real competition. He asked him how one got to travel to some fights in other countries? If they were considered professional or could he still compete in the amateur league? Hero said: "Whoa! Whoa! What is this all about? Why are you so anxious to travel to foreign rings? It can be quite dangerous you know. We don't always know about the opponent, and sometimes it is quite difficult to get the kind of information we need to protect you from getting hurt, especially at your age." Harry looked rather somber and said to him:

"It's not so much that I want to fight in a foreign land, not just any foreign land, I want to go to Algeria."

"*Mon Dieu*, is that all?" Hero was about to laugh but he could see that Harry was very serious and anxious, so he said he thought it would very difficult. Harry asked him, "You remember Yvette?"

"*Oui*!" "The girl that comes to the fights with my mothers?" "*Oui! Oui*! I know who she is!"

"OK! Her father is a diplomat and has to move there for three years and they are taking Yvette with them." He told Hero the whole story.

Hero could see the misery Harry was in about her having to leave. He said he would see what he could do, but warned that it wouldn't be easy and it might not be a good idea, but he would check into it anyhow. Harry grabbed him around his body pinning his arms to his side and said "Thank you Hero, thank you!"

Harry was only able to see Yvette one last time before they left and that was at the train depot. There was only Yvette and her parents. They had other relatives but none of them lived close to Paris, at least close enough to come for the farewell. Yvette introduced Harry to her parents.

"So happy to meet you at last; we know a great deal about you Harry, and it's all good I might add," her father said.

He was a real diplomat but he did seem sincere when he said it and it made Harry's heart jump.

"Yes we have followed your fighting career. I'm a great fan of boxing and I saw your fight, the one before this last one. I enjoyed it very much."

"You were there at the arena? I wish you had come to the dressing room. It would have been a great pleasure to have you." Harry said it with so much ease. One, because he meant it and two, because he was very well schooled in social manners by his mothers and of course Lousier. All of them who had taken great care to see that Harry was a true gentleman and knew how to act like one.

Yvette's father was very pleased with Harry. He saw that he was truly a very handsome young man, intelligent and of course, a gentleman. He told him that if he could get away he would be welcome to come and visit them.

Harry was so stunned he could hardly speak and when he did he wasn't sure of himself and didn't remember exactly what he said. He did manage to say: "That would be a great pleasure sir. I hope I'll have the opportunity".

He looked at Yvette with a grin that could have split his face. She recognized his elation immediately and she too was ready to jump out of her shoes. She had no idea that her father was going to say anything like that and she could have jumped up and kissed him right there when he did.

"We'll be waiting for you in the cabin, Yvette." her father said. He offered his hand to Harry and said: "Good luck."

"Thank you and bon voyage to you both".

As they walked away, Yvette turned to Harry and said:

"I am stunned! I had no idea that my father was so interested in boxing even. You know I don't see him all that often and when I do it's mostly at home unless we go out some place together. I am so tickled that you might be able to come and visit me; it will make the time go so much faster."

"I will come I promise. If Hero can't get me a fight there I will come on my own, and since your father has extended me an invitation it makes it that much easier."

"I would like to hold you and never let you go. I know you must though and I don't want to make a scene here in the station" He took her by the arm and they walked to the train and to her cabin. Her parents were sitting with their backs to them as they approached looking out the window at the crowd. Harry stopped, led her out of the doorway and whispered:

"Don't say goodbye, you know I love you and I will see you soon."

He kissed her softly on the forehead, turned, and walked away without looking back.

Yvette knew that he was always concerned about causing any embarrassment to her or her parents, and she also knew that he was opposed to people making love in public but she also knew for sure that he loved her, and that was all that mattered to her.

They were prepared to take the train to Nice. It was a long way and although the scenery was very beautiful along the way it would be quite tiring. Not for Harry, but he thought it might be for his mothers. However, they were anxious to go.

They arrived in the early afternoon. They talked to a taxi driver to see if he knew where this place was. He said he did so they engaged him for the rest of the day, and on in to the evening, as long as it would take for them to be satisfied for what they came to see. Kathleen had a pencilled map that her friend had drawn for her. The driver didn't know exactly the chateau but he did know the area. They made a couple of wrong turns but they didn't get lost and made it in pretty good time using the map. There was still a lot of daylight left.

When they arrived, the gentleman was there and greeted them with open arms, especially Kathleen. He was a big man, quite elderly but still handsome in a very manly way. His name was Robert and he was very pleasant. He had his helper take the taxi driver to the kitchen and told him to get him something to eat and drink and to make him comfortable because he didn't know how long he was going to have to wait. That sounded good to the driver and he followed along eagerly.

CHAPTER X

Nice

"Come and sit down," he said, as they went into the chateau, and we will have a little wine while I tell you something of this place."

He opened a fine bottle of Beaujolais and poured everyone a small glass.

"See how you like this, my friends, it was grown and prepared right here on this land", he told them.

"This is called a chateau and it is quite old, but since it was built of stone, it is still in very good condition. There are 16 rooms, five of which are bedrooms. I have had to convert some of the rooms into baths because when this place was built they didn't have plumbing as we know it today but everything is quite modern now. There is a wine cellar, which we will go see. It is quite large and holds many great bottles of some of the best wine you can find anywhere. Come, just follow me and we will see."

They went down a flight of stairs from inside the chateau to a beautiful, ornate sitting room with cabinets and shelves all around made of beautiful old hard woods. Shields hung on the walls and there was a carving, which was carved right into one of the walls, a leopard stalking prey. Leading off of this room was a long corridor, divided in the center with shelves on each side and on each wall filled with bottles of wine. It was quite large and about 14 meters long. Three people could easily walk side by side down each isle, and it was lighted just enough to be able to read the labels on the bottles, which were lightly covered with dust, except for those, which were recently turned. Although the bottles were a little dusty, the rest of the place was very clean and cozy. He took them out on the veranda so they could look out over the vineyards. It was a sight to see. Except for some very large sheds where the wine that was produced that housed the vats etc., there was nothing but rows and rows of grapes of several different varieties. It was very beautiful.

Robert took them back into the chateau and showed them the big kitchen first. The cook was preparing some food for the evening meal and the taxi driver was lounging at a table in one corner of the room. Robert said that he took his meals in here most of the time when he didn't have guests.

They went up a short flight of steps and to a short hallway where there was another flight of stairs, which led up to the second floor. There were three bedrooms each and two baths, a storage room, and one that was used for work or hobbies or play like cards, etc. They went up another flight of stairs to the third floor and found two more bedrooms, each with a bath. They were smaller, but not much. There was also a lounging room used for anything one might like to do, perhaps entertain personal guests or family. Back down on the ground floor was the main salon and formal dining room, main entry and the laundry was next to the kitchen, which also was used for storage. They had all kinds of equipment for tending to the yards, the gardens and roads throughout the property.

Robert said as he was pouring another glass of wine:

"Why don't we tell the driver to come back in a couple of days to get you and you can stay here tonight, or longer if you like? I'm sure you will be exhausted if you try to return to Paris to soon."

They were actually planning to stay two or three days. Not necessarily there, but they had to wait for the invitation. They looked at each other, as much as to say do you all agree, and then Kathleen said: "It's very thoughtful of you Robert. We would be delighted to stay. Besides, I haven't seen you in quite a while and it would be nice to have more time to talk."

Robert sent for the driver. Kathleen told him their plans and asked if he would return. He said he would. Kathleen paid him for the day and asked him to be back by noon in three days. Robert had his houseman take all the bags to their respective rooms, instructing him where each one was to sleep.

They had a delightful supper with more great wine, but before dinner Harry donned his jogging gear and took off for a run around the property. He needed the exercise but he wanted to look the place over as well. When he returned, he told Jeanne he was very impressed, with everything. What a beautiful place.

The next day he took Jeanne for a walk throughout the vineyard. They stopped at the big building that housed the vats where they made the wine. The wine maker showed them around and told them a little about how he made the wine and where he learned to process the grapes into such wonderful tasting wines. He said he owed it all to his father, who was a winemaker also. It was very interesting.

"I can hardly imagine us living here. It must be worth a fortune."

"Well Kathleen is handling that end of it, is all Jeanne said."

There wasn't much to do after supper. Harry thumbed through some magazines and said he would turn in He said good night and thanked Robert for the fine hospitality and complimented him on developing such an interesting and beautiful place. They put him up on the third floor. He was asleep in no time.

Jeanne excused herself shortly after and went to her room on the second floor. She bathed before climbing into bed but she too was soon fast asleep. Robert told Kathleen: "I haven't seen you in some time my lovely and it makes me very happy that you are here."

They talked for just a little while and then Kathleen said: "Shall we retire my lord?" and she put out her hand.

"I thought you would never ask!" He said. He put his arm out for her to take it and they headed for the stairs.

The taxi was on time arriving just shortly after they finished eating a late breakfast. They had no trouble boarding the train and after a fairly relaxing trip arrived back in Paris just as the evening traffic was at its worst. But the noise of the horns and the lights of Paris were not hard to take. Jeanne told the taxi driver to go to the Arc de Triomphe, a beautiful area that is especially lovely in the winter time when one could find the vendors with their charcoal burners selling the delicious roasted chestnuts in the snow. Down the Champs Elysees on the way, there were always so many sights to see, and then to pass by the Opera. This was a beautiful route one never gets tired of, they all agreed, and sat back and enjoyed the ride.

Harry was trying to imagine how it would be to live in Nice. Of course he had little to make a judgment on since he hadn't seen much of the surrounding parts or of the city. It seemed so far away from Paris, and his thoughts quickly turned back to Yvette, wondering how she was and when he would be able to see her again, and if she would be willing to come and live there in Nice.

In a few months he would be nineteen. He was taking his final tests to comply with the state so he could be eligible for a "Diploma of School Completion." Lousier had asked him if he had any ambitions to go on to college. He had told him that he really hadn't given it much thought, but that he didn't think that he would, unless it was after he was satisfied with what he could be as a boxer. He wanted to find out if he had what it takes to be a champion. Hero seemed to think he did. Lousier was excited to hear him say this because he thought so too and was also working on some other plans for the future, so he went on to tell Harry about it.

"I'm really kind of tired with teaching, and I have been thinking about other things to do that might make me more money but could offer some fun at the same time. I like to travel and I have been thinking about forming a company of different kinds of entertainment and taking it on tour. Many of the small cities throughout the world do not have much entertainment, and I think that a variety of acts, and things to do, well, you know, like a circus or a carnival. You know all about that don't you Harry?"

"I guess so. That was the first part of my life that I remember. That might be a great idea. I think we should look into it more."

"You mean you would be interested to do it with me?" Lousier asked. "Well, isn't that what you had in mind?" Harry laughed.

"I was hoping that somehow we might be able to stay together. You are kind of like my family after all this time and I thought we could make a good team -partners.

Hero was in full agreement that Harry should be serious about working for the title. It would have to be for the light heavyweight. Now and maybe the next year he could remain in the middleweight class, get more experience and gradually put on more weight. Maybe he would grow a little more too, but that wasn't really necessary, except that he could always use a little longer reach.

"Never mind, we'll make up for it with speed and strategy," he said, "but you've got to work harder on your punch."

Harry began a rigorous training schedule right after Christmas but Kathleen and Jeanne insisted that he must go to visit Yvette over Christmas. They liked to have him there for New Year's Eve celebration. Paris was famous for this occasion and his mothers wanted him to be there, but they knew how much he wanted to see Yvette. They told him how much they would miss him but they thought this would be a good time for him to go. He was elated and wrote to Yvette that same day, October 15, 1925 he hoped he would be able to make it there by Christmas. He didn't know how long it took for the ship to reach Algiers, but he was going to find out right away.

He first went to the steamship company booking office. They told him how much it would cost, the departure dates, the return trip schedule and that he would have to have a visa. They asked him if his passport was in order. He said he wasn't sure but would find out.

It was a blow to Harry because up to that time he hadn't thought about his passport, he never had. The way he came into the country was not exactly legal and he had never approached the American Embassy to see about the validity of his passport. He had to see about it, so he decided to just go to the Embassy and see what they would say. Jeanne thought about it and said she thought it might be best to ask to see the consular in person. Tell him the whole story of your epoch journey and your life up to now, and maybe he can help you get it straightened out.

He did just that. He went to the embassy and had to wait nearly an hour to see the consular. When he finally was seated in the consular's office he began to tell him his whole story. Halfway through he said he didn't want to bore him with all the details, but the consular encouraged him to continue and not to leave anything out. He was engrossed in Harry's story of his life and escape from the Germans, as well as his boxing career.

Shortly after, continuing on with his story, the consular called in his secretary and told her that he didn't want to be disturbed and didn't want to take any calls unless they were urgent.

Harry eventually told him why he wanted to get his passport straightened out and get his visa to Algeria. The consular said:

"Don't worry, I'll personally take care of it; tomorrow you will have your new passport and I will get your Visa to Algeria prepared for you as well."

He also said that he hoped that they could be friends and that he wanted to come to see his next fight, even though he wasn't particularly a fight fan. He was just anxious to see Harry fight.

Harry was beside himself and couldn't thank the consular enough. He said that he would personally bring him tickets to his next fight. He was told to come back the next afternoon to collect his new passport and to be sure to ask for him because he would have it with him.

He was so excited he ran home. Jeanne and Kathleen were up and sitting in their sitting room reading the paper. He was so excited when he entered the apartment they thought something was wrong. He told them what happened at the Embassy and told Jeanne that she really had it right, to go directly to the consular. He went on telling them about the reaction of the gentleman about his life. He said he never considered that what he went through was ever going be of such value to him. Both Kathleen and Jeanne guffawed at his naïveté.

"You don't realize, my love that you have had an experience that few people ever have had or who have ever survived."

"Perhaps," he said, "but most of my survival is due to you two and you know that I love you both very much, not just for my survival though. I don't think anyone could ever ask for better mothers.

He kissed them both and Kathleen said:

"We had better get to the Steamship Company and arrange for your passage." Harry told her that they had time, and might as well wait until he went back to the Embassy to get his passport and visa. He continued, "Besides, we have to wait to hear from Yvette."

The Steamship Company said there was no problem with overcrowding. There were many people going and coming to Algeria but there was always plenty of room. They guaranteed him passage and reminded him to be sure to have a visa.

Harry went to the gym to see Hero to tell him about the events of the day. He had already told Hero that he was planning to go but he didn't know what was going to happen about his passport. Hero was delighted for him and said that he would hold off on booking him for another fight until after he returned. He told Harry to be sure to keep up with his exercise. "I'll work even harder, but I won't be going for awhile, so I'll be coming to the gym until then", Harry told assured him.

Harry finally received the letter he was waiting for from Yvette. It was OK for him to come at this time and she would be anxiously waiting for him. It was signed "With all my love".

He enjoyed the trip on the boat, as he called it. The captain corrected him saying that it was a ship. Aside from his daily workouts he enjoyed talking to many of his fellow passengers. There were people from many places and he was able to converse with most of them in their own language. There was an Italian who was a sports enthusiast and liked to run around the decks with him almost every day. It was nice to have company, and Harry liked using his Italian language. It's easy to forget much of a language if it isn't used.

There were also some Americans and Spaniards travelling. He was asked to do a lot of translating at the captain's table when dinning in the evenings. Of course there were others who spoke more than one language, and the captain spoke French and Italian also. All in all it made for very interesting conversations for them all.

Chapter XI

Fate

When he arrived at Algiers he didn't see Yvette anywhere. He kept looking and looking until it was time to leave the ship, and just before he left the railing he caught someone waving to him, at least it seemed that he was waving to him. He pointed to the man and then himself and nodded his head, gesturing to him to know if it was he who he was waving to and the man confirmed it and pointed to the gangway, to indicate that he would meet him there.

Harry was disappointed that Yvette didn't come to the ship, but then he thought that maybe her parents didn't think it was a safe place for her and he figured that they must have had to wait for some time on the docks. To Harry it seemed like it took forever to get the ship into the dock after they took on the Pilot and then to get it tied up.

The man who met him was named Marceau and he worked at the consulate under Yvette's father. Mainly he was the chauffeur, but he did several other things. He told Harry that he was to take him to the hospital immediately and that he, Marceau would take his suitcases to the consular's home, because they would all be at the hospital.

Harry was immediately shocked and asked why they were going to the hospital? Marceau told him that Mademoiselle Yvette was very ill. He didn't know any particulars, only that she was very ill and that her parents were with her. "My God!" Harry said. He was immediately distraught.

When they reached the hospital, a drab building that looked like it needed more lighting. He asked at the desk for Yvette and they told him the room number. He rushed up to the room and met her parents there. They were waiting outside her room. He father was dry-eyed, but it was obvious that he was in great distress. Her mother had to keep wiping her eyes. The doctor was in with Yvette. They told him that Yvette had slipped and scraped her leg while out shopping only three days ago. Apparently she contacted an infection of some sort, which the doctors were not sure of, but they said that the laboratory tests showed that she had infectious microbes in her blood stream and she was in a very serious condition; life threatening.

"She had microbes in her blood stream. And it was life threatening?" Harry was devastated.

When the Doctor came out he was very grave and couldn't give them any further information regarding her condition. Harry asked if he could go in and see her. He directed his request both to the doctor and her parents. Her father said that she was very anxious to see him and wanted him to go right in.

She was so week and her body was shaking, she couldn't raise her arms to Harry when she tried. Harry gently wrapped his arms around her and raised her up slightly and kissed her a long and loving kiss.

"My love," he said, "you must get well. Do you think you have the best doctors? I know this is a French hospital but I want you to have the best! I love you and I want you to come home so we can be married." A tear came to her eyes and she said: "That's what I want too, oh yes, yes!"

But she was so week she couldn't put her arms around Harry. He laid her back, kissed her again and took her hand in his and held it to his cheek.

Her eyes became droopy and she tried to stay awake but she fell off to sleep. Harry just held her hand and watched her and started to cry silently. Tears streamed down his cheeks. Her parents came in about that time and he looked at them and they too started to cry.

They were all silent however, not being able to do anything about this situation. Quietly, Harry asked the doctor's name. They told him and he left the room. Harry put Yvette' hand down very gently.

He wiped his eyes and asked a nurse outside where he could see the doctor. He was in the next room and when he came out Harry asked him about Yvette's condition. The doctor told him that they had done everything they knew of to do. He asked the doctor if he thought that they could do anything more for her in France, perhaps at a bigger hospital? "No" he said. He was sure. It wasn't because of a lack equipment or technology. It was just that no one knew of any further medication or treatment for this infection. Yvette died the next morning at 5 am. Harry had been with her all night. She had only awakened two times more. The first time she was able to stay awake for about one quarter of an hour. The last time was just before she died. She told her parents how much she loved them and told Harry that she was sorry, but she only wanted him to remember how much she loved him. Harry was the last to kiss her and after she succumbed he stayed with her, holding her hand not wanting to let go.

Her father bade him to come home with them. He had made the necessary arrangements for Yvette. On their way back to France they told him that they would be going home and take Yvette to Paris for her burial. They would love for him to be there with them. They knew that Yvette would want it.

It was the first real tragedy to fall on Harry. Of course it was tragic when his father died, but he was a very young boy and the impact was different. It also was an extremely sorrowful time when he had to leave Gunter in Germany, but that was different than this. Harry just seemed to be in a daze except when someone was talking to him. He had a difficult time concentrating on anything it seemed.

The ship didn't leave for another couple of days and Harry couldn't force himself to do anything. His sleep was erratic and he felt lost.

Finally it was time for the ship to leave. He was just going through the motions. He hadn't even unpacked most of his things from his suitcases. Two of them he hadn't even opened. He brought with him a souvenir photo of a group of the boxers from his gym, and had it signed with respect to Yvette's father. He thought it would be appropriate since he was a fan of boxing and he didn't know of anything else to bring him.

Kathleen had provided a beautiful scarf for Yvette's mother. He gave them the gifts saying that maybe they would remember him as someone who loved their daughter as much as they did.

The trip back home was somber. There were no dinners at the captain's table. He took all of his meals in his cabin except for a couple of times when he had lunch with Yvette's parents. The only other thing he did was to run every day. The way he felt he wasn't sure it was even doing him any good.

The day before they docked he had lunch with the parents again. The father told Harry that he would inform him when the funeral would be. Harry said that he would come to their house the next day since he didn't have a telephone.

It was a very sad time for Harry. When he told his mothers about it, they also cried and that didn't happen very often. He knew that they were truly sorry for Yvette's demise. He was glad that they didn't try to tell him how he should take it or what he should do. They just demonstrated their remorse and asked for the address of Yvette's parents so they could send them a card of condolences. They did ask Harry if he thought they should go to the funeral with him. He was thankful that they wanted to go. The support he felt was good for him.

Jeanne hired a car. They didn't want to go in a taxi. They didn't think it was appropriate. Each and every one of the friends from the Theatre Group was there. Harry told Adrian about Yvette, and he had in turn, told everyone else. They could hardly believe she was gone. They all were very sad. It was a heart-rending service. Literally everyone was crying. They all came to Harry to offer condolences.

Adrian said, "If there was anything he could do—". There weren't a lot of people, but some of the friends from the state department were there. It was a terrible loss for everyone, her parents of course and especially for Harry.

His mothers didn't talk much about it. There wasn't much anyone could say to ease the pain, so everyone was silent on the way back home. They all went in their apartment from the front and Kathleen walked on back to Harry's room with him. She said, "Why don't you try to get some rest? I don't think you've had much sleep since Yvette was in the hospital. One thing you can feel good about is the fact that she didn't die violently, and she didn't suffer. Best of all, you were with her to the end. If you feel like crying, do it! It's best that you don't hold back. I'll leave you now but if you want me for anything just call."

"Thank you." he said as he hugged her and sat down on the bed. Kathleen left.

He didn't go the gym for a couple days. He just stayed in his room, snacked a little, except for the next night when Jeanne brought him in something to eat. He thanked her but said he wasn't very hungry.

He couldn't help remembering the love he and Yvette had together, all the little things they had talked about, and how much she loved to see him in the ring. She said that he looked like a Black Panther. Harry wasn't very black but he knew what she meant, and he knew she meant it as a compliment. It was for her that Harry decided to return to his training regime.

On the third morning after the funeral Harry was out on the street again running. He went to the gym and worked out with enthusiasm but was quite somber, serious, no horsing around, not that he horsed around much anyhow, but he just didn't seem happy working out like he usually did. Normally he would have a smile on his face even when he was sparing in the ring.

Hero caught him when he was leaving that afternoon and said he would like to talk with him. They went into Hero's office and he asked Harry if he felt OK? Harry just said "Yes" without enthusiasm.

He asked him if he still thought he wanted to go for the title. He told Hero: "I'm going for the title and I'm going to win; at least I'm going to do everything I can to win. Yvette would have wanted me to and I'm going to do it for her."

Hero didn't know how to answer him. All he could say was: "I'll help you all I can; we'll do it together, OK?"

Harry nodded his head and said: "bien sur!"

Harry finished all his final tests for his formal graduation diploma with a 98% mark. Lousier was very proud of him and rather satisfied with himself as well. He told Harry that if it was Ok with him he was going to follow him in his quest for the title and that he would like to be his manager. Harry thought it over for a few minutes and said that he thought he would like that very much, but he thought he should talk about it with Hero. It might be a good idea for Lousier to go with him when he did.

"Do you think you know enough about the fight game to be my manger?"

"I have followed the business of boxing for twenty years. I actually know most of the people behind the scenes, and I do know the business. Let's go talk it over with Hero and see what he says."

Hero knew Lousier for several years. They didn't actually associate with one another except at the Gym, but they had had long talks about the fight game and Hero knew that Lousier was savvy about it. He said after a brief discussion:

"I think it is a good idea. If Lousier needs any help he can count on me. The main thing is that you can trust him to do what's right for you every way he knows how and in this game that's important. You two are very close, I know. Lousier brought you here Harry and for that I thank him and wish both of you all the best."

So it was decided they would be partners, at least in the fighting business. Hero of course, was the trainer, and there were none better.

Harry got control of his life over the death of Yvette by concentrating on his training. He went on to have many fights the following two years. He either won on points or knockouts. However he lost two of the first 4 fights he had but only on points and those were very slim decisions. Hero told him not to be too concerned. They didn't expect to win 100% of all their fights, especially when starting out. It does help you to know your shortcomings for the things you have to work on.

Harry learned from each and every fight he had. He got better each time he went out. Just before he turned twenty-one he had to change over to light heavyweight class. He was very anxious to go for the title of the championship of France. He and Hero worked very hard and he fought all the elimination fights necessary and was ready for the title fight. The contender who held the title was a burley, tough and fairly technical fighter. Hero was somewhat reluctant to have Harry challenge him. He was still just into the weight of the class and several pounds lighter than the champ was. But Harry was adamant to go for it.

He and Lousier had been planning their business of the travelling show business since they became partners and Harry told Lousier:

"I want to see if I can get the Title. If I win, I'll continue to fight and we'll make all the money we can. If I lose I'm going to throw in the towel. I'm kind of anxious to start travelling and this show business sounds like a money-maker and a lot of fun. "Lousier was very agreeable with the plan and in fact was just what he was hoping for, and he told Harry. There was a substantial purse for the fight, even for the loser. Harry had already made quite a bit of money. He was a good draw. People liked him. He was tough, yet he was a gentleman, and the crowd could always expect to see some real technical boxing, which was rather unusual. He was a "stand-up" boxer. He moved like grease lightning but stood almost erect. When he danced around, he was very graceful. He put on a good show for the people. Usually in the heavy weight classes, there was a lot of slugging and not a lot of finesse.

Harry and Lousier decided not to tell Hero about what they planned because it all hinged on whether or not he won. They didn't think it was right to cause Hero to worry unnecessarily.

Chapter XII

Title Fight

So the day came. It was 1927 and the Arena was packed. The champ came down the runway and the crowd gave him a roaring welcome, but when Harry came in the crowd seemed to go crazy. No one really knew just how popular Harry was until he entered the arena. Now they knew.

Harry was confident that he was ready for this challenge, whether he won or not. He had trained enough and had enough experience. At 180 lbs, he was much lighter than the champ. But he hoped that his ability and speed would make up for it. The champ was quite a bit slower than he was. The dangerous thing was that he had a powerful punch, more so than Harry. So he would just have to stay out of the way of his right. He put on a good show. The crowd seemed to be with him more and more as the fight went on. Harry was doing well and staying away from the champs right, he did until the ninth round. Harry had fought a great fight. He was well ahead on points, but in the ninth the champ caught Harry with his powerful right as they stepped back from a clinch. Harry went down, not out, but it shook him up enough to throw him out of sync. He took a nine count to try to clear his head, and then, until the bell rang he tried to stay away.

He was OK to re-enter the fight but his coordination and speed were gone. It wasn't that he had a "Glass Jaw" or was afraid; he just couldn't clear his head enough to get back into the fight. Lousier and Hero wanted to stop the fight, but Harry said no, that he was in control and wanted to continue.

Although Harry was able to stay in the fight and counter the champ and not let him hit him again with his right, he couldn't keep him from over taking him on points. In fact if Harry hadn't been the technical fighter he was the champ could have hurt him badly.

So that cinched their decision to leave the fighting game and embark on their show business venture. The following day after the fight, Harry and Lousier went to Hero and told him of their decision and how they had thought about it and planned their future. They apologized for not saying anything about it until now but they didn't know how it was going to turn out..

Hero said, "Fighters don't last forever. You're twenty-one years old. Even if you had won, I wouldn't have encouraged you to fight for longer than maybe 3 or 4 years to stay on the safe side. Unless you're very lucky you could get really messed up and I, for one, don't think it's worth it. I respect your decision to retire and I wish you all the luck. It has been wonderful all these years working with you. I don't think any trainer could have a fighter that was a harder worker or more cooperative than you have been. I'll miss you a lot." And his voice trailed off.

Harry went to him hugged him and kissed him on both cheeks then took his hand in a firm hand shake and said to him: "We'll stay in touch, I'll write to you from where ever I am. There are no words to tell you how much I appreciate all that you have done for me. Please don't forget if there is anything I can do, or if you need me, you only have to let me know."

In August of 1926 Kathleen's friend Robert called her. He told her that he wasn't feeling too well and asked if she could come to see him. He had been in Paris only three months before and they had gone everywhere and done everything that Robert's health and vitality would allow. He had asked her when she thought she might be able to come to take up residence at the Chateau. She told him then that it all depended on what Harry's plans were. She knew, and told him that Harry was training for the championship bout and until that was over and decided she wouldn't be able to make any firm commitments. However she said that she was anxious to see him and told him to take care of himself.

Now things were different. Harry's mothers had helped and discussed at great length with Harry, and Lousier, about their plans for their travels. Together they had devised a relatively foolproof business. Now they would soon be on their way. It would only take two or three months to collect all their trappings, scenery, signs, etc. and Kathleen didn't think she could be of any further use to them in Paris.

She talked it over with Jeanne. Jeanne wasn't quite ready to leave Paris. She felt that she had developed a small but very lucrative clientele. It was as if she was going steady with about ten men and she didn't have to try to recruit any new customers. So she told Kathleen to go ahead and make her plans and when she thought she was ready. She too would join her in Nice and maybe by that time they both would be ready to retire. They both laughed about that. Kathleen said: "How do you retire from sex?"

Kathleen made the first train she could for Nice. She told Harry that if he needed her he knew where to contact her, but that she might be back before he left the country. If not, she hoped that he would be able to come to Nice on his way. She didn't want him to go on a long journey without telling her good-bye. Besides, she wanted him to see Robert one more time. She told him that Robert was willing her the chateau and everything that goes with it, and that one day it would be his, and she wanted him to be able to thank Robert for that wonderful gesture. Harry couldn't believe it.

"You mean that he is just giving all that to you, for nothing?"

"He has no relatives, he's never been married and he has been in love with me for many years. I have never told you about the time that he was a prisoner and a fugitive in Germany. He had been wounded and the Germans captured him. He was being taken to Berlin to a prison camp in a crowded, stinking, old wooden box car but on the way he was able to break some of the wooden slats and make a hole just big enough for him to escape from the train. He twisted his leg (knee) badly when he jumped. That's why you see him limping a little. It was night and no one saw him when he jumped and he was able to hide in the thickets until he was able to walk again with the help of a crutch he made from the branch of a tree. He was nearly starved when after nearly two weeks a Frenchman ran into him in the wood. He was ready to fight with the only weapon he had, his crutch, but the Frenchman told him that he had no need to be afraid. He got him some food and told him to stay where he was and promised to get him some help. The Frenchman came to me and I was able to get Robert to my quarters. I arranged for a doctor to do something about his leg, fed him and nursed him back to a reasonable health and arranged to get him over into France. Except for the injury to his leg, he was a big strong and very manly man. I always admired him but in those days there was no time then for romance.

After the war he went back to Hungry and found that the only relatives he had were dead and had left him a lot of land and a chateau, something like the one in Nice. He sold everything and moved back to France. He lived for a while in Paris, where we ran into one another again. We have stayed in touch ever since. Finally he found this chateau in Nice and decided to settle there.

So that is the whole story, and he feels like I am the closest thing to a relative that he has, and, like I said, he loves me. He wants to marry me to be sure that I retain the property after his demise."

Harry didn't say anything. He was looking down at the floor with little emotion showing.

Kathleen finally asked him:

"What's the matter my love?"

"I was just remembering about the time I was in a similar situation in Berlin and how you and the French people took care of me. I can understand how Robert feels about you. I am the same, and I love you too, but not just for what you did for me then but what you have been to me since, and for all the others you helped that no one but they ever knew about. You deserve much more. You have always been respectable, and I am truly proud of you and our life together. Whether you come back or not I'll be there in Nice. I want to go and see Robert and personally thank him."

"I love you my son." Kathleen responded.

CHAPTER XIII

Enterprise

Harry and Lousier had it all worked out, and they knew just how they wanted the signs made, the portable tents, and all the trappings for their travelling road show. They each went different ways to the carpenters and printers, tent makers, etc. to get them all made. When they reached any of their destinations they would only have to have the two trailers unloaded and hire two trucks to haul them away. They felt that they had thought of everything for any eventuality but if not, they felt sure that it wouldn't be anything that they couldn't take care of wherever they were.

They decided to start their tour on the coast of North Africa, in Morocco then travel along the Mediterranean countries over as far as Egypt. Then they would decide where to go from there. All the population in those countries either spoke Arabic or French, or both. So, they figured it would be a good place to start, and they also figured that those places would be the most starved for entertainment.

They hired a man they knew who was an Algerian. He spoke French, English, and Arabic. The Arabic was the important factor in the first opening of their enterprise. Mustafa was a very clever guy, an entrepreneur. Although he was reported to be of a somewhat shady character, they felt that they could convince him to operate honestly with them. They planned to keep a close watch over his operations. He was needed to go in advance of the troupe to arrange for hotels, bookings, transportation and all the advance operations necessary for a show of this type.

Mustafa was a colorful fellow, incessantly pleasant to the point that he seemed to be overjoyed at all that went on, exuding confidence and professing knowledge of the world and all that went on in it. Harry and Lousier found out that he really did.

They made up scenarios during the time they were gathering things together, imagining what it would be like in actual execution. They had Mustafa go through the motions of how he would handle these various projects. They were confident that he could do a good job and, should he make any mistakes, they would most probably be rectified without too much trouble. They made up lists of things that must be taken care of before they could afford to make a move. It all seemed pretty complete.

One of the most difficult things to overcome was communications. Many places they were planning to go to had little communication facilities except for mail and key- type Morse code. Of course telephones were available in most cities, but in the more remote cities and towns, telephones were a luxury they didn't have or didn't think they needed. Actually, this is what helped to make Harry and Lousier's business a success. The fact that those places were remote and had little contact with the rest of the world resulted in their welcome to each area.

They had to be careful about propriety in the Muslim territories. For example, the women who helped the juggler and the acrobats had to wear long floppy pants to cover their legs and blouses to cover their upper torsos. That wasn't a problem difficult to solve. Another problem was with Harry's opponents.

They had made a sign depicting two boxers facing each other with their gloved covered fists up in the boxing position. This was a "come one- come all" exhibition of three rounds giving the opponent the three rounds to knock Harry down. They paid an entrance fee but if they knocked Harry down they collected a handsome reward. Depending on what country they were in, the reward would be larger or smaller. The problem was that the Arabs didn't want to stop fighting either at the ringing of the bell or at the end of the three rounds. They had to be very careful that they explained the rules in the beginning, but they still had to have extra men there to subdue many of the opponents who didn't want to stop. It was actually a comedy, for the crowd as well as for Harry.

As he promised, Harry did stop in Nice to see Robert before going on to Marseilles to meet Lousier and the rest of the troupe. It was a warm and friendly meeting. Harry said that Kathleen told him about their plans to marry and he thought it was wonderful and hoped that they would be very happy. He also extended the disappointment that it couldn't have happened sooner. They sat and talked for hours. Harry told him all of what he and Lousier had planned. Robert extended his wishes for their great success and hoped to see them back in Nice, not too long in the future.

The troupe was made up of acts speaking several different languages. There were the Russian Cossacks, the Portuguese tumblers and a beautiful Spanish singer and her partner who was a flamenco dancer. They were very popular in Morocco. There were some Chinese acrobats. An accordion player, a violinist, a drummer and a guitarist provided the orchestra or music. The guitarist was exceptionally good and played flamenco guitar as well as popular. He accompanied the flamenco dancer and singer. Harry often played a drum with the musicians. Mostly just so he would have a presence on stage since he was also the master of ceremonies and performed doing a tap dance.

It all worked out to be over an hour show and sometimes more, depending on encores. Over a period of time Harry and Lousier would let an act or two go to make room for new and or better acts they might encounter on their journeys.

The show would normally go on three times a day and they usually had audiences full to the doors. Sometimes the first show wasn't so full but always the afternoon and evening shows were packed.

Mustafa did the advance advertisement very well. He would put up posters all over the city in strategic places and often he would hire "barkers" from the locality to announce in the streets about the shows. It worked very well. Everyone worked hard and the shows didn't run late into the night. Too many people who would like to see it were working people and went to bed early. The last show was over by about half past eight o'clock.

The biggest trouble they had was travelling from place to place. There weren't many good roads, no 'rest areas' along the way, especially from country to country. It was always important but sometimes difficult to find big and powerful trucks that could make it over dirt or sandy roads. Flat tires were always a big problem and they took much time to repair even though Harry always made sure that the trucker had sufficient supplies for the job and extra inner tubes. Whenever it was possible to take the train, it was a very welcome relief, but it didn't happen often. On those road trips, everyone was expected to pitch in and help whenever possible and necessary. It wasn't an easy business in those days but it was very profitable.

It was also extremely interesting and most of the time fun. The people in the troupe were congenial. If there were any acts that didn't get along with the others, Harry would get rid of them. He couldn't tolerate troublemakers. He said life was too short. Be happy. Lousier was a great help to Harry. He kept all the finances straight, paid the performers, arranged for the transportation from place to place, which Mustafa wasn't able to do in advance, paid all the other bills and helped out when they did the carnival routine, which wasn't all the time. They liked to do it as much as they could because it was a good money-maker but sometimes the locality just didn't lend itself for the opportunity. When they did, they often would take bets against the contender. Often the local people thought their fighter was really tough and could take Harry, and were willing to bet on it. They really did make good money then. Once in a while a fellow might get in a lucky punch. Even though at one time or another came an experienced boxer, never did anyone knocked Harry down in three rounds. He was just too fast for them. Harry always won.

It took nearly one year for the show to get to Egypt. They had changed performers twice. In Tunis, they came across another Russian Cossack group that was far better performers than those that were with them at first. Harry made arrangements for them to meet in Libya a month later. Their contracts usually were for month to month. The other only change was the addition of a knife thrower. He was very good and had a beautiful wife who was his assistant. They made a good attraction.

Getting from Tunisia to Libya was a problem. They had done shows in Gabes, a fishing village on the gulf and had gone on to Medenine, thinking they were on their way to Libya, but they had to return to Gabes and hire a boat to take them to Tripoli, (Tarabulus, as called in Arabic). There was really no passable road between Tunisia and Libya that led all the way to Tripoli to accommodate their big trucks. Travel was very difficult, but to Harry it was all part of the game and he made sport of it. As a result, all the people of the troupe stayed in good spirit. A policy of Harry's with Mustafa was to always allow plenty of time to get from one place to another when he booked the shows in the different countries and towns, so there was little pressure on the group.

It was a quite chore getting all the trappings on the boat at Gabes. Everyone had to help. There were no cranes and this wasn't a cargo vessel. It was a large fishing boat. Harry had nearly all the other fishermen and their crew members helping. He was generous in paying for the work that needed to be done. He said it was better to be a little generous than to have workers with ill feelings toward them. At the same time he wasn't over generous to a fault, which could also be dangerous.

It was much easier in Tripoli. They unloaded with the dock cranes. Trucks that Mustafa had arranged for were there to take it all away.

They stayed in Tripoli for nearly two months. There were good crowds and many people came more than once. The carnival action was good also. When they felt they had stayed long enough there Harry and Mustafa would arrange for them to go back on a boat and head for Benghazi. There was little to offer between Tripoli and Benghazi and the travel would have been long and very difficult. The trip aboard the ship was very delightful. Accommodations weren't all that great, but it was very nice to be out on the Mediterranean instead of land for a change. Tripoli was another great success.

They spent a long time in Egypt. Their first stop was in Alexandria. Harry loved it there and they played in several different areas in and around Alexandria. All in all they were in Egypt for nearly one year. When they got tired of working in Egypt they decided to wrap-it-up and pay every one off.

Mustafa, Lousier and Harry took off back to France. Harry missed his mothers. He had written letters to them, but in moving around so much he had only received 6 letters from them and those were all in Egypt, except for one that he received in Benghazi. He told them to write to him to Benghazi, general delivery when he was still in Tunisia. The letters were all over one month old but he was happy to get them just the same. So after nearly two years he was very anxious to get back to what he thought of as home.

CHAPTER **XIV**

Return to Nice

Jeanne had moved to Nice with Kathleen. They had hired a professional nurse to care for Robert. He was in bad physical health, partly from his wound in the battle of Armentieres but now he was quite old as well but his mind and his spirits were just the same.

When Harry arrived at the chateau he went directly to Robert after kissing and holding his mothers for a long time. He had missed being there for their wedding. They said they didn't make it a grand affair. Robert wasn't up to it. It was so good to be with them again. Just the touch of them and their nearness took him back over the years, reminding him of the love they had given him.

Robert was happy to see him. They sat and talked for long stretches about Harry's latest exploits: When the weather was nice, Harry would take Robert out on the veranda. They would sip delicious wine; enjoy the fresh air and talk. They played a lot of chess. Harry had found a beautiful chess set in Morocco made of colorful hard wood. He wasn't sure exactly what kind of wood it was but the grain and the colors were beautiful; they were all hand carved. They were large and exquisite and Harry presented it to Robert as soon as he got unpacked. They were both very good chess players. It was like a tonic for Robert and Harry enjoyed it just as much.

Lousier told Harry one day that he thought he would go on up to Paris and see some old friends. Paris was home to him and he missed it. Harry thought it was a good idea and that he would go along with him because he too missed it and would also like to see some of his old friends. Harry asked Kathleen and Jeanne if they also wanted to go but Kathleen said that she wanted to stay close to Robert. She felt that he needed her, and Jeanne said that it wasn't that long ago that she had been there, so Harry and Lousier took off for some further enjoyable times.

They had already been back in France for 8 months. Mustafa had said hello to Kathleen and Jeanne and stayed just a few days. He made a lasting impression on both of them. They liked him a lot. Restless, he wanted to go on to Paris and have some excitement. Harry kidded him saying that he just came from having lots of excitement. He simply said:

"Paris is different!"

Harry laughed and said:

"I guess you are right. I hope you have a lot of it, fun that is."

After doing so much travelling, eight months seemed like a long time. Their feet were itchy and they needed some action so they were excited to be on their way back to Paris. Harry of course, headed straight for the gym. He hoped to see Hero again and perhaps some of the other fighters there. He had written letters to Hero but never received any reply. The gym was the same except that Hero had retired. He came around to the place once in a while, but had no connection any longer with any fighters. He told them at the gym that he was tired and was planning to do a lot of fishing.

Harry got his current address and went to see him. He was fine and although he looked older and a little tired, he was however, enjoying himself and did do a lot of fishing. He said that he remembered receiving a couple of letters from Harry.

Harry told him about all the things that had happened on the tour through North Africa. Hero was a very willing listener and enjoyed all the stories. Harry didn't stay too long, but they did spend a very pleasant afternoon together. Hero did say that he thought that if Harry had wanted to stay in the ring and have another go at the man who beat him, he thought he might have win. He only had to learn a few different moves to be able to keep the man away from him, and to also improve his punch. Harry told him he had no regrets. He had had a wonderful time in the fight game, a lot of fun and met a lot of wonderful people, like you. He only regretted leaving a good friend like Hero and their close association in parting. He told Hero again that if he ever needed him to just let him know, and gave him his address in Nice.

He headed for the American Embassy hoping to find his friend the consular. He wanted to check again on his passport papers but mostly to say hello to the man who did him a great favor.

As luck would have it, the consular was still there, finishing up his tour of duty with the Embassy and was scheduled to go back to the USA for a new assignment in just one month.

He was delighted to see Harry. They made an appointment to meet at a restaurant near the embassy that same afternoon. He told Harry he had something he wanted to talk to him about.

Joseph, the consular, kept asking Harry about his show and his travels, and the time went on. They left the restaurant and went to Harry's hotel on Rue Grange Batelliere, the Hotel De Jersey, close to where he used to live. There, Joseph told Harry that he had a plan in mind to take Harry to the United States and put him on radio. He had an excellent voice, worlds of experience and he thought he would make a great "Story Teller," a new and very popular programming on the air in the USA.

"Surprised!' was Harry's reaction to this question.

"I never thought of doing such a thing," he told Joseph. "But I will talk it over with my agent, Lousier and I'll let you know in the next few days."

Joseph told him it might be a great opportunity and to consider it seriously. He said that one of his best friends was a producer in New York and he could set it up quite easily. The only thing was that he would have to pay his own way to the US. However, they would pay his hotel expense and guarantee to have a contract ready for him to sign.

Harry caught up with Lousier. They talked it over and Lousier said: "Why don't we go back to Nice and talk it over with your mothers?"

"Bravo", Harry said. I should have thought of that. Harry thought that was very good idea but it did seem that perhaps this was just the thing to give them the change they were looking for.

They told Joseph that they would give him an answer on their return from Nice. He said he would be waiting.

Kathleen and Jeanne couldn't quite imagine Harry on the radio in the United States. But they did say that they thought it should be a great thing for Harry - if he liked it. So after all the discussions and trying to imagine what it would be like decided to take Joseph up on his offer.

They met with Joseph and signed a contract that would allow them live in New York with no money out of their pockets for three months. After that the contract was negotiable.

The Boat trip over the Atlantic was not boring. The food was great, the service was also great and the cabaret was exciting. The girl Harry met in the cabaret was also exciting. She was an American girl who had been studying in France for four years. She was only one year younger than Harry and was quite beautiful. She was from Alabama and white.

She happened to be sitting at the bar after dinner one night next to Lousier. He was sitting next to Harry. She made a remark to Lousier about the show that was to come later on in the evening and started up a conversation with him. But her attention was on Harry. Whenever she could, she engaged him in their conversation.

When the orchestra played an especially lovely tune, she leaned over and asked Harry if he would mind dancing with her.

She wound up in his arms that night and every night of the trip after that. She, however, made it clear that this was her last fling since she was to be married when she returned home. She asked Harry if he would please ignore her when the ship docked since her fiancée would be there to meet her and she wouldn't want him to know about their "shipboard romance." She told Harry that in fact, their affair was giving her second thoughts about her upcoming marriage. Just in case she changed her mind, she asked Harry if he would give her his address in New York. He said he was sorry, but until he landed there he had no address and explained to her why. The only way she would be able to get in touch with him would be through the Broadcasting Company. So they left it at that.

Unknown to Harry, one night Lousier told the Master of Ceremonies of the show that Harry was a professional dancer just back from a tour of North Africa. When the MC announced Harry as a guest in the audience and begged him to do a number for them. Harry gave Lousier a very stern look and said:

"This must be your work!"

But he really didn't mind. He liked to dance and he loved an audience. He explained to the orchestra how he wanted the music played, and the impromptu number was a great success. Lousier was very proud of Harry and the girl was stunned. He made a great appearance out on the floor in his tuxedo. He was wearing one since they were dining at the captain's table. Lousier told him that he knew he could have several other women in the audience if he wanted. Harry just looked at him, smiled, and said:

"You take them."

Actually, Lousier didn't do too badly for himself after all.

Chapter XV

In the USA

They had a telephone number to call on their arrival in case no one was there to meet them but there was a driver with a fine car to take them to their hotel with instructions to be ready to be picked up the next morning by the same car and driver. Harry was impressed. It was the way he liked to do things himself. It reminded him of Mustafa. In fact, he wondered how he was.

Here it was 1932 already and he really missed Mustafa. He told him that he would send him 25% of his regular salary each month until they were ready to embark on another tour. In the meantime he could do whatever he wanted to do, including working at something else if he so desired, but to be ready to get back to work with their advance bookings and travel arrangements when called.

Mustafa was very happy with these arrangements but he told Harry that he hoped it wouldn't be too long. Not for the money part, but because he enjoyed working with Harry so much. He was anxious to get started again. He told Harry that he was going to keep a lookout for some good talent while he was taking it easy. That also pleased Harry.

They got up early and went down to the restaurant to have breakfast. It seemed strange to them to see so many different things on the menu for breakfast. The ham and eggs with biscuits and coffee seemed to be just what the doctor ordered. They both took the same thing and it was delicious. Harry had honey on the biscuits. He told Lousier that if he ate like this every day he would weigh a ton in a short time.

They were in the lobby at the appointed time waiting for the driver; he showed up and took them to the studio. The offices were in a huge building on a major avenue but he didn't catch the name on the sign at the corner.

They were ushered into an office where they met with the producer and director of the show Harry was to do. The producer began the conversation saying to Harry that he had heard quite a bit about his life from Joseph, and in fact would be interesting to hear more. The producer was a fairly non-descript looking fellow. He was pleasant, but no one would think he was the executive that he was. He was thin and a little taller than Harry. His skin was rather white; it didn't look like he got out in the sun often. The texture of his hair was fine and straight, parted on the side, and he had a small moustache.

He continued:

"The important thing now however, is to see how we can get this show going in the right direction. As you know we have written a program of storytelling. It's a one-man show and we think you might be able to add some intrigue to it with your many languages, not necessarily speaking in the languages, but imitating some of the accents when they are called for. We will present the show with background music and some occasional sound effects, but mostly it will just be you and your voice reading these stories. You do read English well, do you not?"

"I think so. I have never had to read stories over a microphone before, so I really don't know for sure.

"We will find out soon. So why don't we go into the sound studio and try out one of the scripts and see what it looks like, just as a bit of a test. Of course you will have a chance to read and study these scripts well before going on the air. For now it will give you a chance to acquaint yourself with the surroundings, and the microphone."

The studio was very small. There was glass on three sides and the microphone was a big round chrome device with a small circular grating sort of a thing in the center of it, hung with springs. It was all on a stand, which went up and down to suit the height of the person using it. It made Harry very nervous. He was told to talk right into it when speaking. He found it very awkward to try to hold the script, read it and speak directly into the thing all at the same time. Not having seen the script before reading it, he just read it as if he was reading a - laundry list so to speak.

After reading a few lines, the director stopped him to ask him if he could put a little more feeling into the lines as he read. So he did a little better, but it was all very strange to him, standing there alone in this small cubicle with the others looking in on him through the glass windows. Actually, before he was finished he wound up reading quite well, with inflection and interpretation, but several times they had to tell him to turn and talk into the microphone.

He read part way through one of the stories and then they gave him another one to read. He was beginning to catch on to the whole operation and was reading well enough, when they told him that would be enough for today.

They said that they thought he would do well. However, it would be necessary for him to come to the studio each day, before the program was to get started, which was nearly one month away, to practice reading for a couple of hours in front of the microphone. It would help him to become comfortable using it. They wanted to have some talks with him about his past so the writers could prepare some various introductions for each show, based on his experiences.

Back at the hotel, Lousier asked him what he thought about being on radio and reading these stories. He kind of laughed and said it was a rather harrowing experience.

"That microphone scared me to death. It's certainly not like being out on the road."

And they both laughed.

Lousier reluctantly said he didn't think it was meant for Harry. He really didn't care for his own part. He could prepare publicity and personal appearances easy enough.

"You could become quite famous I think, but it just doesn't seem to fit you."

"Well I was thinking the same thing," Harry told him. "I could probably get used to the microphone, and I'm quite sure I could read stories as well as anyone, but that studio and the glass enclosure made me feel like I'm in a bottle."

It was funny. "I hate to think about telling them I don't want to do it, and worse, how to tell Joseph. He thinks he is doing me a great favor and I really do appreciate it. I'm going to have a very bad time trying to tell him I don't want to do it. Lousier said that they would talk about how to go about it and he did have an idea that might make it easier.

It was early in the afternoon and they called Joseph to ask if he was free for the night and could he join them for dinner at the hotel? Lousier talked to him and said that Harry would really love to see him, if he could make it. Joseph said he was free and would love to join them.

Harry, always an impeccable dresser, wore his tuxedo. It was European style, very fashionable even in New York. Harry stood out like the star he was when he entered the dining room with Lousier and Joseph, who also were very smartly dressed in their own tuxedos.

Harry ordered some aperitif wine. He was now quite a connoisseur of fine wines and Joseph was impressed with his selection. They had some Hors d'oeuvres and made some small talk, mostly about the trip over.

Joseph was anxious to know how it went at the studio today. Harry told him that he thought it went well. The producer and the director seemed to be satisfied with the interview and "tryout," as it turned out to be.

"Would you he very disappointed if I told you that I don't think I am cut out to be on the radio?"

Joseph was shocked. Everyone was trying to get into the radio business. It was something fairly new and was touted to have a great future. He couldn't believe what Harry was telling him. He asked him what it was that he didn't like about it.

"Joseph", he started. "You'll never know how much I appreciate what you have done for me trying to get me in on this wonderful medium. I'm sure that many would just die for the same opportunity. However, you know pretty well what my past has been like. I'm a traveller, I like an audience and I like to be on the move. I'm really not so enamored of becoming famous. That doesn't excite me. That cubicle and the closed up studio just scares me. I never had any idea what it was like until today. You have been so good to me, especially when you fixed my citizenship and passport. I'll never be able to thank you enough for that. It hurts me to tell you that I can't accept this offer."

Harry was so sincere and spoke eloquently. Joseph could see how difficult it was for him. He really couldn't understand it but he knew that Harry was a man who knew what he wanted. He told him:

"Harry My friend, it makes absolutely no difference to me that you feel that this is not for you. I only hope that you are not making a mistake, but be sure that this will not affect our friendship. I'm sure you would have been a very big hit on the American radio. Perhaps it's only the radio audience who will be the losers. I wouldn't want you to do something you don't feel comfortable at on my account. Now let's have some dinner and talk about what you do plan to do. I'm sure it will be exciting." It was a fine evening.

At the studio the next morning, Lousier and Harry told them of their decision. Harry told the producer that he would be willing to repay him for the expenses. But the producer said that even though he was disappointed, a deal was a deal. But if he changed his mind later on to give him a call and perhaps they could work something out. They told him that they thought he did have a lot of talent.

So now that they were on the loose in America they thought it would be a good idea to have a look around as long as they were in the United States for the first time that Harry knew about. He was too young to remember anything about it before his father took him out of the country.

Looking through the news papers Harry noticed that there were fights scheduled for the next day. He wondered if he could get seats at this late date. He called Joseph to invite him and Joseph said that he was just about to call Harry himself to see if they wanted to go. He could almost always get tickets through the State Department. "Only if you let me pay for them", Harry said. Joseph agreed and they planned to meet there at the hotel.

During the day the two of them walked the streets of New York, took in the sights and had lunch at a hot dog stand, with all the trimmings. They browsed some of the stores. Lousier especially liked the bookstores and could have stayed there the whole day. An attendant in one of the bookstores mentioned that if they planned to go to Washington they might like to go to the Smithsonian Museum. Harry said why not, that should be very interesting. So they planned to do that and proceeded to check the train schedules. They didn't realize that the fight they were going to see was a heavy-weight Championship bout between Jack Sharkey and Max Schmelling when Sharkey defeated Schmelling on June 21, 1932 in Madison Square Gardens. They didn't have ringside seats, but they were close enough to see everything very clearly. It was 15 rounds of excitement.

The next day they poked around New York some more, went to see the Statue of Liberty and took the subway to several places. They got tickets to Washington, took a few things they thought they might need in small hand bags and left the rest of their things in the hotel in New York.

It was hot and humid in Washington and they wished they had brought more of their things and checked into a hotel so they could take showers and change clothes, but they just went directly to the Museum. They stayed for about three hours. They thought the Egyptian exhibition was the most interesting and compared it to the one in Cairo. From there they got back on the train and when back to New York and to their hotel.

They decided to take the first ship available back to France. Luckily they only had to wait five days before the next departure. That gave Harry time to call Joseph and invite him for a final evening of dinner and show before leaving the United States.

The show on Broadway, "Mourning Becomes Electra" with Judith Anderson was a big hit. Judith was exceptional, and it worked out well that they decided to have dinner after the show since it was too early to have dinner before it. As luck would have it, they got to see several of the Broadway actors that came into the restaurant after their shows were over. All three of them had a wonderful time and it gave Harry the opportunity to thank Joseph once and for all for all his kindness.

Harry and Lousier were in a good mood on the way back to France. Harry had taken the opportunity to see what it would be like to live and work in America and it wasn't all bad. But he liked being on the road, travelling, seeing new faces and doing new things. The hardships were all worth the experiences, and the money was also good, but that wasn't the most important thing to Harry. Lousier rather felt the same way. After so many years chained - so to speak - to his teaching, it was like a constant vacation to him, and it was great working with Harry. By this time he felt more like a brother to Harry, although there was a time he felt close to being a second father to him. He was proud also that Harry turned out to be such a fine man because he felt as if he had something to do with it all. They made a fine partnership.

Harry always missed his mother a great deal no matter how long or short they were apart. They were his strength. Their confidence in him is what made him so confident of himself and he knew it. He couldn't imagine what his life might have been if it hadn't been for Kathleen and Jeanne. He just wished he could do something extraordinary to exemplify how he felt toward them. Harry never realized that in fact it was him that gave Kathleen and Jeanne the real happiness and fulfilment in their life, the son neither of them felt they could have. He was what filled the void in their life, something to work for and live for, and the result was rewarding enough for them, because Harry turned out to be exactly what they had wished for.

The homecoming was warm and happy. His mothers were extremely happy to see them both. He had written letters to let them know what was happening, but it wasn't the same as having him home.

"Come. You both must tell us all about what happened in America." Kathleen questioned. "We have often wondered what it was like."

They had many questions that Harry and Lousier tried to answer as best they could. But it was evident that the most interesting thing they saw there was the championship fights at Madison Square Gardens. They talked about that for a long time.

CHAPTER XVI

Chateau De Ville Cabernet

Later, Kathleen told Harry that Robert was very bad. He was bed-ridden and they had hired a full time nurse to care for him. She said that he could go any day. In the face of all the happiness she felt having Harry home, there was still this sadness. Kathleen didn't love Robert fully as a husband, but the respect she had for him was just as intense. He was a very kind man, of stature, knowledge and experience. He was a self-made man who never had time to build a family as he might have loved to do. He adopted this family, just as Harry had been adopted by Kathleen and Jeanne and he was satisfied to find that these people truly felt of him as part of their family. He was also very happy to know that all he had accomplished in his life would be saved and go on to people he knew and loved, for he truly did love Kathleen. Robert felt a real closeness to Harry as well. He thought he was a fine man who, through so much diversity had made it well, not unlike himself.

Robert did pass on after only one month of Harry's return. It was a very sad time. They arranged with a priest to come to the ranch for the burial since Robert's wishes were to be buried on his property that he loved. He was so happy that Kathleen was to survive him. He had prepared a family gravesite on the property. He even had the headstone made, but asked Kathleen to have it engraved after his demise. He wanted the date of his Birth, death and the date of the purchase of this land along with his name and the name of the farm; however she wanted to arrange it. It finally read:

ROBERT SZEMMELROTH A STRONG
MAN OF CARING AND LOVE
LAID TO REST AUGUST 28, 1932
PROUD OWNER OF CHATEAU DE
VILLE CABERNET SINCE 1918

Harry and Lousier stayed on at the farm for some time. Harry didn't want to leave Kathleen alone after such a sad time in her life.

Time and life had been good to both Kathleen and Jeanne though. Although they were not old, as we generally think of old, Kathleen was 49 and Jeanne was 48; both of them still very beautiful, but not the age to carry on with their usual trade. So the time was good for them both. Now they had money they had made and saved over the years, some investments and the farm that Robert left would carry them all very handsomely for many years to come.

Before he died, Robert schooled Kathleen on the management of the ranch. There was a lot to learn. Robert had made the growing of the grapes and the care of the vineyards easily manageable. With the help of the farm boss, the wine-maker, and the workers who knew just what to do, the biggest job for her was to take care of the paperwork and the sales of the product. That also wasn't all that difficult for Kathleen or Jeanne.

They treated the help, as Robert did, very well. They paid them more than any other rancher did but they also made them feel as if they were part of the family. None of them ever gave a thought of leaving. The sons were taught the business as they grew and other young people were also trained to take the place of those who would leave or soon retire. The chateau required little upkeep as it was made of stone, only a little maintenance was necessary once in a while. Quality grapes and quality wine was the goal of De Ville Cabernet. They often won first prize in the local wine contest, but always their wine was rated in the top of the class. Kathleen and Jeanne enjoyed going to the wine meets. It was a happy gathering and much fun. They met a lot of nice people during these events, and occasionally some very handsome men, usually attached but occasionally not and that too, was very nice. They too gave some well-attended parties at De Ville Cabernet and the people they invited were fun, joyful and a good time was usually had by all. Kathleen and Jeanne spent a lot of good times planning these parties. They especially loved New Years Eve but the summer time was probably the best time of the year for parties.

Now after many months Harry and Lousier decided it was time to plan their next adventure. They both had been very intrigued with South America. Harry spoke Spanish like a native and he was sure that the Portuguese they spoke in Brazil would be easy to pick up. They got out the maps and charted a course. Then they went to the different embassies or consulates to get some idea of the population, types of businesses, and the general demographics so they could determine, more or less if those locations would be profitable or not. But of course, Mustafa would also check into these things, which was part of his job when he made his advance survey prior to booking them into any town or city with on-the-spot-observance.

Harry called Mustafa's number and left a message. It took a few days before he returned the call. The number was a "drop" call where he could always be reached, but one never knew exactly when. He was delighted to hear from Harry. He said that he had almost given him up and thought he would never call and right away he wanted to know where they were going. Harry laughed. It was good to hear his voice. Nothing seemed to faze him. He was always in a good mood and ready for anything that came up. If one could use the term "Happy go Lucky" for anyone, it would be for Mustafa. But he wasn't a dummy by any means. In fact he was a very shrewd businessman. It was his personality that threw people off. He got the best of the bargains and made them like it. He was indefatigable in doing his "homework." He knew what things were worth before he started the bargaining because he had already done his research. South America sounded great to Mustafa.

"When do we get started," he asked?"

It's already 1934". Harry laughed again saying:

"What's the matter? Haven't you been making any money on your vacation?" "Sure" he said, "but it's not as much fun alone as it is with you Harry."

"I want you to meet me soon and I will let you know where in just a few days. So stay where I can get hold of you, I don't want to wait for nearly a week again. OK?"

"OK," was the reply, "with pleasure"

He laughed again and said "*ma'assalama*." – go in peace.

It was a long way to South America from Nice. They decided that they must organize their show and all the trappings needed after arriving somewhere on a northern shore. They planned to go from North to South on the South American Continent. They thought Brazil would be a good place to start. In any case, they would have a lot to decide on after reaching there. Perhaps Mustafa should do some advance casting of acts prior to their arrival.

Now it was the unpleasant business of saying good-by again to his Mothers. As much as he could, he always tried to make it easy for them but it was never ever easy for Harry. Aside from the great hurt he still had inside him for the loss of his love, Yvette, the only thing he regretted in his travelling was being away from Kathleen and Jeanne.

He and the ladies went over every aspect of the running of the farm, their finances, as well as proper papers to direct the legal transfer of the farm, should anything happen to either Kathleen or Jeanne. Of course, it was in the name of Kathleen Szemmelroth, but that didn't have anything to do with all of them sharing in it. Their desire was that Harry would keep and care for the farm for the rest of his life. They also hoped that one day he would have an heir to pass it on to.

Harry always transferred all of his money to the bank there in Nice with Kathleen and Jeanne's name on the account as well as his. Trust between them was no question. Should anything happen to Harry there would be little loss of his assets. He would prefer them to go to his mothers in any case.

So all was ready and time for the good-byes. Kathleen and Jeanne arranged for a magnificent dinner for Harry and Lousier. They invited just a few of their closest friends and it was a happy, yet sad occasion, good-bye dinner. Everyone however, preferred to say "*a bientot*," hoping to see them back sooner, than later.

Harry called Mustafa. Fortunately, he returned the call in just a few hours. Harry told him he would send him money to his bank and he was to proceed to Rio de Janeiro. He told Mustafa there wasn't a great hurry since it would take them several weeks to get there. In the meantime he was to scout for all the supplies they would need, i.e. tents or tent makers, trucks and flatbed trailers, sign makers, tailors and any other artisans he thought they might need. As well, he wanted him to scout out for talent, not just from Brazil. In fact, he would prefer that they not be from Brazil. On the way he wanted Mustafa to go to Portugal and find some good talent, musicians, a good singer, and tumblers, acrobats, knife throwers and whatever he thought might make up a good show. He would keep in touch with him by telegram. He was not to leave until he received the money, and when he did, by that time Harry would be able to tell him which ship he would be on and how to send him messages.

Before he left he told him to go to Egypt. He wanted him to see if he could find an exceptionally good magician. Harry thought it would be a good attraction to have an Arab Magician. With the right costumes, presented the right way it could be more mystifying than just the magic he performed. Mustafa said that he had already found the best there is. He was an Egyptian, and he was here. "Good, sign him up." Harry was elated.

Although they knew it would take some time to reach Rio, it really didn't distress them too much since it was so nice travelling aboard ship. They both loved being on the ocean and most of the people aboard ship were interesting and there was always much to do. The time would also allow them to further plan their production and Harry could work out and get in top shape. He always did his runs, in Nice or anywhere they were, but now he would concentrate on his boxing again.

Harry reached Mustafa when the ship was about halfway and when they arrived in Rio, he was there to greet them.

"Ahlan wasahlan!" (Welcome) he cried before they descended the gangway. He was so happy to see Harry and Lousier and they too were happy to see him. He was kind of like a ray of sunshine. Mustafa was talking a mile a minute, telling them of all that he had accomplished. Harry said:

"Attendez, attendez. Whoa. We have plenty of time to go through all of that. First I want you to tell me what you have been doing since we last saw you?"

He said that he had spent much time in Alexandria at the beach and enjoying a lovely lady he met there, a Tunisian girl of twenty-four years, with silky sandy colored hair that fell down her back and blue eyes, and warm lips.

"So you fell in love, did you?" Lousier asked.

"Yes and no" he said.

"We had a wonderful time but she finally told me that she had to go home. She was married with two kids and had been on a vacation. When I looked somewhat stunned, she explained that her husband travelled a lot and she knew that he had women all over the world, so she decided to have some fun of her own for a change. *Haram!* - Pity. What a lovely woman. I could have loved her, yes!"

"Too bad," Harry said.

Mustafa shrugged his shoulders and said:

"There's plenty more where she came from."Now I want to tell you about the people I found."

Mustafa, excited as ever told Harry and Lousier all about his search and success in finding some great talent. The magician form Cairo, the tumbling act from Portugal, and also a wonderful juggler who rides a bicycle at the same time. His wife is a lovely young lady, who also works with him; a singer who sings in four different languages, a real beauty and an orchestra that he found here in Rio that could read and play any kind of music you want. He also told them about finding trucks and much of the tenting and other equipment they needed.

Chapter **XVII**

Odyssey

"So," **Harry said, "seems like** you have been quite busy Mustafa?"
Shaking his head, Harry went on:

"I appreciate and am very happy with what you have accomplished
so far, but now we must take stock and see what else we need. Are all
the people you have found here now waiting to go to work?"

"No, not all of them" Mustafa said.

"The people from Portugal are on their way; they should be here
in about 4 days. The magician is here and so is the lovely girl singer
but except for their expenses, they don't get paid until they start to
work, that is until the show opens. The orchestra is working now
but will finish their contract in one week and they will be ready to
start any time after that."

Harry said: "Good, that's good."

Harry met all the acts that Mustafa had gathered together and
was quite pleased with all of them and thought they should make
a box office show. He had each one of them perform for him so he
could see their talent. Mustafa had done well.

When all was ready, they all climbed in the trucks Mustafa had purchased and started out on what would be a most hectic, fun, profitable, and fateful odyssey of South America.

It took many months to get to Santiago, Chile. On the way there were many successful shows and fun people to play to. Harry did a lot of dancing since it was really an oddity to most of the people in the towns they worked, and everyone seemed to enjoy his tap dancing immensely. All the other acts worked out very well also. Mustafa picked some very good talent, but probably the Egyptian magician was the biggest attraction of them all. His act put people in a trance. The combination of the lighting and the stage setting, his costume and his manner just seemed to hypnotize the audience.

They all worked real hard. There was a lot of physical work to do whenever they moved, but they all pitched in and helped one another, so it made it pleasant even though it was lots of work.

Santiago was an interesting place and the people were kind to them at the shows; they enjoyed it and applauded wildly for all the numbers. The town was interesting as well and they took advantage of the day time hours to have a look around.

Harry and Lousier were walking along the wharf in Santiago one day when they noticed a sign in a window which read in big letters - "GOLD"- and under it read:

Wanted
Prospectors
Everything Supplied Including Mules
"You find it - we dig it."

They looked at it for a long time then Lousier said to Harry: "Do you think there is gold around here?

"I don't know, but why don't we see just what they are talking about?" was Harry's reply.

The mining company offered what they called a "grub-stake." They supplied all the tools, mules, food and everything needed for nearly a one-month's trek into the mountains of the Andes. But they also had maps that indicated where gold veins were most likely to be found. Harry asked them how they knew about the where the gold should be. They said that prospectors in the past had found small veins and some larger veins, but geologist had studied all the various findings and figured the most likely places, which are indicated on these maps: This Company even provided proper clothing and blankets to survive the cold. There is almost always a lot of snow as well as a lot of dangers. First aid kits were also provided. It did seem to be a very legitimate offer. Harry told them that they would think it over and come back if they had any further interest.

The show was starting to slow down there in Santiago and the performers looked like they were beginning to tire also. They were all doing a good job but it had been a long, long trip of nearly two years. They also had made quite a bit of money, all of them. Harry and Lousier had urged them all to save their money, as much as they could and not throw it away, to spend it wisely. For some of them he banked money in their names and only gave them enough to have spending money. The Egyptian sent most of his money home to his family. It would last him a long time in Egypt, perhaps even put him up in business. He, along with most of the others, was rather anxious to get home. It was a difficult decision to make, when they were all making such good money.

Harry and Lousier talked and discussed over and over again about the prospecting proposition. Both of them were adventurers and found it hard to pass up any adventure they hadn't tried, especially if it seemed to be profitable.

They went back to the mining company and asked to see the contract they were offering for the finding of gold. Both Harry and Lousier had good knowledge of legal jargon and understood the proper wording of contracts quite well. They read the offer put in front of them and decided it was a reasonable offer. It said, among other things, that they would share 15% profit of all gold found. That the company would do all the mining operations and their overhead expenses would come out of their eighty five percent. There was a clause also which allowed them to "cash out" if they wanted to. A survey would be made as to the richness of the find and the company would make an offer. If they accepted they could walk away with a large sum, depending on how rich the vein was, or they could wait for the gold to be mined. It was by all indications a legitimate contract.

They decided to close up the show, sell off all they could, except one truck and their personal things. They would pay everyone off, buy homeward bound tickets for everyone, and go prospecting.

They told Mustafa about the scheme and asked him if he was interested to go with them. They would have liked him to accept because Mustafa was a very pleasant person to have around with his talk and his attitude, besides being a good businessman. But he said, right away that this kind of adventure was not for him. He would prefer to go back to his old haunts and perhaps even get married and raise a family. Harry and Lousier both laughed. "Mustafa, you do not seem to be the type to settle down," Harry teased him.

"Who's talking about settling down? I just said I would get married and raise a family, not settle down!"

They laughed again, but didn't take this conversation very serious or pursue it any farther. It all seemed too complicated.

They put up signs that the show would close in two weeks. Harry told Lousier that they really should have a big party before everyone parted and went their own way. They were almost a family, having become such close friends and living so close together for the past two years. It was going to be a little sad to see everyone split up, but of course, it was inevitable.

So a party they had. Harry told Mustafa to pull out all stops, the best food, plenty of drinks and to hire some other good entertainment for them for a change. Everyone could invite a few friends if they had or wanted to. Both Harry and Lousier thought it would be more fun if there were some outside friends to share with them. There were the people who made signs, women who the girls had do their hair, favorite taxi - drivers two of them - some people who came to see the show several times whom they got to know and just a few friends the entertainers had become acquainted with. In all, there were enough to make it a very good time for all, a party none of them will ever forget.

But there was someone special who Harry invited. A beautiful girl he met at the jewellery shop. He wanted to give all his people something as a souvenir but he wanted it to be something of good value as well. He and Lousier went to look for something at a jewellery shop in town and met Isabelle. She was from Brazil. She was a very good jewellery designer. The shop owner who had seen her work at a show in Rio persuaded her to come and work with him in his shop. She was dark skinned, with blue eyes, jet black hair, skin as smooth as silk and a beautiful figure. Harry was stunned when she walked up to them and asked if she could help them. Speaking in her own language, and with his warm gentle voice, he told her what his dilemma was: that is, to find something suitable for both men and women, of good value, a souvenir, a memento of many months working together under good and sometimes difficult situations, for my employees. "We've been travelling for over two years since we arrived in Brazil, with our travelling show. We're closing our show now and they are all going home. I want them to have something nice to take with them".

Isabelle could see the tenderness in Harry. He was handsome and it wasn't the first time she had seen him. She had gone to see the show one night and she recognized him right away when he walked in the door.

"Oh, that's so sweet of you to think of your people. I saw your show two weeks ago. I thought it was wonderful. Now let's see if we can think of something nice."

Harry said:

"Thank you." I didn't see you there. I don't know how I could have missed you."

He was sure she knew what he meant by the remark.

They looked over the counters and on the wall cabinets but nothing seemed to fit the occasion exactly. Then Isabelle said:

"You know I might have something in the back that will do nicely. Excuse me for a moment."

She retreated to the back room and when she came out she was carrying a case that seemed to be quite heavy. Harry jumped and said:

"Here let me help you with that."

He took it from her and set in on the counter. She opened it and inside lying in their own recesses was beautiful gold coins about the size of a Florin and weighed exactly one ounce each. She said that they had individual boxes for them, lined in velvet that made beautiful display cases. Harry looked at Lousier, who had been quite silent till now, seeing the play going on between Harry and this beautiful girl.

"What do you think Lousier?" he asked.

"They are very beautiful and if need be, readily spendable. One never knows when gold will come in handy in an hour of need."

"Exactly," said Harry.

He didn't even ask how much they were, he just said:

"We'll take them but please put them in the boxes like you said and wrap them up in some nice gold wrapping paper. He told her how many they would need and said that she would have to bring them to the party herself—as his guest, "Please?"

She realized that he was asking her to join him now. She looked at him with her blue and captivating eyes and said:

"Yes, of course, I will."

There was an inflection in her voice that told him they were going to be close friends. "Ah! Wonderful, I will come and get you" He said laughing.

She laughed and said:

"That would be very nice."

Lousier paid for the coins and they prepared to leave, Harry saying, ...
.... "I'll pick you up at 8:00 O'clock." "I'll be waiting."

As usual, when someone starts out on an adventure never taken before they are a little apprehensive. That's the way both Harry and Lousier felt after getting all their instructions, packing up their mules and striking out on a very new and perhaps dangerous journey.

CHAPTER **XVIII**

Gold

They kept the one truck, but it took three weeks to get rid of nearly all their accoutrements from the show even though they nearly gave everything away. Saying good-by to Mustafa wasn't easy either, but he departed in good spirits as usual so it made it easier. Harry and Lousier gave him one of the coins but they had it made into a necklace with a heavy gold chain, typical man's style. He loved it. It also gave Harry a chance to be with Isabelle again. They did some shopping for a little extra warm clothing and a handgun. They had to pay dearly for it because it was against the law to own one. Since they were going on a hazardous journey, they might have been able to get permission from the government, but it was still unlikely and they didn't want to take a chance on them even knowing that they wanted one. If they couldn't get permission, they thought they might ultimately be searched and the gun found, if they were suspicious of them getting one anyhow. It made them feel a little safer. They considered that where gold was concerned, there could possibly be people who were interested in it also, only the kind of people who didn't like to work for it.

They were also able to get ample ammunition and hid it in several places throughout their packs, but Harry carried the gun on him. He fashioned a loose cord to the handle of the pistol and tied it around his waist, leaving enough room to use the gun if necessary but making it so that he wouldn't drop and lose it while hiking or working.

When they were in a fairly small city in Argentina, Harry and Lousier got acquainted with one of the government officials, whose very close friend was the chief of police. It all happened when Mustafa went to get permission to produce the show in their town. This official became rather excited about having the show come to town and not only gave the permission without question but was anxious for it to open and said he wanted some tickets so he could bring his friends, the chief and their respective wives. He wanted to know how much the tickets were. Mustafa, being a "cool operator" said they didn't need tickets and to just let him know when they wanted to come. Mustafa introduced them to Harry and Lousier before the first show. The Chief invited them over to his home for some food and drinks for a little get together after the show.

They were very impressed how well Harry spoke their language. The official was a fairly nondescript man. One could tell he was an office worker. His skin was rather pail and his hands looked like they had never done any work and had never gotten dirty. The chief on the other hand was completely different. He wasn't too tall but he was burley and powerful. He had strong hands and a gruff but pleasant voice. He liked to laugh a lot and acted like he was rather starved for something new in his life, adventure, and friendship. He asked Harry if they ever took a day off. Harry told him that they didn't do the shows on Mondays. It was almost always a slow day and he thought it was good for the performers to have a little rest, as well.

"Good!" said the chief, "We will go hunting. Do you like to hunt Harry?

Harry told him that he had never been hunting, but that he had been taught how to handle a gun some time ago in France.

Harry's mothers, wanting Harry to be knowledgeable in all things, had arranged to have him take some instructions at a shooting gallery in Nice after moving there. They thought it would be good for a little extra protection around the farm. He was taught how to handle a shotgun and a pistol. He was quite good at it, since his hands were strong and his coordination was excellent.

He told the chief that he would love to go if he would promise to teach him what he didn't know about guns and hunting. The chief said:

"I will teach you everything, and there is no better one to do it than me; you will see, my friend."

He took Harry to his gunnery. It looked like he had about any kind of gun one could imagine.

"I have bought many of these guns, but a lot of them I have taken from criminals. Some of them I had to kill first, but they were very bad men. "Do you like to run?" he asked.

"I have been running most of my life and yes, I do like to run. Do you?"

Harry was a little sceptical that this burley man who looked a little over weight would be much of a runner.

"Absolutely! Sometimes I have to run after someone and sometimes I have to run away from someone." He laughed. "Let's run tomorrow morning. What time would you like?"

Harry was quite pleased with his offer, the chance to go hunting, and this new acquaintance. He noticed also a rare and fiery gleam in this man's eyes; like he couldn't wait to live. He smiled constantly. Harry said he would be ready any time he got there after seven o'clock.

"Fine, I usually run between seven and seven thirty myself so I'll see you in the morning and we will have a nice run."

Harry was really surprised at the speed and the distance the Chief could run. He was in very good shape. They ran about 3 Kilometres, all at a good pace and the Chief didn't seem to be worn at all. Suddenly he said:

"That is enough. I just want to work out, not to get tired. I never know when I am going to be called on to run after some very bad hombres and I don't want to be too tired to do it." Harry laughed and said:

"You're quite right!"

That was a Tuesday morning.

The Chief said: "Now don't forget next Monday. We will go hunting and get us some good eating."

Harry told him that he would be looking forward to it.

The next Monday morning they stopped at the edge of the forest and the Chief said:

"Let's set up a little target practice and see how you handle my guns."

He had brought several guns with him; shot guns, rifles and pistols. He brought a belt and holster for Harry, a bag with a shoulder strap to carry shells for the shotgun and the rifle and he had the same for himself.

He set up some targets, paced off about fifty steps and said:

"Now load the rifle and let's see how many of those targets you can hit but do it as fast as you can. Sometimes you don't have much time to take a good aim with an animal on the run."

Harry did as he was asked, and much to the Chief's surprise he hit nearly all of the targets and his time was quite good also.

"Good, good" he said. "You need practice, but that was very good. Now let's see how you do with the shot gun."

The Chief walked out to the right of where they were standing and picked up a small limb, a little over a foot long and about the thickness of a forearm.

"Now get ready, for when I throw this wood I want you to shoot it. Pretend it is a bird."

"Ready?"

Harry held the gun in ready and said: "THROW."

When he saw the limb leave the Chief's hand he pulled the gun up quickly, aimed and fired. He missed. He could see the shot passing just behind the limb. The Chief said:

"Don't forget you have to shoot just a little in front of the wood, er, bird."

He picked up another limb and said:

"Now, ready?"

Harry was ready and said:

"THROW."

This time Harry shattered the limb and the Chief gave a '*Campo Howl,*' "*Hay ya yiee.* That was great" he said. "You are a natural born hunter, or you were kidding me about not hunting?" he said with a sly look in his eye.

"I wasn't kidding", Harry said.

Next was the pistol. Harry needed more practice for that, but when the Chief said now let's see how well you can do shooting from the hip, he did almost as well as the chief.

The fellow who taught him in Nice told him to act as if he were pointing with your index finger at what he wanted to hit, which he did, and he did quite well.

They let the target practice go and went hunting and came back with several kinds of game. Harry really enjoyed himself and the chief was delighted that he was such a good hunter, especially for his first time.

So Harry wasn't exactly a novice with a gun. Before they got too far into the wilderness, on their gold hunting expedition, they stopped and tried out the pistol they bought. It turned out to be a pretty nice gun. They both did a little target practicing, but didn't want to linger too long shooting in case there were some army or police who might be in hearing distance and come to see what was going on. On the other hand, they didn't want to attract any unnecessary attention from anyone.

They walked until they could see the sun starting to go down, stopping ever so often to get aquatinted with the maps and their direction. They had a compass and were careful to keep going in the right direction. They stopped and made camp under a great fallen tree. They gathered a lot of leaves and spread them out to put their sleeping blankets on and extended the leaves out around the parameter. They made sure the leaves were good and dry so they would make noise if some animal might come near. Harry also had the gun handy, just in case. They didn't actually know what to expect in this wilderness.

It took them five days to get to the base of the mountain where the maps indicated the veins of gold could possibly be found. Finding the paths shown on the maps was another big problem. There was snow now and quite deep. Landmarks were hard to locate. An outcropping of boulders covered with snow just looked like snow. They did see a huge mound off in the distance at about 2000 yards. Lousier said that could be it, but we will have to go and dig around some to see if it is boulders to be sure. The problem was that the snow had drifted up to the base of the out-cropping and made it look less high than it really was. As they approached they could see the snow was getting deeper and deeper so they moved out on the right side of it and tried to come to it from the opposite side. It was only about 300 yards long and as they came upon the other side the snow was less than half the depth. Besides they could see some of the boulders since the snow didn't cling to the boulders as it did on the other side.

They found what they thought was the right inlet to the mountain valley. Actually it wasn't much of a valley, more like a "V" where the two mountains came together, but after they had gone away, they could see that there was another mountain that intersected the first two, which made up a kind of a triangle of the mountains. It wasn't clear on the maps except for now as they looked at all three mountains, the one in the center was some distance from the entering "V" shaped area, which actually created the valley.

There was supposed to be a cave of a sort somewhere on the mountain in front of them, the third mountain. Finding it was going to be something else. There was so much snow. It was early afternoon now so they decided to make a camp and get some rest before getting started in search of it. Lousier said that he thought it would be kind of nice to be in a cave, instead of out here in all this snow. Harry laughed, "You can say that again," he said.

They found some fairly flat ground, covered with snow of course, and there was one big tree. Except for a couple of saplings, it was about the only tree in the whole level area. There were of course trees on the sides of the mountain. This big tree offered some protection from the falling snow. They decided to tie up the mules there and leave them. They surely didn't want them wandering off, so they made sure that they were quite secure.

They had packed some dry wood the people at the office told them they would need, but they also picked up more choice pieces along the way before they reached the snow area. All the pieces were fairly small but big enough to burn until they cooked or heated their food before they burned out. There was a single burner coal oil stove in their pack but they thought they had better save it in case the wood ran out, besides they didn't have a lot of coal oil; it was too heavy to carry very much.

They made a small fire and warmed up some food. They were both quite hungry with all the walking they had done and the mountain air seemed to give them more of an appetite.

After a breakfast snack the next morning, they headed out in search of this cave. The map indicated that it was not at the base of the mountain but up the mountain a ways, so they started looking from where they were, which was about fifteen yards up from the base. They would hike along in as straight a line as possible, poking into the mountain to try to see if there was any indentation at all. Several times they stopped to dig away the snow thinking they had found it, but to no avail. They traversed the side of the mountain for about 100 yards, then climbed up farther and came back doing the same thing. It was pretty slow going.

They decided to leave the mules where they were. When feeding them that morning they realized that from the mountainside they would be able to see the mules most of the time, and they seemed rather comfortable where they were. It was the only protected area around.

It wasn't until the third day after traversing the mountain back and forth many times that they found what looked to be the entrance to a cave, but it was so small they couldn't be sure. Also it looked like one of them would have to crawl on hands and knees to be able to get through the opening, if that's what it was.

It was well past noon and both of them were hungry, but they were anxious to see what this cave looked like, if it was a cave, and if it was big enough for them to stay in instead of out in the snow.

Harry dug round the opening some with his shovel, but the ground was quite hard and the snow didn't help matters. Lousier said:

"Let me at it with my pick."

After about one half hour digging they had opened up the entrance where one could crawl through. Lousier could stand up in the cave but Harry had to bend over just a little, since he was taller than Lousier. It didn't take long to figure out that this would be a much better place to sleep than outside in the snow.

They made the entrance a little bigger so all they had to do was to bend over some. They didn't want to make it too big in hopes that a smaller entrance would keep out some of the cold. They had to get their gear from the mules. The first things they got were some wood and food. They also threw their blankets over their shoulders and went back to the cave to eat. They would have time to get the rest of their gear, feed the mules and prepare themselves for sleep before it got dark after eating.

On their last trip to the mules they checked that the ropes they had them tied up with were secure and headed for what proved to be a much more comfortable night of sleep. Lousier started preparing the breakfast the next morning while Harry took off to go and feed the mules. It wasn't exactly an easy trek down and back up the mountain to feed the mules. It was a good 45 yards, a 135 feet, which had to be traversed in a zigzag pattern. Never the less, it was worth the trip because the mules were in good shape and looked quite comfortable. Harry thought to himself on the way back, that it might be possible to get the mules into the cave once they found out how deep the cave was, and if they opened up the entrance more. By the time he got back, Lousier had the breakfast ready. Although the breakfast consisted of canned vegetables mixed with dried beef, it made a meal good enough for two hungry people. Lousier had gathered up some snow to use for making coffee with and to drink. The coffee was the best part of the breakfast.

The cave was dark after leaving the entrance. They had what is called "carbide lamps." They put a few pebbles of carbide into their carbide lamps that were fitted to their heads like a cap. The carbide, when mixed with a little water produced acetylene, which when lighted made a usable light which lasted for some time. A little more water would allow it to burn even longer. Then when it burned out, it would have to have more carbide.

After eating, they took their shovels and small picks with them and began a search into the cave. They had only a rough idea as to what to look for. They had studied instructions before setting out on this adventure however, reading about what to look for and actually trying to identify the signs of gold and other precious material in a cave was another thing.

They picked and dug into the sides of the cave for some distance, not finding anything they thought looked like what they read about. They hadn't really kept track of how far they had gone or how long they had been working. Harry said:

"You know Lousier, we had better take stock of our time and where we are now."

They stopped and looked around and found that the cave had become a little larger. The air was a little stale but not bad. They noticed that the lamps were burning just as bright as when they lit them up close to the mouth of the cave, so it was evident that there was sufficient oxygen and they had no trouble breathing either. They decided to head back to where they started from and count the steps as they went, not looking further for gold but only to get their bearings.

They found that they had gone 16 steps. Not long strides but an average of about 45 to 55 centimetres each. That would mean that they had worked about 29 feet, up to where they stopped working. They couldn't see the end of the cave yet. Lousier said:

"I wonder just how far it does go."

On their way back they kept their eyes open as to the condition of the cave also, the flooring and walls to try to determine if there were any signs of anyone having been there before them. They could see no signs what so ever of what looked like any humans, but there were some bones close to the entrance where an animal might have taken some refuge. At the same time they realized that the floor was quite uneven, rocky, with loose rocks laying all around, in fact they had to be a little careful stepping so as not to stumble over any of the loose rocks. On their way in, going slow and chipping at the lining of the cave in their search, they didn't notice these things so much as when they were walking straight and counting their steps. Lousier said:

"I think we are going to have to go a little slower next time and search deeper into the rock. We could easily be missing something."

"Yes, I think your right about that," said Harry.

"Those men at the company said there was supposed to be gold producing ore in this mountain, and this seems to be a very likely place for it. I think we are lucky that we found this cave, instead of having to dig outside into the side of this mountain."

They had snuffed out their lamps and made some tea which went down nicely.

"Let's go down and feed the animals Lousier. By the time we get back it will be time to have something to eat and get ready for the night. Tomorrow we'll start a real search for what we came for."

"*D'accord*" said Lousier, we must be more systematic."

Before going down to the mules, they investigated the possibility of enlarging the opening in thought of perhaps bringing the mules into the cave. They hadn't had a bad snow storm as yet, only light flourishes, but there was always a good chance there would be at any time, and they didn't know how well the mules would take it being tied up there by the side of the mountain, even under the tree. The skies looked pretty clear for now, but they picked around the overhead of the entrance some just the same, to see how hard it was. They didn't want the opening to cave in on them either. It didn't seem too hard to break away pieces of the earth and rock. They decided that since it looked like there was no storm pending, they would wait until at least tomorrow to try to bring them up. They cleared away the rubble from the entrance and headed down to the mules.

While they were feeding the animals, Harry thought he heard some strange noises somewhere in the distance. It seemed to come from one of the other mountains, but it was indistinguishable. He couldn't tell if it was the wind, which wasn't very strong, or an animal, or something else. They both listened for some time, but heard nothing else, so they dismissed it.

They had a good night's sleep, the best so far. They were both ready to start to work after a little breakfast . Harry took one side of the cave and Lousier the other. If they saw anything that looked discolored, like a vein of any kind they would dig into it until they could see what it was. They could only work a couple of hours because of the lamp's duration, but it was time to take a rest anyhow after two hours. It got a little dusty as well and they had to give time for it to settle. They just couldn't work too fast, as fast as they would have liked to.

After their second refill of the lamps was just about gone, they went back to the entrance and had something to eat. They worked until early afternoon, and decided to go and see about trying to move the animals, as they had planned. On inspection of the sky, and the calm weather, they decided it wasn't yet necessary to do it, maybe another day or two. It snowed a little during the night and early morning, but now the sky was clear again. They brought some samples out with them to inspect in the light of day. It was difficult to tell for sure about colors in the light of the lanterns. On inspection, some of them looked interesting enough to go deeper into the vein. They wanted to go back to work, so they prepared to feed the animals and work till later in the day. After all, the cave was dark during the day anyhow, so as long as the animals were taken care of, they could work until they got tired. The sample from the vein they inspected turned out to be nothing

The next day, going on a little farther into the same hole, Lousier came upon a vein that really seemed to be what they were looking for. Both Harry and Lousier started digging into the side of the cave and something fell out of the hole they were digging in. Harry picked it up to look at it and the two of them could see right away that it was a large nugget of gold. Not some fine grains in a clod of coal or such, but a big hunk of pure gold. They couldn't believe it. They just looked at it and looked at it. Harry handed it to Lousier. They were quiet for several minutes, just looking at this beautiful piece of gold. Then they looked at one another then started to dig more. They were now excited and after a couple of minutes Harry said:

"Hay! We better take it easy. Whatever is here has been here for a long time, and we better be careful we don't cause a cave in."

About that time, they found another nugget, not quite as big as the first but still big enough to cover about half the palm of Lousier's hand. The two pieces weighed over a half pound. Harry put them in the pouch he carried around his waist. It was getting late, so they stopped working and went back to the entrance to prepare for the night. They were both so excited they had a hard time getting to sleep, even though they were both quite tired.

The next morning they talked about how they should proceed. Lousier said that he woke during the night and in a dreamy kind of twilight sleep he became afraid about finding the gold and all the implications such as how far should they go. Gold is heavy and even if they do have the mules to carry it, what if one or both of them should go lame or die, or whatever, then they would have to carry it. What do they do with the gold then? Should they bring the mules up to the cave to load the gold instead of carrying it down to them? If we had a lot of it, it would be very heavy to carry to the mules? Would it be dangerous to leave the gold with the mules to come back to get the rest of it? And he had some other questions but he couldn't remember all of them. At first Harry thought it was a little comical, but as Lousier went on it began to sink in that they surely had made a significant find. No telling how much gold there was, and there were things to consider, as Lousier was mentioning.

"OK! Lousier, I think you're right about the need for a plan. Suppose we open up this entrance just enough to get the mules in, for one. We'll bring them up here. Then we go and see if we can find some more gold. We make markers and mark the layout of just where we have found it. We will have to step it off again. We don't take too much, so in case we run into trouble, such as you have described, or any other, we would be able to carry what we have back to the mining company.

We can divide the gold up between the two mules, but keep it so that only one mule could carry all of it, just in case we should lose one of them. Then, at last I think it would be wise to think about the possibility of bandits, robbers."

Chapter **XIX**

Tragedy

"Oh! God, I hope we don't get tangled up with that!" said Lousier. "I didn't think of that.

That sounds like a good plan Harry, so let's get started, the sooner we get back to civilization the better."

"You mean you aren't having fun?" Harry laughed.

"Oh Come on lets go," and Lousier started to pick at the entrance of the cave."

Harry pitched right in and in no time they had what looked like enough height and width for the mules to get in.

Getting the animals up the slope through the snow, zigzagging was no easy task, but they figured it would be somewhat easier going down, hopefully. The snow was quite deep it hadn't snowed heavily for all the days they had been there except for late at night and early in the mornings. But it had snowed for about two hours fairly heavy that morning.

"I guess it's a good thing we decided to bring the animals up to the cave today" Lousier said, "If the snow came again soon it might have been impossible to get them up here."

When they reached the cave, they were pretty worn out. They stopped to position the mules so as not to get them jittery about going into the cave. Harry said:

"I'll hold this one and you go into the cave first and see if you can get yours to follow you. Try to be as calm as possible about it."

Lousier went into the cave, pulling the reins of the mule after him and the animal followed him in easy, with no hesitation. As it turned out, they had made the cave entrance plenty big enough.

Harry, holding the other mule, waiting for Lousier to get into the cave, thought he heard another noise like the first one he heard the other day. It just wasn't clear enough to tell what it was.

It was quiet as the mule entered the cave, only the crunch of snow from his hoofs made a noise. The noise Harry heard was faint and seemed rather far away. It was hard to tell. It sounded a little like an animal, but then again, it could have been someone calling. He entered the cave with his mule and they made stakes from the wood they had for fire and secured them to the side of the cave, and fed them. Harry said:

"I'm going outside and listen a while and see if I hear that noise again."

"I'll come with you," said Lousier.

They stood outside for nearly one half-hour. Neither of them talked, they just listened, but there were no strange sounds. They also looked hard over the surrounding terrain. There were some low clouds hovering around some areas of the nearby mountains so visibility wasn't all that clear but they could see nothing. Finally Harry said, "We might as well go on and get the rest of the work done."

Lousier said:

"Well how about us having something to eat first?"

Harry laughed, and said:

"Oh, I had forgotten all about eating."

"Well I hadn't" Lousier said, as he patted his stomach.

Harry took out the gun he carried, still in the holster slung around his waist.

"I think it would be a good idea to clean and oil this thing just in case we should need it, heaven forbid. I haven't had it out of the holster since we tried it on the way up here.

When he was satisfied the gun was in good condition, they proceeded to count off the steps to the vein of gold they had found. Twenty-two paces was all it took to reach the location.

"Let's skip a few feet in the direction of the vein before we start digging again; just to avoid the possibility of weakening walls or roof. We don't want a cave in."

They did just that, and it wasn't long before they found more nuggets. Many were small but some were a good size, but not as big as the first ones. Lousier said:

"I think we must have about six kilos or more now, what do you think about calling a halt?"

"I think you have a good idea. We're going to turn this gold strike over to the company anyhow, so we'll let them dig it. We'll have this and our share, and that will be plenty."

On their way back to the entrance, they decided to make everything ready to pull out in the morning after feeding the animals. They prepared the maps for the company, and decided on what they would take and what they would leave behind; things they wouldn't need any longer. They figured one shovel, and one pick would be all they would need in the way of tools. They still had quite a bit of wood left so they would leave some of it. It didn't take them nearly as long to find gold as they anticipated so there was still plenty of food and wood left. They did keep the food with them.

Everything was divided up and made ready to load onto the mules. After they had a light breakfast and fed the animals, they loaded it all up dividing the gold and the rest of the gear between the two.

The morning was clear and very brisk, cold yes, but rather dry. It was light but there was little sun to be seen. It had snowed during the night and the snow hung heavy and deep. They had to go quite slow going down the mountain. They covered up the entrance of the cave as best they could. It was hard since they had opened it up so much to get the mules through. They found and piled up rocks as high as they could and then threw snow all over it, until it was completely covered. When they looked back on it, it looked pretty natural.

When they came close to the bottom of the mountain, the snow started getting so deep they had to cut over and try to stay on firmer ground. About that time Harry heard the same noise he had heard before. He looked back over his shoulder and saw three men coming over the same mountain they had just been on.

They were big and burley men in heavy snow gear. Looked like typical mountain men.

Just as Harry looked around they were levelling their guns at them. One of the men shot and the bullet grazed the mule that Lousier was leading. The mule reared, pulling the reins out of Lousier's hands and in its panic started running as best it could in the snow. Oddly enough, it was heading in the direction of the strangers. Instinctively Lousier took out after the mule. At the same time Harry's mule took off in the other direction while Harry was pulling his pistol. Harry's mule was heading up the adjoining mountainside. Lousier and the mule were nearly chest deep in the low mountain snow. Harry got his gun out and fired at the men. He took good aim and was sure he had hit one of them. Lousier had regained the reins of his mule, and the men had backed off some out of the site of Harry's fire. Harry turned and was trying to make it to his mule, not wanting him to get away, and as he was heading up the mountain he realized that there was a great noise coming from high up on the mountain.

He looked up and saw, with amazement, what looked like the whole mountain coming down towards them. Avalanche, of course. He had never seen an avalanche before and didn't immediately realize exactly what was happening or the danger that it carried with it. He was awe-struck but at the same time lurching up the mountain after his mule.

He quickly realized the danger Lousier was in. He called to him:

"Lousier, get out of there, come up the mountain, hurry!" But he had no sooner said it than he realized it was too late.

"I'm coming Harry," called Lousier.

It seemed that the whole damn mountain was falling down.

Harry was probably 40 or 50 feet above where Lousier was, but when the snow stopped coming down Harry was also covered. He kept climbing up the mountain as the snow was falling and the only thing that saved him from being completely engulfed in the snow was the valley between the two mountains. The rushing snow kept flooding through this area instead of piling up on Harry.

It had been the shots of both the robbers, if that's what they were, and Harry's shots that started the movement of the snow. It took Harry several minutes to wiggle his way out of his snowy tomb. When he looked over to where he last saw Lousier, the snow was almost level with his eye. He instinctively started to go to Lousier, but one step and he sank into the soft snow over his head. There must have been fifty feet of snow covering Lousier.

He was, for the first time in his life, in a panic. All he could do was to hold on the reins of his mule and stare at the site. He thought for a moment that he might be able to get around from the other side of the mountain, but even if he could, it would take hours and the shovel they brought with them was with Lousier. Harry had only the pick.

Realizing the enormity of the situation and the obvious death of the man who was like a father to him, and the fact that he could do nothing about it, he started to cry. He just stood there and the tears became profuse.

CHAPTER XX

Lament

He didn't have any idea how long he stayed in that spot. It was as if he was frozen. He was trying desperately to think of something he could do, knowing all the while, in his heart how hopeless it was.

He became angry, thinking of the reason they were there in the first place: the damn gold, and those bastard men. If it hadn't been for them this never would have happened. At least he was sure that they died in the avalanche as well but that was little consolation.

He didn't want to leave but there was no alternative. It was well past noon before he finally brought himself to start in the direction of the city. He was still crying, and he felt as if his gut was turning upside down. He kept looking back, although he didn't know why. It was a great effort to put one foot in front of the other.

He didn't go very fast, but he kept on moving until it was almost dark. A natural instinct for self-preservation took him to an area where he could make a camp of sorts. He moved like a robot He couldn't keep his mind on what he was doing. He tied up his mule, threw down his bed pack, gave the mule something to eat, erected a small shelter over his bed pack, crawled in and finally went to a very restless sleep.

He awoke with a start. He didn't even realize where he was for an instant. He looked around for Lousier and suddenly realized the disaster of the day before. He lay there and started to cry all over again. Finally, he gave the mule something to eat but couldn't stand the thought of making a fire to heat up or cook anything to eat for himself. He didn't even feel hungry. As soon as the mule finished eating, he headed out again, this time moving as quickly as he could. He wanted to get out of the forest and the mountains. He tried not to think about Lousier. He tried to concentrate on what he was going to do. He just couldn't keep his mind thinking straight. He would lose his train of thought, and have to start all over again.

What should he do? He dreaded the thought of going back to the mining company and tell them what happened. If he did, should he tell them about the gold, some of which he still had on the mule? What would they demand of him. He couldn't stand to go back and show them where it was now. He thought that even if they could recover a body 50 to 70 feet below the surface, and do it by hand and shovel, it would take many days. It may not even be possible now with such deep snow all around. Yet he dreaded the thought of leaving Lousier there, it seemed like such a lonely place.

He mulled it over and over in his mind all the way back to civilization. He was heading back to the mining office, but as he approached the town he turned off the path. He found a place where he could sit. He tied the mule to a tree, sat down, and started to cry all over again, silently but the tears rolled down his cheeks.

He finally decided not to go back to the office. He planned to write a letter to them telling them all about what happened. He thought that he would tell them that if and when there was a thaw of the snow and it was possible to get to the body, they could contact him and he would return and lead a team to go and get Lousier. That way they would know that they found gold, where it was marked out on the map they gave him, and they might help him retrieve his friend. Yes, that's the thing to do. He would tell a little lie about the mule and the gold that he brought out with him. It wasn't a big thing, but he just couldn't go back there now. He had to get away. He longed to be home again. God, it had been over two years, since he last saw his mothers. Yes, he had to get away.

He gave the mule to some children whom he could see were quite poor. He also had some food left over which he left in his pack with the mule. They were very happy for the gift. They asked him to come to see their parents, so they could thank him, but also so that they would know that they had not stolen the mule. He did and the parents were very grateful.

He made arrangements for passage on a ship that took him through the Panama Canal. Before he left he thought about seeing Isabelle but he just couldn't bring himself to see her, or anyone for that matter. He would have to tell her all about the misfortune and he didn't want to talk about it. He knew though, that he would never forget and he didn't want to forget the man he loved like a father, but he did wish he could get the awful picture out of his mind of that avalanche coming down and Lousier trying to move out of the way of it over and over he could hear him saying:

"I'm coming Harry," over and over. No, seeing Isabelle wouldn't help at all.

He tried to keep himself busy getting his things together, selling the truck and making ready to set sail. This time he wished he could fly and get home sooner but he knew nothing about the airlines, or even if there were flights he could take but he didn't even feel like finding out.

He avoided seeing anyone he knew and he boarded the ship, took one look back, a quick one, closed his eyes and leaned against the rail until the cabin boy came to take him to his cabin.

It was a very long and boring trip. The same trip would have been wonderful if Lousier had been with him, and not back there lying under tons of snow. As it was, he spent most of his time just sitting on deck, looking out over the sea. Just as a habit, he did run every day but it was labored, it wasn't fun and for the first time he got tired.

He sent a telegram to Nice several days before arriving and his mothers were waiting for him with open arms. He hadn't told them about Lousier and he hadn't written a letter since it happened, so they didn't know. They were all smiles and so happy to see him and he was very relieved to see them as well. Of course it wasn't long before they asked about Lousier. At the mention of his name, Harry almost broke out in tears. He choked his tears back and it took him a few deep breaths before he could get it out.

He explained:

"Lousier isn't coming home. There was an accident. He's dead. Please, let me tell you all about it after I have bathed and changed clothes. I really hate to think about it. It's a very sad story I have to tell you."

"Of course, don't think about it now Harry, we can talk later, Kathleen said.

Jeanne agreed and they hugged him and Harry said:

"It's so good to be home and to see you two. Oh! How I have missed you"

Harry eventually told them the whole story, from the beginning. It was hard to get it out but it was chiseled into his memory as if it were happening all over again. He could hear the sound of Lousier calling again, "I'm coming Harry," like a record playing over and over in his head. Then he could see that horrible mountain of snow crashing down, with no time to do anything at all about it.

"Fools! Fools we were to go up there."

The tears came back in his eyes and his mothers knew how hard it was for him to remember. They couldn't think of anything to say to try to ease his pain. For days he would sit and look out over the vineyards, or walk out among the grapevines. Aside from his daily runs he just couldn't get himself to get interested much in anything to do. He sat down one day to write to the mining company. It took him nearly one hour before he got one line written. After starting over three or more times he finally found the right wording and wrote an exact description of the events, including the would-be robbers. He gave a fairly good description of them as well, and asked them if anyone else had ever been attacked by them before, that they knew of. He told them where and how to find the cave and to look for the rubble of rocks they had piled up in the opening. He was sure they would have no trouble finding it. He made a copy of the map and sent them back the original that was all marked. He made it clear that he would return to retrieve the body of Lousier when the snow would allow it. If they would just give him time enough to get there he could show them in person exactly where the cave was.

Somehow after he finished the letter, and it was quite long and very detailed, he seemed to feel a little relieved.

Several weeks passed before he got an answer from the mining company. They thanked him for his letter and for his directions to the gold. They would set up a plan for sending a party to further investigate the value of their find. Also, according to their contract, at that time he could decide whether he wanted to cash out or take royalties from the mining of the gold.

He hadn't even thought of the contract he and Lousier had signed with them, nor did he even consider gaining anything further from it. It had completely slipped his mind. But they made it clear that they were bound by the contract and would honor it. Harry didn't want the money, not that he was so rich, but somehow it didn't seem right since he couldn't share it with Lousier. Oh, how mixed up everything was. It was so hard to think about the right and the wrong.

Harry showed the letter to his mothers. They both read it through before saying anything. They sat for a while, and Jeanne finally said:

"Well you do have the contract. They will go and find the gold, and as you say it looks like a rich vein. If it is and produces a lot of gold, you might just as well get your share. Otherwise, you leave at all to the mining company. That doesn't seem very faire either, since Lousier gave his life for it."

Kathleen pitched in and said:

"Yes and you know very well that Lousier would want you to have it whatever it is, just as you would have wanted him to have it if the situation was reversed."

Harry was silent for a while.

"I guess your right about that, he told Kathleen. That's the kind of person Lousier was. If there is any amount of money coming from it, I could use it to go and get him, bring him home to his own land, and give him a fitting burial with it. I think he would like to be here on the farm with us. Perhaps that way he might be sharing in it just a little" and tears began to swell up in his eyes.

They didn't talk about it again. However, the plan seemed to take effect. Something positive, and now he was hoping to hear from the mining company soon. It might not be long to wait since the snows should have started to thaw by now. Although they said that there was almost always snow in the mountains, maybe not just as much.

Harry tried to keep himself busy with his mothers, tending to the ranch, doing some business, and trying to stay in shape. He began to feel a little better after a while. He did finally realize that Lousier's death was, if not a total accident because of the robbers. At least it wasn't his fault. He just had a hard time dealing with the fact that the firing of his gun might have been what helped to trigger the avalanche. There was little else he could have done though, and that seemed to become more evident to him as the days went by.

Finally he received a letter from the mining company. They were sure that by the time Harry could get there the snow would be at its lowest level and they would be ready to send a party with him so he could show them where the gold was found and they would also help him with his friend.

CHAPTER XXI

Lousier comes home

Harry made reservations right away, and prepared to leave. Jeanne said the night before he left, to be careful but she was sure he would feel much better when he returned with Lousier.

"Yes, I think your right, I feel better even now for the opportunity to go after him."

The people at the mining company were happy to see Harry and congratulated him on the finding of the gold. Of course they said that they were very sorry to hear about his partners accident and that they would do all they could to help him.

It took a couple of days for the mining company to prepare for the trip into the mountains after his arrival. In the meantime, he thought he should go and see Isabelle. She was surprised to see him and asked him where he had been so long and had he been in the mountains all this time?

He said he would tell her the whole story, but it was a long one and would be better told over a dinner. She looked a little sheepish and said:

"Harry, I hate to tell you this, but since I last saw you, I have become engaged to be married."

It took Harry very much by surprise. For him the time had passed quite quickly, but it had actually been several Months.

"I've known my husband to-be for a long time. He is from my hometown. It was never very serious, although I have always had a close relationship with him. He asked me to marry him and I accepted. I'm sorry."

"Don't be sorry. I'm very happy for you and I hope you both will be very happy."

"Thank you" she said, "but I would like to know what happened on your trip to the mountains"

"If you and your fiancée will meet me here this evening, I'll take you both to dinner and tell you. I'd like to meet him anyhow".

"She said, "I'll arrange it and we will be looking for you, and thank you for your understanding."

"I am disappointed, but what else could I do? Things seem to work out for the best" he said, as he gently put his hand on her cheek and continued, "I wish you all the happiness."

The trip into the mountains was very labored for Harry. Oh, he was physically OK, but it was the thought of seeing Lousier, as he imagined he was, and it was heavy on his mind.

When they finally reached the area, there was still a lot of snow but much of it had melted. The man in charge of the party came to Harry and told him,:

"It would be better if we waited to find your friend until we are ready to leave. I know you must be anxious, but if we take him out now, he might begin to thaw, and that wouldn't be good."

Harry thought for a moment, and said, "Of course."

He showed them where the cave was and the veins. They took a few samples and did a little digging. They carried quite a bit of some kind of sophisticated equipment with them. Harry didn't see what they did with it.

They told Harry they thought it looked good. But they weren't there to do any mining, only to investigate, and report back to their office. They spent the night in the cave and the next morning

descended the mountain and prepared to look for Lousier. Harry
knew exactly where he was. It was fastened in his mind, as if it were
yesterday. By this time in the year he was only about 15 feet below
the surface, but the digging party still had to start from a lower level
beside the mountain down from where he was entombed, almost
like tunnelling. When they came upon the mule Harry cautioned
them:

"Be careful digging now, because Lousier would be very close
by."

After clearing more snow off the mule, they found Lousier's arm
around its neck. Harry remembered that he was trying to lead the
mule away from the robbers back to where he was. He must have
grabbed the mule around the neck when he realized the avalanche
was so near. If they had to dig fifteen feet to get to Lousier now,
more snow than Harry imagined must have covered him. When they
finally cleared all the snow away, they found that he was huddled up
close to the mule, as if to stay warm from its body.

It was a terrible sight for Harry to see. The man told Harry to
go and wait for them. They would pack him in snow and wrap him
with a big tarpaulin they brought and carry him on a sled behind
their mules. They did come prepared, and Harry appreciated their
experience and their consideration.

When they returned to the city, Harry had Lousier's body
embalmed at an undertaker. He bought a casket for him and made
arrangements for the trip home. When he returned to the mining
company, they told him that they could give him three choices
offered in the contract. One, he could wait until they started mining
the gold and they would send him his royalties; two, he could wait
until they made further exploration to determine better just what the
find was worth; or three, they would settle with him now. Harry said
right away, that he would rather settle now and have done with it.

The gold that was in Lousier's pack was equal, or nearly so, to the
amount Harry had taken in his pack. Before the rescue party reached
the office on their return, he told the lead man, that he would like for
them to have it, and share it amongst his men for their kindness and
attention. They seemed reluctant to accept, but Harry insisted.

The man called over all his men and told them what Harry wanted them to do. He said he would sell it in the city and divide the proceeds with them all, but he then turned to Harry and said he wanted Harry to go with him when he did. Harry agreed. It made the men very happy and they all thanked him.

The mining company offered Harry a cash settlement of seven thousand five hundred dollars. He told them that if they would pay him in French Franks he would accept. He might have gained much more had he waited, but he already had over three thousand dollars worth from the first load he carried out, and he didn't want to have any further attachment with this company or this country. It flashed through his mind though, that if things had worked out differently with Isabelle, he would probably have had a lot more to do with this country.

The trip home was uneventful, and as usual he was very happy to get home. They held a memorial for Lousier and buried him in the graveyard that Robert had prepared. It was a great load off Harry's mind. He seemed satisfied that he had done all he could do. The head stone they had prepared for him read:

Lousier Villant
Professor, Tutor, True Friend
Laid to Rest November 24, 1937

It was just about one month to Christmas 1937, and the climate around the house turned a little more joyful. Things started buzzing about the Christmas party. Kathleen and Jeanne knew just how to plan a good party after so much experience and it wasn't hard to get people to come.

Times were quite uncertain in these days due to the political situation, with the government rocking back and forth with the Socialists, Communists and royalists of the third republic and the depression when many people were hurting. The friends of Kathleen and Jeanne jumped at the chance to get the government and all the problems off of their minds.

Harry was happy to be at home again. He thought many times of his earlier years in Paris, but now he really did think of Nice as his home.

Kathleen and he talked one day before the party. She asked him if he had plans to take another show on the road.

"It hasn't crossed my mind as yet." He said.

"You know Lousier's death really gave me a Sunday punch; the memory of that avalanche and his death still haunts me at times. That reminds me I haven't told Mustafa about the accident yet. I must get in touch with him. We were all very close friends as well as business associates."

"Yes of course," was all she said.

"No, I'm not planning anything now. I have been away from you two for too long and I want to stick around for awhile, if you'll let me." He laughed and she hit him a little slap on the face. "You bad boy,

we missed you so much, but when you're doing the things you enjoy, and you're not having accidents, it also makes us happy. We read your letters over and over."

Chapter **XXII**

Christmas 1937

"Well, are we going to have a party or not?" he asked, with a lilt in his voice and a wink in his eye.

"You bet, and I'm going to see to it that everyone has a very good time!" She stood up and further said: "I'm sending out the invitations today."

Actually none of the invitations were mailed. She had them delivered by car, foot and by bicycle. The person delivering them was to wait for an RSVP. Neither Kathleen nor Jeanne liked to be kept waiting.

Jeanne told the houseman to round up all the extra blankets and have them handy. There surely would be people who wouldn't, or couldn't go home, and would spend the night there. She was right. The morning after the party there were people sleeping all over the place, some had a little too much to drink, but no one was rowdy or caused any trouble. They just didn't have the ability, or the desire to make it home. Kathleen and Jeanne enjoyed having them there and told the cook to be sure to have plenty to eat when they came alive again.

By the way Jeanne said: "Harry isn't here," talking to Kathleen quietly.

"Oh! No? You mean he has taken that ugly girl home?"

That ugly girl was the daughter of another vineyard rancher and businessman. She was twenty-seven years old, and a raving beauty. She had never been married, but had had many men friends over the past few years. Kathleen invited her to the party, thinking that perhaps she might just enjoy meeting Harry.

Jeanne said: "I guess you were right." and they both laughed.

Harry came in that afternoon. He said he had a date for that night and wanted to get freshened up. He asked both of them:

"I don't have to tell you with whom, do I?"

They shook their heads no at the same time and then they all laughed. Christmas Eve was the next day and Harry said:

"I'll be here tomorrow, for sure. I have something for both of you that Santa Clause gave me.

"Ooh!" They said, "Santa Clause La?" With a serious face, he just nodded.

After he had returned home and started feeling better, he decided what he wanted to do with at least some of the gold he had brought back, there was quite a bit of it.

He took it to a Jewellery maker and had two necklaces made, one for Kathleen and one for Jeanne, both identical. He had the jeweller fashion in an artistic but unusual design bunches of grapes on the vine. They were fairly heavy, but not bad for the neck. They turned out beautiful.

Since Christmas was a family affair, they invited all the workers and servants to come and bring their families. They had the kitchen help prepare all the food, but Kathleen hired several outside workers to come to serve it all and clean up afterward, so her own help didn't have to, and they could all enjoy Christmas together.

Kathleen and Jeanne had gone shopping during the year, looking for gifts for all the people especially the children. Harry shopped nearly every day after Lousier's burial. They had collected together many different and wonderful kinds of toys for Santa to pass out to the children. One of the single men, who worked on the farm in the vineyards, acted as the Santa. He was a big man, and with the costume that Jeanne found, he was perfect for the job. He also passed out all the other presents for the rest of the people. But the best presents they gave were envelopes with money. They didn't pass them out however, until everyone was leaving, either going home or going to their quarters where they stayed at the farm.

When all had left, Harry said that he thought that Santa had forgotten something. He went to the wall and from behind one of the drapes he brought out two packages, all wrapped in beautiful paper and large bows.

"I think these are for you two," he said looking at his mothers.

As they opened them they found a beautiful box made of hand rubbed teakwood. When they opened the lids, the beautiful 24 K gold necklaces presented a glow that was dazzling. There was a lot of ooing and awing. Harry helped each one on with them, and they both stared at themselves in the mirror.

Jeanne said: "We don't have to look in the mirror; we just have to look at each other, see. They are both exactly the same."

"You naughty boy, so this is what you were talking about when you said that Santa Claus had given you something?"

"Yes, and he said he hoped you would both like them."

They hugged him and kissed him, but they both said in unison that they had found something that they thought Santa had left for him, as well. They left the room for a moment and came back with several boxes, large and small. First you have to open the big box, they said. It was a gorgeous set of dress tails, black mohair. They had gone to his tailor and had him make it. The tailor knew the exact measurements, and when they insisted he try it on, it fit perfectly, but they made him take another smaller box with him which was his shirt, tie, and studs. When he came back into the room he had everything on but shoes. They handed him another box.

"Open it" they said, and when he did he found some beautiful shoes; dress slippers which were all the rage.

"Now so you don't feel too undressed, you can open this last little box." It was a gold watch.

"Well," he said, "I think we should just step over to Monaco since we are all dressed for it." They laughed, as Harry started to do one of his "Soft Shoe" dances without music. He was so graceful and they loved to see him dance. Jeanne put some music on the Victrola, and when he finished, each one danced with him. They lingered a while longer, dancing and loving being together. Finally, tired and it being very late, or early in the morning, they kissed and said good night.

Life around the farm resumed on the day after Christmas. However, things got started a little slowly. The families around the farm were still much occupied with the children and all their toys. Harry went out and played with many of them. They flew little model airplanes, and sailed toy ships in the ponds around the farm. Some of them had sails and others were propelled by a small candle which made steam to turn the propeller, they were quite fascinating.

With New Year coming up, great parties were in store. Kathleen and Jeanne usually had a lot of people at the chateau for New Year's Eve parties, but this year the father of the young woman that Harry took home from the Christmas party had invited all of the people that were usually at the chateau, and others. It was to be a fabulous gala. Of course, everyone would be wearing their finest, jewels and all.

France still was not in the best shape financially, but these people had money from long years past. Some of them had fought in the war, and all of them had contributed both money and time. Some of them had done some resistance activities, as Kathleen and Jeanne did, working in different places throughout France. Many intriguing stories could be heard from time to time. Now few people wanted to talk about it but some still wanted to hear more. It had been such a horrifying time in France, for the country and for the people, everyone was just happy that it was over. The celebrations were testimonials to their relief.

Although well into their fifties now, both Kathleen and Jeanne were still beautiful and also very shapely. They kept themselves in good shape by doing exercises, steam baths and massages regularly. When they appeared at the party with Harry, dressed in his new finery, they made a striking scene.

Kathleen, with her salt and pepper black hair and blue eyes, wore a long white evening gown with spaghetti straps, cut quite low, but not inappropriate. Around her neck she wore the necklace Harry gave her.

Jeanne with her blond hair that she had touched up to hide the gray, and her hazel eyes wore a stunning long black gown, with the same cut as Kathleen's and she too had her necklace on. Everyone remarked about how unusual and beautiful the necklaces were, and the story of how Harry had found the pure gold in the mountains in Chile made them even more interesting. They didn't get into the misfortune of Lousier's demise; some of them knew about it, but those who didn't were not told.

Most of the people in the crowd around Nice knew and liked Kathleen and Jeanne, and most of the men loved them, in one way or another. There were several single men there at the party and they were all devising different tactics and approaches to get next to these two lovely ladies, yet trying not to be too obvious. The two ladies danced with just about everyone there, but they and not the men chose the one to be with at the midnight hour. Of course it was customary for everyone there to kiss on New Year's, but the kiss with the men they wound up with lasted a little longer.

Harry, danced with most all of the women, but most of his time was taken up with the beautiful daughter of the man who threw the party. The Gentleman knew Harry. Actually he knew of Harry, he had only met him briefly one time. His daughter's name was Yvonne. He and Harry were getting acquainted and having some Champaign. He said to Harry:

"Yvonne tells me that you are an entertainer."

Harry said that he was. He explained how he and his partner put together "travelling shows" and took them to different parts of the world.

"That must be an interesting undertaking," he said. Harry told him that it offered a world of education,"p eople in general are most interesting. If you speak to them in their own language, it's unbelievable the things you can learn."

"You speak several languages don't you?"

"I feel that I am quite fluent in 10. I learned 5 languages here in France in school. I can never thank my mothers enough for giving me the kind of education they did. My life has been extremely interesting and my efforts were made quite easy because of it."

"Would you do me and my guest a big favor and perform a dance for us?"

Harry tried to beg off, saying that he thought the guests would prefer to do their own dancing. But the man insisted, and attracted everyone's attention.

"All of you know Harry. Some of you know that he is a great dancer, but most of you have not seen him dance. I am one of those. I have asked him to perform for us tonight"

A big applause rang out, and some of the people nearby, said, "Oh yes Harry, please do."

Harry looked at his mothers, shrugged his shoulders, and stepped out into the center of the dance floor. He told the small orchestra that he would do a soft-shoe, and he wouldn't need any music, but if they wanted to pick it up somewhere, it would be OK. The orchestra was just a few pieces but they were a very professional group. About halfway through the dance they started playing along with Harry in soft music, and stop-time. When he got ready, Harry told them how many more bars left to the end of his dance, and they all ended together. It made a splendid performance, and everyone howled and applauded. They wanted more, but Harry got their attention and said:

"At our next fund-raiser for the wounded war heroes, I will do as many dances as you will pay for, but until then, I want you to do your own dancing."

They all laughed, and as the music started playing, they rushed to the dance floor.

The Host thanked Harry and complemented him on his performance. He said he wished he could do that. About that time Yvonne came over, put her arm through Harry's and said to her father: "You have hogged this man long enough, now it's my turn."

She dragged Harry to the floor and they embraced, moving gently with the music, cheek to cheek. They made a stunning pair.

Chapter **XXIII**

Yvonne

As it neared midnight, the leader of the orchestra gave a warning. Harry took Yvonne by the arm and said that he wanted to go over to where his mother's were.

"I've missed kissing them on New Year's Eve too many times, and I'm not going to let it happen tonight. I do want you to be with us though, will you please?"

"Try to get rid of me?" she said, as they worked their way through the crowd.

Kathleen and Jeanne were looking for Harry too. Each of them seemed to be attached to one of the lucky men who had won the pleasure of their company and he caught their eye just as the countdown started. Ten, nine, eight, at the count of zero, they all embraced together and after many kisses, and many happy new year's. Harry said to them all: "I guess I am the luckiest man in the world right now."

The other two fellows said, "Me too," almost in unison.

It was humorous, since they were actually a little shy, but quite excited. They all had a good laugh. As the music played they all sang and traded off dancing with one-another. When Harry danced with Kathleen and Jeanne, he told each of them how very beautiful they looked. Jeanne remarked;

"It looks like you have another beauty to look after as well?"

"It's been a long time since I have had much real feeling for any of the ladies I have known, but this one," and he hesitated, "I don't know, she really does something to me.

"Yes, we can see that," she said, holding back a laugh.

"I guess we had better get these two gentlemen to take us home, No?" He answered:

"Oui, je suppose!"

Kathleen saw them having a laugh and said: "What's going on?"

Jeanne told her that she would tell her later, as she let Harry go to dance with Yvonne again, but she whispered in his ear as they broke: "Have a good time."

Soon after, Harry and Yvonne snuck away, quietly. They headed for Yvonne's apartment. Her father had offices in town and she worked for him doing almost anything that needed to be done. She was an accomplished businesswoman, and a great asset to the business.

Her apartment was close and convenient to the office. It wasn't the first time Harry had been with her there but with his excitement it made it seem as if it was. He paid the taxi and they started up the stairs to her door. His anticipation of taking her in his arms and having her this night, with all the other excitement was a little overwhelming. Before she opened the door, he took her by her both arms and turned her to him. He looked at her for a long moment, he said:

"I'm very happy." They embraced with a long warm kiss.

Harry kicked the door open, bent down and picked her up, carried her right into the bedroom and gently laid her down on the bed. He leaned over her and she said to him, in a soft, whispery voice:

"Make love to me Harry, please make love to me."

For many days after, Harry mulled over the prospects of asking Yvonne to marry him. He couldn't get it straight through his head. He had been a bachelor for such a long time it was difficult to visualize what it would be like to be married.

He kept seeing Yvonne every other day, at least. They never got down to any serious discussions about their future together, they just had fun being together and doing different things. They would go horseback riding, boating, and swimming; spend time on the beach, and dancing. They even made it over to Monaco for a long weekend, but no serious talk.

Finally, One day, Harry asked Jeanne and Kathleen to sit-down and have a talk with him. He told them of his dilemma. They were sympathetic and they listened to all the things that seemed to trouble him. Yet in all, they could not see that he really had any problems.

He kept saying how much they liked to be together, that they had mostly the same interests, and so on, they couldn't find any contradictions with what he was saying.

Kathleen asked him, after listening to him:

"Do you love her?" The question rather caught him off guard. He didn't answer for some time, seemed like an eternity.

"I guess that is the trouble, I don't know." "Well that is a big question," she said.

"Yes, I think so too." Jeanne chimed in. Harry looked at one and then the other.

"I guess I don't know what love is any more. I thought I did, I knew I loved Yvette. I thought I could get over losing her. I thought I had, but maybe I hadn't. Maybe I'm afraid to. Could that be the problem? I can't tell. I don't know what it is."

Jeanne brought up a question that no one had thought of as yet. She said:

"Do you think Yvonne wants to marry you? Do you think she wants to get married at all? She has had lots of chances. I know that several men have asked her, nice men. Maybe she is not yet ready to settle down with one man."

Harry looked quite surprised, puzzled.

"You know, that question hadn't entered my mind. What a fool I am. Why would I think that all I had to do was ask? We fit so well together. I guess I just took it for granted that she's mine for the asking how foolish of me."

"*Alor!*, that's all you should have to do: to ask, that is" Kathleen remarked. "But it is something to think about."

Then Jeanne said:

"If she was going to marry anyone, there is no reason she wouldn't want it to be you, but there again, she may not want to get married. Would you be hurt if you asked her and she said no?"

"To be honest, I hadn't thought about that denial. I guess I would be disappointed. I don't think I would be hurt with her rejection but I have to think about it. If it came to that, I would hope that we could remain close friends, as we are now."

His mother's both agreed that that would be great and the way it should be.

Harry didn't see Yvonne for a couple of days after that. When he did decide to make another date with her, he went to her office where she worked with her father. Yvonne's mother had died when she was quite young, and her father and she had become very close. He hadn't re-married although he had thought about it several times. He wasn't a womanizer but he wasn't a prude either. He and Yvonne experienced a great life together as a loving father and a devoted daughter. They had almost no secrets from one another. Their life went along smoothly day by day.

Yvonne was happy to see Harry. She took him into her father's office to say hello. He greeted Harry cordially, offered him a drink, or tea, or coffee. Harry refused graciously. And they visited for just a short conversation then Yvonne and Harry went back into her office. Harry asked her if she would care to go to Monaco again on the weekend. She said but of course, almost without thinking about it, as if to say, why do you have to ask. He was delighted.

"We'll leave early on Friday, Is that all right with you?" "Yes, she said, let's do get an early start."

Monaco was a beautiful place. They decided to take a tour to see the capitol atop a rocky promontory called Monaco Ville. It seemed majestic. They stopped at a lookout, and gazed out over the Mediterranean and they could see nearly all of Monaco. They went down to the Oceanographic Museum, which was established in 1910, 27 years ago. Louis II, ruler of Monaco, continued the tradition of making Monaco a place of interest and beauty. France approves the successor to the throne of Monaco which is mostly a formality. It is just on the border of Italy.

One could find the very essence of wealth and beauty in Monte Carlo. It was a romantic place. Just the setting that Harry wanted when he turned to Yvonne, hesitated a moment, took her hand and looking at her warmly said:

"I have wanted to ask you something for a long time."

She was silent.

"I think you know that I love you. I would like to make you my wife, if you'll have me."

She said nothing. She reached over and kissed him, a long and lovingly warm kiss. When she finally broke the kiss, she didn't break the embrace. She stayed close and spoke in his ear, in almost a whisper, but her voice was soft and clear.

"You know I love you, I love everything about you, and when you make love to me it is like heaven. You're so gentle yet strong, all the things a woman could ask for." She hesitated. "I am so flattered that you want me to be your wife."

She broke way now and looked at him. "I just can't marry you Harry, It wouldn't work."

A thousand thoughts raced through Harry's mind; was it her father, her job, because he was black or that he was an orphan. Did she know about his mothers and their work? He was suddenly panicked and his breathing started to be labored.

"I know myself Harry dear" She used the words, *"Mon Cherie"* "I'm not ready to settle down. As we are, we are happy, lovers, happy go lucky, no commitment, only to make it as grand as we can. I like that, and I would like it to continue like that, for as long as it last."

Harry was at a loss for words. He thought right away how happy he was that she wasn't angry with him for asking her, but he wondered what the future would bring. He was dreadfully disappointed, but somehow in the back of his mind he wasn't too surprised. This beautiful, carefree woman, with total abandonment, whom he had been with now for some time and made disparate and wonderful love to, was surely a thing of passion, with no commitment, like she said.

"Well will you at least think about it while we are enjoying this life?"

She laughed and kissed him again with a little peck.

"Silly," she said, "I think about it all the time. Now come on, let's go play some games and mingle with the beautiful people, and above all, let's find our hotel room."

She laughed and they kissed again a passionately.

Of the many things Harry was, he was a businessman. To idle away his life playing wasn't something that gave him the greatest satisfaction.

Oh, he was enjoying himself all right, especially being with Yvonne and their lifestyle and being around his mothers. He tried to busy himself with some of the business of the vineyard, but it wasn't something that either Jeanne or Kathleen wasn't very capable of doing themselves. He began to get nervous, more ill at ease. He was accustomed to being on the road, travelling and engaging himself in exciting business.

He told his mothers that he thought it might do him good to go up to Paris and see some of his old friends. Jeanne asked him:

"What about Yvonne?"

"The thought just came to my mind, and I haven't had time to think about it. I suppose I could ask her if she wanted to go along."

Kathleen said:

"On the other hand it just might be good to be away from her for a little while. Both of you might find out whether you can or can't live without each other."

"You might have something there," Harry said with a surprised look. He got up and wondered off in deep thought.

Jeanne and Kathleen chuckled with one another as to the way Harry took suggestions and conversations they often had. They would often nearly put him in a concentrated trance, like now. He just got up and walked away, deep in thought

"I guess that is one of the things that make him so special; he doesn't argue, he thinks."

A couple of more weeks went by and Harry was on the verge of taking off for Paris when a letter came for him. Kathleen called him from the chateau. He was engaged in a conversation with the ranch foreman about an irrigation problem they were having in one quarter of the property. It wasn't serious, but it seemed as if a new well might have to be dug.

Hurry Kathleen called waving the letter. It's from Mustafa. When he heard her say that he wheeled around and bounded into the chateau with great excitement. He hadn't heard from Mustafa for several months. He thought to himself how strange it was that Mustafa had been on his mind for some time, and now here was a letter from him.

"Listen, I will read it to you" Harry told Kathleen. She was delighted that he would be so considerate; she really did want to know what was in the letter.

Through the first part, it was just cordiality and expressions of how much he missed the fun they had on their various excursions, and what he had been doing since they ended their tour in South America.

He did get married as he said he might, and he already had one child. He was engaged in the management of a cabaret in

Algiers. He described it in much detail. The owner was old and had taken a liking to Mustafa. He had no sons but he did have a couple of daughters that were themselves fairly old but had absolutely no ambitions to be tied to a cabaret.

Chapter **XXIV**

Algeria

"Would you have any interest in going into a partnership with me in this business? We can have it for a song, and I would dearly love to have you for my partner; at least I know you could protect me." And he added "Ha-Ha."

Suddenly Harry's heart started to pump stronger. He had a sudden rush of excitement. He put the letter in his lap and stared out into nothingness for a long moment. Kathleen knew that look. She had seen it many times before when he was deep in planning. He could, at this moment, be out in the middle of the Sahara, for he was oblivious of anyone around him.

Finally he turned and looked at Kathleen,

"What do you think of that?" he said, in a soft voice that was not exactly a question.

Kathleen was quiet, thinking that she would let him answer his own question.

"This presents a very interesting situation and question. You know I have been terribly uneasy lately because of nothing for me to do but play. I have needed something to do. I wonder if this could be it."

Kathleen said:

"Maybe it would be a good idea for you to go and take a look see."

Harry looked at her for a moment, then leaned over and kissed her, looking at her again, his eyes full of love and said:

"How is it that you always seem to know how to say just the right things?" It brought tears to Kathleen's eyes.

"It's easy to be good to you my love. You are such a devoted, loving son."

Jeanne entered the room about that time and they told her all about the letter, and explained what they were discussing.

Jeanne said:

"Why don't we go with him?"

"Voila! Now that is a thought." said Kathleen.

"What a wonderful idea." chimed in Harry. We had better think it over seriously, was everyone's opinion.

Jeanne said:

"In the meantime, I will start making reservations," then laughed, sure that they all would be going.

Mustafa had asked Harry to try to give him an answer without too much delay as the owner friend was very anxious to retire from a business that he had owned for over twenty years. Besides, he wasn't in the best of health. Of course, the letter instead of a telegram meant that it wasn't a crisis situation but Harry decided to reply by telegram, just the same.

He told Mustafa, in his reply, that he was interested and was coming to look things over. He couldn't give him a definitive answer until he did. But, he did like the idea, and the thought of being in partners with an old friend was certainly something worth considering.

They did decide to all go together. They weren't worried about the operation of the farm for a few weeks anyhow because the people managing it were just like family and had proven their loyalty many times over. Kathleen, Jeanne, and Harry went to the bank and explained to the bank manager that their plans would keep them away for a few weeks. They would allow the foreman of the ranch to draw a reasonable amount of money for salaries and any kind of emergency. The bank manager could contact them at an address that they would send to him as soon as they arrived, for any conformation he might need.

Their arrival in Algiers and seeing Mustafa was very happy and exciting. Mustafa wanted them all to stay at his villa. He said there was plenty of room, and he and his wife would be delighted to have them. They thanked him graciously but said that they thought it would be better if they stayed at a hotel but they did want to spend a lot of their time together.

Mustafa had a lovely villa. Actually it was Moroccan style architecture with lots of arches and beautiful sandy and orange colored stones. Marble floors and hand carved furniture. It was quite large and they had two or three servants. The cabaret wasn't the only business Mustafa was engaged in. Harry knew that he always had many things going at the same time. He was a true entrepreneur. Harry was delighted to see that he was successful, although he never had any doubts about that. He had always been very happy with the way he handled his tours. Yes, he though, if he was going to be a partner with anyone, it was good to be with someone he trusted and who had the acumen to make a business successful.

They spent some time there with Mustafa's wife and their young child before going on to the hotel. She was quite a beauty and very cordial. She spoke French as well as Arabic and seemed to have a decent education. She was pregnant again, but in no distress. Harry and his mothers liked her right off. Of course it was the first time Harry had ever met her but since he and Mustafa were such old friends, it was as if he had known her for a long time. He was very happy to meet her and gave her kisses on each cheek in respect of their custom.

Algiers wasn't a very pretty city. It was interesting however, and it held many strange tales. On arrival, Harry couldn't help thinking of that horrible experience of arriving only to find out that the girl he loved so dearly was sick.

The town was rather dark most everywhere one went; only dim lighting lit the streets where there were lights at all. At night it seemed almost sinister, and gave one the feeling that there was danger.

They stayed at the Aletti Hotel. It wasn't grand, but it was one of the better hotels and it was accommodating and in one of the better lighted areas of the city. It wasn't too far from where Mustafa lived. After their first night, having rested up from their trip, they all went to the cabaret.

They served a fabulous Moroccan menu. The food was one of the reasons why Mustafa became acquainted with the owner in the first place.

Mustafa had been doing some business with a man who took him there one night when they were talking over some negotiations. He introduced the owner to him, whose name was Hussein Abd Al-Karim and they just seemed to strike up a good relationship from the start. Mustafa went there several times after that and his wife went with him and that also set well with Hussein. Now Mustafa wanted to introduce Harry to the cabaret.

There was a small orchestra that played soft Arabic music most of the time and featured a man who played the *oud*; a musical instrument much like the lute or mandolin. When they were resting, there was a violinist who played classical numbers and roamed the large room. The bar was quite large and was separated from the dining area by a mosaic wall about chest high. One could only see part of the backs and the heads of the patrons sitting at the bar. There was little or no noise to be heard from the bar area, which was good. Harry was getting some ideas in his head about how they could liven things up, yet still keep a soft atmosphere. The food was great, and the decor was appealing. The service could possibly be improved on but it wasn't bad if one was just having a leisurely evening.

Even though Hussein was quite old, he was a modern man and liked to live a relaxed, non hectic life. His wife had died several years before. They had a loving, long marriage life together. He missed her very much and never married again. He had devoted himself to the business of running the cabaret and often stayed there at night after closing. Hard work and long hours helped to ease the pain of losing his wife. He had a loft built over his office after she died, and although small, it was quite adequate and comfortable. There was even a beautiful French bathtub in one corner of the room, and in the other an Armoire for changes of clothes.

He decided that he would like to devote the rest of his life to his own children and his grandchildren. The cabaret didn't allow him enough time to do that. Besides, he figured that he had owned it long enough, and he was getting a little tired.

During one of Mustafa's many visits to the Cabaret, Hussein told him about his decision. In the following conversation, he asked Mustafa if he had ever had any experience in the restaurant business. By this time he and Hussein had become quite close friends. He told him that he had never had much to do with food, but that the restaurant business, entertainment, and the operation of a bar was his forte. Mustafa proceeded to tell him about Harry and all their travels.

In the end Hussein said:

"Why don't you take over the 'Fez,' as it was called, and make it your business? You have the personality that this place and my customers would like. I will let you have it for an exceptional price, and you can pay for it out of the profits. I don't need the money but if I should die before it is paid you will have to continue to pay the balance to my grandchildren."

Mustafa was amazed by his offer. He almost thought he was kidding, but when he looked into his eyes he could see that he was dead serious.

"You mean that you want to walk away from here completely?"

"Yes. I've made up my mind. I've had enough, and I want to spend time with my family, which I have had little time to do in the past. Perhaps I can make up for some of those lost years".

Mustafa was now in deep thought, not knowing exactly how to react to such a generous offer.

"I am a rich man," he continued. "I own everything I have: my villa, land, everything, and if you take this place, I will also have the money from that. I can give my family, I think, much enjoyment by having the time to spend some of my money on them but doing it with them in person, which I have not been able to do before."

"Before I give you my answer, and believe me I appreciate your offer, I want to talk with Harry, my partner of whom I have told you. I would want him to be with me in this. If he isn't interested, and doesn't want to join me in this enterprise, it would weigh heavily on whether or not I would want to undertake the ownership of such a fabulous place. If and when he comes here you will meet a man like no other you have known. I know you will like him immediately. I will contact him right away and then we will see."

Hussein said that he understood and that he wasn't in a big hurry. He said he would be anxious to meet this Harry you speak of. He was hoping, without saying it, that this Harry would accept the offer.

"Two people who have been together as long as you two have would surely be successful here at the Fez. That is my wish: that it remains as I have made it, a place for people to enjoy. I would like to think that you and Harry can keep it so."

Mustafa was waiting for them outside of the cabaret. They were all so excited just to be together again they couldn't get their remarks to come out right and each one was talking over the other. Mustafa held up his hand and said:

"*Bas! Khalas!-* that's enough- my dears, we have important business to tend to tonight. You will meet Hussein, who is a lovely man. He is offering us a New World, at least a New World of business. And he is doing so at our price, practically. At least he is making it so easy. All we have to do is say yes. I have told him the whole story about us and about Harry. He wanted to hear the whole thing. He was very intrigued. I can't wait for you to meet him, so let's all go in."

Hussein was in the Kitchen when they arrived. The headwaiter showed Mustafa to his usual table but another table had been added to it to make room for all of them. The waiter told Mustafa that he would tell Hussein that he and his guests were here. Mustafa thanked him.

Hussein came in right away and looked quite excited. One of the reasons that he was such a success with the Fez was because he had such a likable personality. He was a fairly big man, a little over weight, but a meticulous, clean dresser. His smile made you want to smile. He had a dark complexion, and looked as if he had just been scrubbed. He held out both arms to Mustafa as he approached. Mustafa did the same and they embraced, as was their tradition. Then Mustafa introduced everyone to Hussein. Looking over at Kathleen and Jeanne, Hussein remarked to Harry:

"I can't believe how lucky you have been to have two mothers as beautiful as these. Oh, don't worry, Mustafa has told me the whole story." He shook his head and said, "What a life you have all had."

Suddenly Harry was missing Yvonne. He had an ache in his heart. He felt that she should be here with him. He had asked her if she would like to accompany him and his mothers and she had said right off that she didn't think she would want to be away from her father's business at this time. He really depended on her for many things and thought it would be an imposition to ask him for the time off. She was certain he would say it was OK, but she didn't think it would be right. Harry had offered for her to just come for one week, but she said one week just wouldn't be worth the trip. She had said that she would miss him terribly, and hoped that he would be back soon. If he decided to stay and engage in the business, then she would consider another arrangement along the lines that they had discussed in Monaco.

Whoa! That made Harry's heart jump. Could she actually be contemplating their marriage? That's what came to his mind now. Oh, how he wished it were so, and how he wished she were here.

"Now we don't want to waste time. Let's have a look at the menu and let me serve you some of the best Moroccan food you have ever tasted. Our chef has been with me for 15 years. All the recipes and instructions are in my safe. If anything happens to him, *la samahallah* - God forbid, the food will not change. Perhaps Mustafa can recommend something. If you will excuse me for a moment, I will go and make sure everything is in order."

He returned almost immediately, with some of the most delicious wine, saying:

"I hope you like red wine. If you do I'm sure you will enjoy this,"

The wine was truly delicious but the food was even better. Mustafa ordered a variety of plates so they could have a good idea of what they served and how good it was. The plate they all chose as the best was the Couscous; it was served with an assortment of vegetables and some delicious, tender lamb roast *Au Juice*. All the other plates were probably just as good but that one stood out above all others.

They ate and talked, and after some exquisite desert, Hussein turned to Harry and said: "Now, Harry, tell me, what do you think of the Fez?"

Harry was already sold on one thing, and that was that the food was for sure, the best he had ever tasted. Harry was the one that had ordered the couscous with lamb. The meat and its sauce were spiced superbly, and the vegetables were exceptional. But that wasn't all that was good about the place. The location, the ambiance, the size of the building, and the condition of everything he could see so far seemed to be kept in pretty nice shape.

"I am deeply impressed. So much so that I can't imagine that you would walk away from it. Mustafa has told me your reasons, but it must have been a very difficult decision to make." Hussein said:

"I anticipated it to be, but when I met Mustafa and he told me of his, and your experiences, I knew that if I could get him, and now you, to take over, I could leave knowing that the Fez would be in good hands.

Mustafa has told me so much about you that it is as if I know you for a long time even though we have just met. Please think it over carefully. I know it's not an easy decision to make but I am sure of one thing: you will enjoy owning and operating the Fez."

Harry turned directly to him and said in all conviction:

"I will be considering your offer very seriously. If I decide to stay, you can be sure that your Fez will continue with its good name. That is a promise I think we can keep."

They agreed to come the next day to the office and look over the books and the inventory, to inspect the rest of the building, and most important, to find out about getting their permits. It was important to know about whatever licenses they would need, and if there would be any problem with Harry being a foreigner. Hussein said that he was certain that there would be no problem, but that he would take them to the proper offices and they could find out for themselves.

After they said good night to Hussein, and thanked him graciously for his hospitality, they all went to the Aletti Hotel, Mustafa included. Mustafa told Harry that he knew all the ropes about permits and licenses and he knew that there would be no problem.

Harry said that he knew that this was Mustafa's forte and if anyone should know about such things, it would be him.

Mustafa asked Harry what he thought about it. Harry said:

"As I told Hussein, I am very impressed. I just want a little time to think about it." Mustafa said that he knew exactly how he went about deciding such things. He said good night and left.

Both Kathleen and Jeanne said that they didn't think they should discuss it any further tonight. It would be better to sleep on it and talk about it again tomorrow. They all agreed and besides they were all full of good food and a little tired.

Harry's thoughts were of Yvonne as he was preparing for bed. Oh how he wished she was here tonight. He hoped that he would dream of her.

The licensing and permits for the Fez proved to be no problem as Mustafa had expected. They inspected the building with a fine-tooth comb, and could find nothing to be concerned about. There would be some painting and a few minor repairs, but nothing more than regular maintenance.

Harry told Mustafa:

"It looks as if we are going to be partners now." Mustafa's eyes lit up, but being the shrewd businessman he didn't want to show too much elation, he just extended his hand to Harry and said:

"It is an honor and such a great pleasure."

Of course, he had talked it over with his mothers after all the information was collected, and they too thought it was an exceptional offer. They also thought that Harry and Mustafa could increase the business greatly by making a few changes and adding more entertainment to the activities of the club, and that was truly their business, and they knew it well.

Hussein agreed to continue attending to some of the business and to show his face at the club until his old customers became acquainted with Mustafa and Harry, and until they made contact with all of the vendors that serviced the club.

Since the cabaret was quit large and it already had a small dance floor, even though no one ever danced on it except at private parties, it allowed room to expand to prepare for the entertainment Harry planned to present to his new, and the old customers.

Chapter XXV

The Fez

They began almost immediately to draw up plans and get bids from contractors for the remodelling of the club. Harry told Mustafa that since scouting for talent was his job and doing it very well, he thought it a good idea for him to go and hunt up some exquisite talent to open the first show. t

Between them they decided that they should have a singer, a beautiful woman. A woman dancer who danced the traditional Harem dances, but extremely beautiful and very talented. The small orchestra they already had could easily take care of providing all the music required. He thought also that perhaps they should have a duo or trio of ballet dancers, maybe from Spain or Italy and should be quite colorful. They agreed on the type of talent they would be looking for and Mustafa said that he didn't think it would take long finding them. He thought he knew where to look.

Kathleen and Jeanne did some sightseeing while Harry was busy and after a few days, said that they thought they would return home. They weren't worried about the ranch but they thought that they had given Harry all the moral support he needed and in fact, they were a little homesick.

Harry decided not to contact Yvonne direct, but thought it better to send a letter with his mother's to her saying that they could tell her first hand what it was like here and would she please come. They said that they would contact Yvonne immediately on arrival.

Jeanne and Kathleen saw that his deep infatuation for Yvonne was quite reminiscent of what he once felt for Yvette. They hoped he wouldn't have another disappointment.

Work began on the cabaret in just a few days, and after only a couple of weeks it was finished. They installed lights and dimmers for the audience. They installed some beautiful table candles with shades so that the people eating could see and continue eating while the shows were being performed. They removed the short wall that divided the dining room from the bar. It allowed them to make the dance floor bigger and oval shaped. They installed drapery that closed off the bar but could be opened during floorshows.

To arrange further privacy for the dining guests they carefully arranged some very beautiful and large potted green plants around the dining room, and made sure that they placed them so as not to block the view to the floorshows. Toward the rear of the dining room they built platforms to raise the tables and the eye level of the customers so they also could see the performances. The arrangement not only enhanced the ambiance of the room but offered more privacy to customers who enjoyed privacy while dining.

When they were finished, it looked beautiful. The lighting, the candles, and the colors made a romantic setting.

They designed new costumes for the waiters of traditional Moroccan styles, only fresh and new material that gave a clean and bright look. Everything from the shoes to the fez they wore on their heads was new. The new costumes even gave the waiters a bright new lift. Harry gave them some new instructions on how to service their customers, nothing drastic but more efficiency when ordering and delivering the food to the tables. It all worked out very well.

Harry and Mustafa garnered much confidence with the help when they saw how well their changes worked. They could add nothing to the food. It was perfect. However, Harry did buy and install some new equipment in the kitchen, which helped the cook to speed up the preparation of the food.

For the bar, Mustafa bought a new set of glassware. He had some new napkins made with the Fez name on them, had the stools padded with rich Moroccan leather, bought new shakers and strainers for the bartenders to use and gave them a few new recipes. He had new, colorful menus printed for the bar. Nearly everyone wanted to try the new drinks, especially the women.

So now they not only served the best food and drink anywhere, with excellent service, but their customers could also revel in the finest entertainment offered anywhere.

Harry was getting very lonesome for Yvonne. He was wondering when he would hear from her. Finally, a letter came saying that she would arrive in only a few days. Harry almost dropped the letter as he got so excited. She said that her stay might be rather short, two or three weeks at the most. It was a fairly slack time for her father's business so her leaving now would not put him in a bind. That part about her short stay was disappointing, but at least she was coming now. It's been a long time.

He took another big double room in the hotel. The view looked out to the Mediterranean. The only thing that marred it was the railroad yards between the hotel and harbor. It was nevertheless, a nice view.

When she arrived, Harry had a hard time controlling his excitement. He held her hands and gave her a big hug but no kissing, never liking to make a scene. Harry was also aware of the customs of the predominately Muslim population and that was something taboo in public. It was however, done by many of the foreigners that were there in the country. Harry thought it an insult to his hosts. On the way to the hotel, Harry told Yvonne that he thought it best if he registered her as his wife; if she thought that would be OK?

She said:

"Why not, no one knows mc here." But she asked if he thought it might bring some repercussions on him later, since he was in business there? He didn't think so and for that matter, he didn't care much for himself, he wasn't a lawyer, or a politician.

He told her how much he missed her, and in the horse drawn carriage that Harry hired to take them to the hotel, he could only hold her hand and look at her and tell her over again how much he missed her and how beautiful she was. Harry thought that the carriage would be romantic and a nice way for Yvonne to get a first look at the strange city of Algiers.

Yvonne was truly very happy to be there with Harry. They always had a wonderful time together and his loving was so warm and gentle. They finally finished with the porters and hotel servants. It was customary for the hotel room servants to unpack the bags, hang up the clothes, shine the shoes, prepare the bath, and even scrub your back if you wanted them to. This service was learned from the Shepherds Hotel in Egypt, who used exclusively the Nubian men from northern Africa trained for the service. There were none better anywhere in the world.

Harry thought they would never finish fussing around, but after they left, he poured two glasses of champagne, held one out to Yvonne, and said:

"Here's to missing you."

"And you too," she said. It was slow and gentle, but their loving that night was probably the best ever.

They slept late the next day. Harry left strict orders the night before not to disturb them until he called. He called them after they finished making love again. Yvonne thought that the morning was a special time, and making love was one of the best ways to start the day off right.

Their breakfast, or brunch according to the hour, was brought up and they ate heartily. "Funny how one can work up an appetite, isn't it," She wondered. They both laughed.

Harry wasn't exactly pleased with the food at the Hotel, but breakfast was convenient to have in the room. He promised Yvonne that she would have some of the best food she had ever eaten tonight.

"I can hardly wait," was her reply. "But perhaps you can show me more of Algiers first!"

"*Avec plaisir Madam,*" he said as he bowed low, with a great gesture of his hand. He emphasized the madam since she was supposed to be his wife; something he would prefer.

It was a fun day. First they stopped by the Fez to introduce Yvonne to Mustafa, and to tell him of their plans for the day. Harry wanted to know also if everything was OK at the cabaret and if Mustafa needed anything. Mustafa told Harry in the kitchen, in a low voice, that he didn't want Harry to even think about business.

"Don't think about business!- Repeating it. Come tonight for supper and we will have a wonderful time, but don't think about business, not today or any day while that beautiful lady is here with you."

"She is beautiful, isn't she Mustafa?"

"*Wallah*" – by God - he said with his hands pressed together, "She is like a soft cool breeze in the desert sunset. Go now!"

Harry threw his arm around Mustafa and they walked out into the bar. Harry told Yvonne:

"Mustafa won't let me do anything but eat and drink while you are here. What do you think I should do?"

"Well, I think you should eat and drink, after you take me sightseeing, Right Mustafa?" "*Bien sur Madam, d'accord!*" he said, with a terrible frown on his face. Yvonne reached over and kissed him on the cheek and said, "*Merci, a tout d'ailleurs,*"

They toured the town all afternoon. They stopped at a small coffee shop and had some exceptionally good Turkish coffee. The proprietor came over and asked Yvonne if she would like to have her fortune read. She said:

"Only the good part though."

He laughed and took her cup that she had just finished, put the saucer on top of the small cup and turned it upside-down. He waited a few of minutes, then carefully picked up the cup and peered down into the many different figures the dripping mud of the coffee made as it spilled down along the sides of the cup.

"I see someone is looking for you, or waiting for you. It is a man, but there seems to be no urgency, only concern. You have a loving nature and you will be filled with love in your life." Harry tightened the grip on her hand in his, a little. "You will be going on a journey, not now, but a little later."

Yvonne said:

"But of course, I must go home soon."

"Ah! Yes, but I don't mean your return home, smetime after you return home. Not a long journey, but a pleasant one." "Bon!" she said.

"You are a happy lady, and a very beautiful one, but now I don't read that from the cup."

He said that with a sly grin on his lips.

She laughed and thanked him, and they left.

"So, I wonder where I am going," she asked Harry. He chuckled and said: "Perhaps you are coming back here to be with me."

"Oh! I don't think you would like that," she said, teasing him. "My wish," is all he said.

They dressed and went to the cabaret. Harry, always the most meticulous dresser, looked exceptionally handsome. He had all his clothes made to order by a wonderful Indian tailor he found in town. Yvonne wore plain, but exquisitely made clothes of the finest quality materials. The dress she put on was low cut and although she wore a bra, it was made of silk and so thin that one could see the nipples of her breasts through the dress. The dress came well below the knees, but clung to her so that every curve of her body showed prominently, and since she didn't wear any panties, it was only the body that could be seen and what a body it was. She wore a necklace that Harry had given her and one beautiful ring on her finger that matched it. Her blond hair hung down loosely just over her shoulders. The proprietor of the coffee shop was right. She was a very beautiful woman.

Mustafa came and sat with them at their table and took his supper with them. They reminisced a little about some of their travels. Mustafa was careful not to bring up anything to remind Harry of Lousier. He didn't want to spoil his evening. Yvonne and Harry told Mustafa about some of their trips to Monaco. Quite seriously he said that he must go there someday and bring back some of their money. "No?"

The food was delicious, and the entertainment was wonderful. The house was full of people, which made for an exciting evening. After the last show, Harry and Yvonne decided to leave. Mustafa told them to wait for just a moment. He left and soon came back with two very delicious drinks, two brandy snifters with a little strong coffee and some Crème-de-Cacao, some heavy cream covering the top portion of the liquor. The cream was carefully poured into the glass so as not to mix together with the coffee and liqueur. A Maraschino Cherry with a tooth pick stuck through it was positioned on the rim of the glass. It was beautiful and delicious, as well.

When they rose to leave, Yvonne took Mustafa's hand and told him how much she had enjoyed the evening. She leaned over and kissed him on both cheeks, turned and took Harry's arm and they started to walk out. Harry turned his head and winked at Mustafa. They both smiled and Harry waved good-by with his hand over his head, looking away while walking out the door.

Mustafa had found some very talented acts for their shows. The ballet dancers were from Spain who had been working in Morocco. The harem dancer was a beauty and her dancing was performed just as beautifully. She was from Egypt and quite well known there.

Nadia, the singer was from Lebanon. She had a mysterious aura about her. She was a mountain peasant girl, refreshing in her simplicity. Her beautiful jet-black hair was long and hung down her back. She wore but very little makeup, only the lipstick, and the eyeliner *kohl* (antimony), used in Lebanon and in many of the Arab countries and India. She had a perfect body and wore dresses that could be described as like the one Yvonne wore and they clung to her body as did Yvonne's, except that her nipples didn't show. The only jewellery she wore was a dozen gold bangles on one arm. One could see even from a distance that they surely were hand-made but of exquisite in craftsmanship. There was no doubt that she was a beauty but she sang, and the songs she sang electrified most of the people, women, and men alike. There was a wild kind of vibrancy and quality in her voice, and rhythm in her music. She only sang in

Arabic and French but that was all she needed, especially in Algeria. When some of the English speaking patrons heard her and couldn't even understand her language, they too had a hard time keeping still in their seats.

After hearing her only a few times, Harry decided that he would play a drum for her. It was a drum held under the arm and played with the fingers called *"Doumbek."* It was a traditional drum that was used in Lebanon and her numbers called for it, so Harry thought. He was right, and Nadia was very appreciative of him for wanting to do it. They practiced together and it produced an emphasis to the words of her song when she sang.

Naturally, she also had the accompaniment of the orchestra. All this didn't happen until Yvonne had left to go home. Harry didn't have much time to do anything but see to it that Yvonne was entertained, and loved a lot. He was devastated when she had to leave.

"You know I am going to miss you an awful lot," he told her. "I thought hard about taking this business opportunity just because of you. I hate not being able to see you. We desperately need to work something out. Don't you think so?"

As she hugged and held him tight, she said:

"Harry, Mon Cheri, it will all work out somehow. I know you love this business. It has been a great part of your life, but I'm glad knowing that you will miss me because I know I will miss you too. We'll have to see what can be worked out.

He felt quite abandoned for a while but being busy now and letting Mustafa have some time to be with his family, helped to calm him down. He liked to receive their guests that came to the cabaret. It was not only good for business but he enjoyed seeing and being with people. Often he would order a bottle of some good wine to be served -on the house-for good customers, or for some he wanted to cultivate. He did enjoy doing the show with the singer Nadia. In fact he was also trying to pick up some of the Arabic from her. People in Algiers spoke Arabic but being a French colony, they also taught French in the schools. Many of the Algerians long ago learned to speak French, especially businessmen, so there was little need to learn it to be able to get around. That didn't suit Harry. Being a linguist it haunted him that he couldn't speak the language. Of course he could have learned it from Mustafa, but the thought never occurred to either of them. Mustafa, an Arab spoke French and English also, but they weren't always together on their tours, and when they were they were invariably quit busy.

Chapter XXVI

Nadia

Nadia was originally from the Hauran Hill in Syria called the "Jebel Druz" (Jebel is mountain). This hill country has always been pre-dominantly inhabited by the Druses - a people whose religion is based in a sense on Islam, but their beliefs vary considerably from the Shiite and Sunnite doctrines. They have their own beliefs that are not very well understood outside the Druze sect. Nadia moved to Lebanon with her parents when she was just a baby. She didn't have an extensive education, but she did know how to read and write. Her lack of a complete formal education was no drawback to her. She had lived as a carefree girl from a loving family who are still the bakers of their village.

She described for Harry once just how they baked bread in the clay ovens. They made what she called *"Khoubz,"* the staple that everyone loves all over Lebanon and much of the Middle East. She explained that it wasn't the only kind of bread they made, and went on to describe the various other types. Some were used in place of dishes to hold the food being served or eaten. One of the delicious flat breads they make is used to pack rows of *"kufta,"* (lamb finely chopped up with onions and parsley and garlic and other spices packed on a skewer and cooked over a charcoal flame) folding it over with each row of the meat. When serving it at the table, they tear off a row at a time for the diner. "I'll show you one day", she said. She told him also that they did not make the French loaf type bread like they have here in Algiers.

When she talked, her soft, strange accent and demeanor, as well as her grace were very pleasant to Harry. He asked her if she would mind trying to teach him Arabic.

"It is a difficult language." She said.

"I suppose it is. However, I speak 10 other languages now, so it might not be too hard for me to learn." He told her.

She closed her big beautiful eyes for a moment then looked at him in astonishment and repeated: "Ten languages?"

"Yes, I have had the opportunity to learn them because I have lived in several different countries. I also studied some in school when I was young."

While they were talking he noticed her hands. She had long slender fingers with the nails cut so they weren't too long but beautifully shaped. Her skin had a dark olive complexion and was as smooth as silk. He enjoyed spending long periods with her. He didn't plan to get romantic with her however. For one thing, he was in love with Yvonne; second, he had always held to the idea that it wasn't good to become romantically entangled with people who worked for him, even though most of them became close friends. Still, it was very pleasant to be around this strange girl.

Harry received a letter now and then from Yvonne. He was always happy to get them, but she wasn't a particularly good letter writer. The problem was that she didn't tell him things he wanted her to say. He would have liked for her to tell him that she was coming back to Algiers of course, as well as other loving messages, but they were conspicuously absent. He on the other hand would tell her how much he missed her and longed to have her there with him and mention about some of the times they had together, nothing too personal, however In case, someone might possibly have the chance to read them.

Their relationship went on like this for some time. Harry was almost getting accustomed to being without her except for the times when he was alone, or something that reminded him of her and things that they did together. Those times, he would get a kind of sick feeling in his stomach, but it began to happen less often.

The cabaret was doing very well. The people working for Harry and Mustafa loved them as their employers. They paid them more than any other restaurant or cabaret and they made very good tips. Mustafa set a rule that the waiters had to share some of the tips they made with the kitchen help and busboys. They made decent salaries, but the kitchen help could make the waiters life easy or it could go the other way, as Mustafa explained. The share amount was more or less on a voluntary basis. It depended on how good the business was. However, they did have to share something reasonable, and they did. The camaraderie amongst the help seemed to get better as time went on. They were a pretty close nit family of friends.

Mustafa and Harry really didn't have to do much other than keep watch on everything and bank the money. One day Harry and Mustafa were having lunch together and Harry mentioned that he really missed being on the road. He missed Lousier, and all the great times they all used to have. He told Mustafa about the girl, Isabelle, and how he had imagined that he would ask her to be his wife.

"We have had some wonderful times together, but losing Lousier just about did me in," he said. "I have almost come to terms with this tragedy, as well as the one with Yvette."

Mustafa knew all about Yvette. Lousier had told him the whole story of their romance and her demise.

"You know about it, Lousier said that he told you, when we passed through here before." At that time it brought back sad memories and I still think of her once in a while. It wasn't the same when I decided to come here with you this time however. So I guess I have hardened to the fates."

"You have lived through many difficult times Harry, It's no wonder you are as stable as you are. Anyone who has lived a life like yours is either stable or crazy, and you are not crazy! Are you happy here now, with what we are doing?"

The question was something that Harry hadn't asked himself and it stopped him for a moment.

"It's great being here and working with you. The cabaret is doing very well and we have made many wonderful friends. I guess you could say that I am happy, although I hadn't actually thought of it until now. I miss my mothers. I miss Yvonne and I must say that 1 rather miss our travelling around, like we used to do. Other than that, I would say 1 am very happy!" They both laughed, as it did seem a little humorous.

In Nice, Kathleen, and Jeanne both noticed that Yvonne had been seen by them and by others with a man they all knew. He was the son of a large landowner and businessman. The family was quite rich and he was handsome. They waited for some time to see if their togetherness was just a temporary thing or if it seemed to continue into something permanent. As time went on and friends kept reporting seeing them, it seemed that Yvonne had found someone to take Harry's place.

At the same time, the letters from Yvonne were few and far between and seemed to take on a rather cold impersonal message. She would write of her activities in the office of her father, and general daily activity, but the old warm attitude was not apparent as before.

Harry took this to mean that she was just trying to look for something to write about without saying the same old thing over and over. He was a little disappointed each time he received a letter, and now even that was beginning to be less frequent.

Kathleen and Jeanne were quite worried as to what to do about this situation. Should they tell Harry or should they let him find out for himself. But how will he know unless someone tells him, or unless Yvonne does. His letters to them were the same. He would tell them about the cabaret and little things that went on in his life never ever mentioning anything about Yvonne one way or the other.

He did tell them about Nadia and of her interesting background, and what a great entertainer she was. He would also tell them about the other entertainers. He told them nothing that seemed like he was personally interested in Nadia.

Kathleen and Jeanne devised a plan for Harry to be able to find out for himself what was going on. They went to the bank and told the bank manager, who was a close friend of theirs, including Harry, that they were looking for a good excuse to ask Harry to come home for a while and possibly a forced vacation, which they thought he needed.

They asked him to draw up some papers regarding the disposition of their property in case of any eventuality. They already had lawyers do this some time ago, but they made some changes to include the people working for them and their families, as long as they were still working for them when anything did happen. They thought this was a good enough reason for Harry to make a visit home and he could have a nice vacation as well.

Harry received a letter saying such, and that they thought it was a good time to come and see them anyhow as they were getting quit lonely for him. They simply said that there were some papers that needed to be signed but didn't go into any detail, but there was no urgency, "Come when you can," was the wording.

Harry thought it was a bit strange, since he had been away for much longer periods before and he had never received a letter such as this. He threw it off however, thinking that it was probably because he was actually fairly close by, just a hop across the Mediterranean.

Yes, he thought it would be good to get home for a little while, and he could see Yvonne, something well entrenched in his mind.

He talked it over with Mustafa. Together they decided that there was really nothing to keep him from going. This was Mustafa's home and the work that had to be done at the cabaret was minimal. They would miss him at the club, but since it would be just for a short while, no matter. Harry told Mustafa that Christmas time wasn't too far off, the only critical period, and that he would be back long before time to help him get things ready.

It was just turning August 1938. Christmas was a big time for the cabaret. Hussein had told them how busy they would get each year. New Year was even busier. Of course almost all of the customers were foreigners since the Muslim community does not celebrate Christmas even though they do recognize the birth of Jesus, but New Year was just about the same for everyone. What it was was PARTY TIME.

For the first time, Harry decided to try the airplane. He sent a telegram to his mothers telling them when he would arrive. They were there to meet him of course, and the same loving greeting they had for each other was still touching. Right away they asked Harry if he would be able to stay for season parties.

"No, I'm afraid not this time. Mustafa will need me at the Cabaret and it is my duty to my partner to be there to help him make a success of the biggest time of the year."

"Yes, of course, Ma Cheri," Kathleen said, "but it will be very dull without you," pouting and in a sad voice.

"OH! I will never believe that." He said, laughing.

"Have you seen Yvonne?" he wanted to know. "She hasn't been over." Is all they said. He didn't pursue it. Yet he realized that they didn't actually answer his question. Well, I will see her in the next day or two, after we have become acquainted again. They had another laugh. Of course, he would have gone over right then to see her had he been alone, but he would never hurt his mother's feelings by rushing away. Besides, he did want to see and spend time with them

The next afternoon a friend of theirs came over to discuss what they were planning for the holiday parties. He was a long time friend, wealthy and happy to be a bachelor. He had many love affairs but refused to "tie-the-knot." He used to say: "Why get married and make only one woman happy?"

He was a happy-go-lucky sort and humorous, a good person to be around. He was delighted to see Harry. They were all together in the great room as the maid showed him in. He kissed Kathleen and Jeanne then turned to Harry.

"Bien Venue, Mon Cher Ami" He said, "We miss you. How's Algiers? I saw Yvonne just the other day"—and as he said it, Kathleen, who was behind Harry, held her finger up to her lips and gestured to Jan Paul not to say anything. He broke off, somewhat confused, but being well experienced in the business of romance, realized there was something going on and changed the subject quickly. Harry made no notice. Jan Paul simply said: "When do you plan to see her?"

Harry replied that he wanted to spend some time with his mothers and would get together with her soon. It was difficult for Harry to be there in Nice and not call Yvonne, but he didn't want to call her and not be able to go to her immediately. He thought it'd be better to wait until he was ready to go and see her in person.

The next morning they had a date with the banker, just before noon. As they were leaving the bank, Harry caught sight of Yvonne in a street cafe across the street from the bank. She was sitting with a man whom Harry thought he recognized but wasn't sure. She didn't see Harry as she was turned slightly away.

At first, Harry froze at seeing her, then realizing she was with another man, gave him goose bumps. He thought of simply going over to say hello, thinking to himself that the fellow was perhaps a friend of her father's or someone that was at the cafe, and they decided to sit together. However, this wasn't the kind of meeting he wanted, a chance meeting, and in public at that.

No! He wouldn't go over, but he decided right then to call her that evening before she left work. Kathleen and Jeanne were watching his reaction as he turned to them and he said: "Let's go. I don't want to see her here on the street"

When they were in the car he asked them if they knew who the man was with Yvonne. They didn't want to lie to him but they also didn't want to say too much about it. They just said that he was the son of a Monsieur Gautier, a prominent local family, and that they didn't know him personally, nothing more. Harry said:

"I think I will call Yvonne tonight."

Jeanne said, without any inflection in her voice:

"Yes, perhaps that would be a good idea."

Harry called the office where Yvonne worked and asked for her. The receptionist said that she wasn't there, that she left this afternoon to go to Monte Carlo for the weekend, and that she would be back on Monday. Were there any messages? Harry was silent for a moment and then said:

"No, I'll call again Monday. Thank you."

It seemed evident that the receptionist didn't recognize his voice.

Now he was worried. He thought for a long time wondering what could be going on. First he thought about the fellow he saw with her, then about the letters he had been getting that seemed rather cold. He asked himself if she had found someone else to replace him, or was she just lonely and needed some diversion. He couldn't answer these questions, so after thinking on it for some time, he decided to wait and to see her as soon as she got back.

Kathleen and Jeanne didn't say anything or ask him any questions. They figured that if he wanted to discuss it, they would do their best to try not to hurt him. Yes, they would wait until Monday and find out just how everything stands.

Harry busied himself over the weekend checking out things at the ranch, discussing little problems that had to be attended to. There was nothing major. The foreman and his crew of workers were all capable people and kept things in good repair. All the while his mind was on Monday and the return of Yvonne. He could hardly wait.

Even though he knew fairly well that Yvonne would return Sunday night, he decided not to call until Monday morning.

At about 9:00 o'clock that morning he picked up the phone with trepidation and dialled the number. The receptionist passed him through to Yvonne but she hadn't asked his name, so she didn't know who it was. When he said:

"Hello Yvonne," She hesitated for just a moment then said:

"Harry darling, where are you? Where are you calling from?" Harry said:

"I am here. I am calling you from my home here in Nice."

"I don't believe it. What are you doing? Can you come over right now? I'll tell my father that I must take off; don't have a lot of work to do anyhow. Please come."

Harry chuckled a little, happy that she found it pleasing that he was there. "Yes, I can break away and come now, if you want."

"I'll be waiting."

He hung up the phone and just sat there for a moment trying to collect his thoughts. How come she was so happy to hear his voice when she just got back from Monte Carlo with another rich handsome man? He couldn't answer his own question.

When he arrived at the office Yvonne was waiting for him in the entrance. She threw her arms around his neck, kissed him and said:

"You bad boy you, why didn't you tell me you were coming?" she said as she broke away.

"I wanted to surprise you," was all he could say.

"Well, you certainly did that. Come on lets go. My father is busy with some people and you can say hello later. Let's go and have some lunch."

There was a nice cozy little restaurant close by, so they walked, holding hands, but not doing much talking. She asked Harry what prompted him to come at this time. She wanted to know if he was going to stay for the holidays. He told her that his mothers asked him to come to sign some papers. It wasn't' urgent hut he wanted to do it before the Holidays, so he could get back and get ready for the holidays there.

"Oh!" She said with a sad tone in her voice. Then you won't be staying!"

They reached the restaurant at this time and took a table in a quiet corner. Harry ordered Pernod for the two of them, and when the waitress left, Harry asked Yvonne what she had been doing besides working, a leading question. He was very anxious to hear what she would say.

"I just returned from Monte Carlo with the most handsome man."

She looked at Harry when she said it quite provocatively. "Aren't you jealous?"

"Extremely! Who is he?" She gave him about the same description of Michael as his mothers did. She continued,

"My father has been doing some business with his father, the family actually, and he has asked me several times to have lunch or go places with him, and I have accepted, but now I have to tell you something that you must keep just between us, OK?"

"Yes I guess, if you say so, but please continue, this is getting interesting," he said with some chagrin.

Yvonne could see that he was getting quite concerned. She reached over and took his hand.

"Don't be too concerned, *mon cheri*, you will see when I tell you why I have accepted his invitations. You see this handsome rich man is a homosexual."

She had a look on her face of expectant amazement and a big grin. A thousand thoughts ran through Harry's mind instantly. He imagined what might have happened, but he wanted Yvonne to tell him all about it.

"Mon dieu! Please, tell me how you got into this," he said with a smile.

"Well, one day when they -he and his father- had been discussing some business at the office, Michael, that's his name, asked me if I would go to lunch with him. You know I can't turn down a nice luncheon, now can I?"

Not waiting for an answer, she continued:

"You can imagine for me, it was the same as a business luncheon. However, at lunch he said he wanted to tell me something that was very personal, and hoped that I would understand and help him. At the time, I couldn't imagine what he was talking about. Then it came out, he said:

"I have a lover and it's very difficult for me to be with him."

"When he said him, I immediately understood what it was all about." Then he went on saying:

"I apologize for asking your help, but I know you are a woman of great compassion, I have heard it from several people. I really don't know where else to turn. I don't think anyone else knows about me. Will you help me?" He asked.

"What could I do, Harry? The poor fellow was pouring out his heart to me; such a confession, and to me whom he hardly knew."

Harry thought to himself that his mothers didn't even know and they of all people should have guessed.

"It looks like he has kept it a pretty good secret."

"Yes, and I hope for his sake it doesn't come out. He really is a nice fellow," She said.

"I can understand how you feel, but it sure is a shame a fellow finds himself attracted to another man in a sexual way. I don't suppose they can do anything about it though, do you?"

"I don't think so either. Now to go on with the story, we went to Monte Carlo to the same hotel you and I stayed at. Michael went to the hotel phones and asked the operator to speak to his friend. When he found out which room he was in, he checked me into my room and we went up, together. He asked that I go with him to meet his friend. I was incredulous when I met him. He was even better looking than Michael, and very manly.

They asked me if I would like to have a drink, or something to eat, but I made excuses that I wanted to freshen up and change clothes. I didn't see them again until we were ready to leave and come home. I had a very nice time though all by myself. I even won at the tables, how about that!"

"Well, you seem to have had a rare experience, and you deserved to have won at the tables!" He smiled.

"They should go off somewhere so they can be together and not worry about people knowing them. That might be rather hard to do however; it is such a small world. In any case, I'm happy that you weren't any more involved."

"Well what did you think?"

"Oh! I only meant that you didn't have to do anything else for them. You know what I mean?"

She squeezed his hand. "You're not jealous are you?" He smiled saying: "I could be, but not of those two."

Harry's heartbeat returned to normal. He was terribly relieved after hearing this story. He wanted to do something exciting. He couldn't think of anything offhand at that moment, so he asked Yvonne:

"Let's do something, something wild."

"Like what?" she quarried, with a surprised look on her face.

"I don't know but I feel like doing something we haven't done before."

They both sat there for what seemed an eternity, and then Yvonne said:

"I know, let's go to Paris. I haven't been in ages."

"I haven't either, and that is a great idea. I will show you where I used to live, and where I almost won the boxing title of Europe. Sometimes I wish I had continued on. I think I could have eventually become the champion."

"You didn't tell me you were a champion boxer Harry."

"Didn't I? I don't think it would be right to say I was a champion, but I almost was. I fought the champ, and nearly won- If I could have only stayed away from his right."- He laughed. "I guess that is what all the losers say."

"Harry, you are not a loser, in any sense." She leaned over and kissed him. Let's go, shall we? *Allons!*"

Harry dropped Yvonne off at her apartment. They decided it was better to call when either of them was ready to leave, but Harry was to make the plane reservations for the earliest time possible and let her know. They would fly, instead of going by train. Both of them enjoyed travelling by train, but they didn't want to take the time.

They arrived in Paris just after dark. Harry directed the taxi driver to take the rout that Jeanne always preferred, by the Tour Eiffel, the Arc de Triomphe and through the Champs Elysees. The crowds and the noise of the taxis on the Champs were sights and sounds, which brought back fond memories to Harry. They cut through by the Opera House and over to Rue Grange Batelliere and when they arrived at the place where Harry lived for so many wonderful years, he asked the taxi driver to stop. There was virtually no place to park, and Rue Faubourg Montmartre was always very busy, so the taxi pulled onto the side street. He made the tour on the one way street past the Folies Bergere and pulled up to the corner and stopped.

Harry pointed out the old private entrance to his apartment. They stayed just a couple of moments. Harry was silent remembering and visualizing how he use to go out running every day, and many of the wonderful times he had living there. Yvonne could sense his reverie and she put her hand around his shoulder and gave him a little hug. He came out of his trance, turned to Yvonne and she could see that his eyes were misty.

"You must have had a wonderful life here," she said.

"It was wonderful, every bit of it"

He thought to himself however, the part about Yvette, not how so wonderful she was, but only about losing her. The rest was magnificent. He remembered the first time she kissed him in the taxi. It made a little shiver go up his spine. He didn't mention anything about that though.

They went on to the hotel and checked in. The clerk simply wrote down his name and double occupancy, two persons. The concierge ordered the room clerk to take their bags up to the room. They followed and when the bellhop left, Harry asked Yvonne if she wanted to freshen up before they went out to have some supper.

"I am going to freshen up, but we're not going out to eat, not now." She said.

She looked at Harry for a long moment, then went to him, and said:

"You silly man, don't you know how long it's been since we've made love?"

She kissed him before he could say anything.

"Now you unpack while I take a bath, then you can take one, and then we will see what happens."

"*Bien sur*! Mademoiselle," he said, rather sheepishly, but with a smile and a sense of sudden arousal.

When Harry came out of the bathroom he saw a beautiful woman rising up from the foot of the bed, in a black negligee, so thin he could see right through it. She held out her arms to him, and when he approached her she pulled the towel he had wrapped around him so it fell to the floor. She put her arms around his neck, held him in a kiss and they slowly sank back onto the bed. Their loving was even better than ever, if that were possible. Oh how this woman could make love, Harry thought to himself. Yvonne was probably thinking the same of Harry. They made love for a long time.

"Let's rest a little while. I'm going to have to bath again after that workout," she said, "Then we can go out and eat, or whatever."

"Whatever is right, we came here to have some fun and excitement, and that's what we're going to do, whatever it takes." They held one another close, and in a few minutes they both fell asleep.

They decided to take a taxi and tour the city before deciding what to do next.

"Let's see what changes have been made since we were here last. How long has it been for you Yvonne?" Harry asked.

"About 5 years, I think." I came here with my father on a business trip about that time."

"Well it has been about the same for me, so I really would like to look around, and we may as well go over to the Right Bank and see what's going on over there."

After about an hour of touring around they came to the Champs Elysees, and the Arch de Triumph.

"Look Harry there is a nice looking restaurant there, do you know it?"

Harry was silent for a moment. The restaurant she was looking at was the first restaurant that he had taken Yvette to, with his mothers. He felt a little hollow inside. For a moment, remembering how he felt that night, his first date with a beautiful girl, winning his fight and how she looked at him when they sat down to eat. He just couldn't bear to take Yvonne there.

Then he broke the silence saying:

"Not exactly, but others have told me that it seemed a little small and cramped. Let's look for another. Before we eat though, maybe we should go and make reservations at the Etoile. We could eat there as well, but the food is not the greatest. We could eat and then go and see a show, what do you say?"

"*Magnifique.*" She cried.

They had a nice time. They saw a very good show at the Etoile. A little risqué but neither of them were embarrassed, and it didn't seem that anyone else was either. Some very beautiful girls performed on stage. Yvonne remarked how beautiful they were.

Before they slept that night, Harry said that if she didn't mind, in the morning he would like to go to the gym that he used to train in to see if any of his old friends were still around.

"How long will you be, do you think?"

That he wouldn't be long and he would probably be back before she got up.

"It's three in the morning, what time are you going to get up?"

He laughed, and said:

"Well I'm not going to get up at six, like I used to, but about 7:30 or 8 O'clock, I guess. You can sleep late if you want to. I'll run over there and run back, like I am accustomed to, and I won't be long at the gym."

"Well don't run too hard, I don't want you to be all tired out when you get back." She said, with a pouting look on her lips. Harry kissed her and said "Never fear!"

CHAPTER **XXVII**

Hero

Arriving at the gym the next morning, Harry found out that Hero had died. The people at the gym told him the he had suffered a heart attack and went in his sleep, nearly a year ago. Harry didn't know these people, but they said that Hero would come in occasionally and everyone knew him. They knew who Harry was also, by his reputation and from Hero who had told them all about him.

It was very sad news for Harry. He asked them where he was buried. Harry knew the place and planned to visit his grave before leaving Paris. He noticed that there were many men coming into the gym in uniform as well as in civil clothing. It looked as if the military was beefing up for a conflict. With what was going on in Germany again and in Italy it was no wonder France was concerned and preparing for a defence.

He told Yvonne about Hero and that he would like to go pay his respects. "I'll be happy to go with you, if you want *Cheri*."

"Yes we can stop there when we are out."

He proceeded to tell her about how Hero had made him into a near champion, and what kind of a man he was.

"I think you loved him very much?" She said.

"I really did! I only wish I had known before now, but I guess it wouldn't have done any good. You can't be of any help to anyone after their dead."

That afternoon when they were out, Harry took some flowers to Hero's gravesite. He talked to him for a few minutes. He said he was sorry that he didn't get to see him again, and thanked him for all that he had done for him. It rather eased the pain that way, and made Harry feel a little better.

For the three-day's they were there in Paris, they had a very good time. They took a boat ride on the Seine, mounted the Tour Eiffel, went to the flea market, and visited the Bastille. One night they went to Pigalle, the Moulin Rouge, and the Cirque. They also visited the "BAL TABARIN," a huge club with a review of beautiful, near naked girls and young men dancers who put on a wonderful show. They thought it was even better than the show at the Etoile.

Yvonne told Harry:

"You should be dancing with them." He smiled and said: "Yes it probably would be great fun."

Harry tried to broach the subject of Yvonne going back to Algiers with him but nowhere in any of their conversations could he conjure up a discussion that worked. He decided to let it lay until they got back to Nice. He figured she would be asking him when he would be leaving, and then he would ask her.

Harry took Yvonne to his home. They and his mothers all sat together while they told Kathleen and Jeanne all that they had done in Paris. They were saddened to hear that Hero had died. Kathleen recalled the first time they met him, how reassuring he made her feel. She was confident then that Harry would be in good hands with him.

Later that day, Harry sent a telegram to Mustafa asking how he was and how everything was going.

He wrote back:

"Have everything under control-stop-looking forward to your return- stop -looks like a big holiday season- stop -lots of strangers in town- stop -hope you're having fun- stop -Regards, Mustafa

They all laughed, and Harry said:

"I really have to be getting back. It's a big job getting ready for these holidays."

"Yes I know," Jeanne said.

"Do you have anything special planned?"

"Nothing other than the seasonal music, some Christmas food and color, most of it will all be inside the Fez. We don't like to display too much of the Christian influence externally. We feel like it is a bit of a "slap in the face" to the host country, which is Muslim. Those who want to celebrate with us are free to take part, and we are happy that there is enough freedom to do so. There is a lot of politics in running a restaurant."

"*D'accord!*" said Kathleen. "That's very wise. But isn't Mustafa Muslim also?"

"Oh yes he's Muslim, and I think he is a damn good one, but he doesn't see anything wrong in other people having the freedom to believe whatever they wish, for that matter, doing whatever they want to. We talked about it once and he said that he really thought that there should be one universal religion, realizing that that would never be possible. He knew never-the-less, that if it were so it would tend to stop people from hating one another because of their differences, and every man could call each other brother.

He decided to accept each man as his brother, not knowing, or caring what his religion was. To love each one, until and unless they proved they were not worthy of his love. He believes that one's religion should be a private thing, to love and worship his God in his heart and his mind. No need to broadcast it to the world or to judge others. In any case you see that Mustafa is a man without prejudice. That is one reason why I like him so much."

Harry was to leave the morning of the second day. He wanted to spend the last day with his mothers, so he called Yvonne and said he wanted to take her to dinner. She accepted and he selected a cozy restaurant that served very good food and lulled the patrons with an excellent violinist and a piano accompanist.

Eventually, Harry asked Yvonne when she thought she might be able to come to Algiers.

"I really don't know Harry. You know it's not so bad for me to take a vacation away from my father and his business. His business could get along without me just fine, but He and I have been alone since my mother died. We support one another in every way. It would be hard for me to leave him for any length of time."

"Is that the reason you won't think seriously of getting married?" asked Harry.

"Not entirely. I suppose I could marry and still be close to him, but I guess I am just a little afraid of marriage. I can't say why. I will come and see you again, I promise."

She touched his hand and smiled a beautiful smile. Somehow it softened the dis-appointment for Harry

"Let's have a glass of Champaign and a toast to our next meeting. What do you say?"

She smiled and blinked her eyes, "Let's do."

"Waiter," Harry called, "Two glasses of the best Champaign in the house."

Harry told her he would miss her, and she said likewise.

"It's been wonderful, I'm so happy you came."

Only his mothers were at the Airport so see him off. That's the way he wanted it. He had spent the whole day with them and they had dinner at the same restaurant as the night before. They talked of many things, but one thing that made Harry happy was that they said that they would come again to visit him in Algiers. They had a wonderful time when they were there before and would enjoy doing it again.

"Who knows? Maybe we will meet some nice men there," Kathleen wised off as they left.

They all had a good laugh and Harry watched them through the window of his plane until they were out of his sight.

He and Mustafa plunged right to work setting up things for their regular guests that they expected over the holidays, their regulars and the tourists alike.

Unexpectedly, in the evening when Nadia came in and saw Harry, she came over to him and threw her arms around his neck and kissed him on each cheek. She said that she had missed him so much. She looked at him with her big black eyes when she talked, and he loved her Lebanese accent. Arabic -was her mother tongue. She had learned French much later in her teens but she wasn't very much older now. The greeting was a surprise and very pleasant. He had a hard time pulling his own eyes away from hers; they were enchanting.

Harry and Nadia resumed their stint for the show. It was a hit with all the people and Harry enjoyed doing it. He decided to try something different for the show during Christmas. He thought it would be good to do a Christmas song and through a little dancing in with it; rather a humorous number; not comedy, just humor. He rehearsed with the orchestra and had a Santa's hat made. The idea was that he would have some sleigh bells ringing off stage, the music would start, and then he would start singing as he entered the floor. He would be carrying a bag of small wrapped presents, nothing expensive but appropriate. He would walk around the tables while he was singing and distribute the packages to each table. Then, when the song was finished, he would do a short dance and the ending would take him off stage. He and Mustafa would have to put their heads together and figure out what the presents should be.

A week went by and no one could think of just what should be in the presents. Oh! They thought of many things, but none of them seemed to be just right. Nadia was the one who came up with a good idea. In Lebanon they feel that carrying an amulet of Turquoise brings good luck. They wear it many ways, but she thought it would make a nice key ring. They are not expensive and if it could be done in time, you might put the name of the cabaret on the back.

Harry asked her if she knew where they could find these stones. She did and she said that she knew where it was and that she saw these stones there one day.

She and Harry went together. He bought all of the stones the fellow had, over a hundred of them. He wasn't sure that would be enough, but with all the work to be done on them, a hundred would take some time. They also had to be wrapped and that will take some time as well. They had a little over two weeks to get it done.

The Santa number was the last on the show and needless to say it was a big hit. They did it on Christmas Eve. It was such a hit they figured it would be nice to do it on New Year's Eve. Now that they knew where they could get everything done, they might be able to have it ready for then. Of course he wouldn't be wearing the Santa costume but he would be passing out the souvenirs again.

Harry remembered that he wanted to send a New Year greeting telegram to his mothers, which he did on the 29th. He wanted to be sure that it was delivered before, or on the 31st.

New Years was a little sad for Harry, thinking of the great times he had with his mothers on those nights. He wished they were here. The house was packed for New Year's and the gifts and the horns and the confetti and the singing made a great night for all. The "Fez" made a lot of new patrons over these holidays. Not all of the guests were French and they weren't all Christians, but everyone had a great time.

Life resumed to some kind of normalcy after the holidays. Business too was a little slow for a few weeks after. It seemed as if people had to have some time to recover from the two big nights. The weather wasn't so hot and there were a lot of new customers coming in though and that was very encouraging. Many of them mentioned what a good time they had on either Christmas or New Year's. Some were there for both.

Harry and Nadia began to work out some new songs. He loved to listen to her sing her native songs they were inspiring. He also did a lot of dancing working out new routines. He worked before they opened for lunch or before any customers arrived. He did it mostly for the exercise but he also wanted to be ready to have something well rehearsed for whenever he did feel like performing.

Instead of running every day, he began to walk briskly, but he noticed that there were several streets that had inclines to them and the streets had interesting shops on them as well. He could get a good workout just walking up hill and looking at everything. Running, he didn't get a chance to see much

All the rehearsing brought Nadia and Harry together a lot, she was a quiet girl, never saying very much unless she was actually engaged in some conversation but at such times she displayed good intelligence. Harry liked her reserve but it didn't make her seem subservient, which is a lot like many of the Middle Eastern women are except perhaps in their own home where they are very often the boss.

Business and activities levelled off to a normal pace. Everything became rather ro utine. Harry and Mustafa occasionally tried different things to keep the customers interested and coming back, but other than that, routine was the name of the game.

They would occasionally change the acts in the show so the customers didn't' tire of seeing the same thing over and over. Nadia however, stayed on. She was so well liked, people invariably wrote notes of request for her to sing, some French, and some Arabic. No matter what she sang, all the customers enjoyed it, regardless of the language.

Several months went by and Harry exchanged letters between his mothers and Yvonne; he missed them all

Restless, he asked Nadia if she would like to go with him for a drive out of town on a Monday when they didn't have any shows, just for a change of scenery. She didn't hesitate and answered yes immediately. She said that she would love a change of scenery.

They drove out to the edge of the desert, got out and began to walk into the desert. It was near the coast and they came upon a patch of green and found that it was a huge vine of black grapes. It was partially covered with sand, but the grapes were huge and sweet. They picked several bunches of them and sat down on a small dune to eat them and talk and watch the view over the ocean.

Harry asked her if she had made friends with anyone since she had been in Algiers. She said that except for her neighbors where she lived and only two women at that, she didn't know any one that she could call friend. She felt that most of the people that came into the cabaret were her friends.

"Do you get lonely?"

"I miss my family of course, but I enjoy working at the Fez for you and Mr. Mustafa so much, I don't get too lonely."

She said it so sweetly and when she did she looked at Harry with those big beautiful eyes.

Harry had to restrain himself from taking her in his arms. She was so desirable. He wondered, to himself, how it was that some handsome gentleman hadn't swept her up by now. Finally he said:

"Perhaps we had better start back, but let's pick some more of these delicious grapes before we do. We can take them to Mustafa's family."

The ride back was quiet and peaceful. Each one of them pointed out different things they saw along the road to one another. Other than that there was little conversation.

They stopped by Mustafa's home on the way and dropped off the grapes. The kids were happy to see Harry and it was the first time they had seen Nadia. Harry introduced her to them and right away they asked

"Is she your new girl friend?"

Nadia laughed, and Harry was perplexed. He laughed though and said:

"What a question! She is the singer at the cabaret," but he didn't say she wasn't his new girlfriend. Mustafa wasn't at home. He was out with his wife so they left the grapes with the kids. They played with them for a little and left.

When they reached her place, she said thank you for taking me on such a nice outing. At that she reached over and kissed Harry on the cheek. As she was getting out of the car, she said, "Would you like to do any rehearsing tomorrow?"

Harry thought for a moment and said:

"Perhaps it would be a good idea to work on something new if you like." "Yes, I like," "tomorrow then."

It was a strange feeling Harry had after driving off. He had waited for her to go into the building, watching her. She walked with a gait that was as smooth as a leopard, lithe and very feminine. Actually he was a little befuddled. Before he reached his apartment, where he had moved into after he returned, he was aching to see Yvonne again. He decided to call her. What would he say? Would he ask her what she was doing? That might seem to be a little intrusive, like trying to check up on her. Should he tell her how much he missed her, again for umpteenth time? He could tell her how well the cabaret was doing, he was sure she would be interested in that, or maybe he could tell her how nice it was to take Nadia for an outing today. That thought popped into his head too, he was surprised that it did, but it did.

He really had a nice time today, very relaxed. He felt good, he felt good and relaxed. No! He wasn't' relaxed. He had a good time but now he wasn't relaxed, he couldn't get Nadia out of his mind.

He forgot about calling Yvonne. He lay down for a little rest before getting ready to go out to get something to eat. He wasn't tired, it was more of a habit, but he couldn't even close his eyes. It wasn't dark yet, so he hurriedly dressed into his jogging gear and went out for a run. Funny how a run can clear your head, he thought, but in fact it really didn't. He couldn't get Nadia off his mind or Yvonne either, first one and then the other.

He came to the conclusion that although he thought he loved Yvonne and wanted to marry her, they had no promises between them, they weren't engaged; there really wasn't anything to keep him from spending some time with anyone he chose to, if he wanted to; did he want to? The question continued in his mind unanswered.

He took a bath on his return from his run, dressed into some of his nice sport clothes and went out to take a leisurely walk and stop somewhere to eat. He walked toward town and passed a small but interesting looking bar. He went in and on entering was intrigued by the decor. It was complete in every Moroccan detail he could imagine, even the smell, the semi sweet odor of *bakhur*, a resin or wood incense that when burned over a hot morsel of charcoal gives off a pleasant odor.

The bartender was dressed in traditional garb, and a musician was playing the *oud*. He played soft pleasing music, where a melody is not always easy to follow.

Harry went to the bar and was pleasingly greeted by the bartender. What is your pleasure sir? He asked.

"I'll have some of your *arak*, if you please, if you have it" Harry asked.

"With ice monsieur" he wanted to know.

"Please".

Chapter XXVIII

Tarik

The bartender brought him a glass with the aperitif with water and ice on the side. Harry poured the water into the glass with the *arak* and then put the ice in.

"*Bon!*" replied the bartender; you do it the Arab way."

"Oh, you mean by putting the ice in last?"

"*Bien sur Monsieur*" he said, "it is the right way, the only way, no?" "I think you're right, yes."

The bartender offered Harry some pickled beans that look like big lima beans, a little salty and very delicious. They weren't new to Harry. He had eaten them when he was in Morocco. He held one between his fingers and squeezed, popping the meat of the inside into his mouth with the skin of the bean left between his fingers.

"*Alors!* You are no stranger to our ways. Tell me where have you learned about our food and customs?"

He was a jolly fellow with kind eyes, and Harry took a liking to him right away. He told him of some of his travels through North Africa. He didn't tell him then that he was an entertainer.

"How did you happen to do so much travel along the coast of the Mediterranean?"

Harry told him then about the shows that he and Lousier had presented all along the coast, from Tunisia to Egypt. They just had a casual conversation, but it was relaxing to be talking to this fellow who seemed interested and himself interesting.

He told Harry that he used to be a boxer in Morocco, several years ago and that if he had known about the show when it was there he probably would have come to challenge Harry. They laughed about it.

"It would have been a good challenge, I'm sure," Harry told him. "You know what we should do? We should find a gym where we could work out and do some sparring together, what do you think?"

The fellow's name was Tarik.

"That's a great idea, and I know just the place. I go there all the time to keep in shape, but there is no one there for me to spar with."

So they made a date to meet there at the bar and then go to the gym the next day.

The next morning, Harry met with Nadia at the cabaret to rehears some new songs for the show. It was fun and the songs that Nadia brought to sing were exciting like most of her songs. The music of the Lebanese was full of fire and melody. When they thought they had it down well, Harry said:

"Let's break and get a bite to eat".

Then he told Nadia about going to meet Tarik for their workout.

Nadia begged Harry to let her go with him to see. She said that she had never seen a boxing (the way she said it) and never watched anyone "exercise" (as Harry mentioned that that is what it was) that way.

"OK, I guess Tarik won't mind if I bring you along."

Tarik was delighted to meet Nadia and welcomed her to watch. He said jokingly, "Maybe you will want to join in."

Harry laughed, but Nadia didn't realize how absurd it was.

Tarik and Harry did some workouts to warm up and limber up, and then they put on the big sparing gloves and began to go at it in the ring. They started slowly at first checking one another out. It had been some time that Harry had done any boxing. Actually not since before he and Lousier started on their tragic journey. He had however, stayed in pretty good shape running and dancing. They threw a few blows at each other and worked some strategic moves. Neither one of them was going to get hurt with the head gear and the big gloves, but as professionals go about their profession, so they did with their boxing.

Nadia was tense with excitement when she saw what was about to happen. She didn't realize what boxing was all about. The two men in the ring were pretty fine specimens, neither of them showed any fat on their bodies, and although very well built they didn't look like weight lifters. Their muscles were long and supple. Both men were fast in their action, and sometimes it was hard to tell exactly who was hitting whom.

They had a timer and they took three-minute rounds. They talked a lot and didn't get all that tired. They used the rest period to discuss how each one was doing. Tarik was a good boxer, but so was Harry. Harry probably had more experience than Tarik, even though Tarik had boxed professionally. There was no winner of their bouts; they were just getting some exercise. They stopped after the sixth round. It was fun, and they both enjoyed it immensely.

Harry said: "I will probably be sore tomorrow.

Tarik laughed and said: "Yes I think me too."

They showered while Nadia waited. When they came out Tarik asked her again if she wanted to go a couple of rounds? Now she had a good laugh too.

Harry asked Tarik when his day off was, and invited him to come to the Fez and have dinner with him. He thanked Harry and said he would love to, on Tuesday.

"I'll be looking forward to it". "Make it about eight thirty OK?"

Tarik said he would be there.

Harry took Nadia home so she could get ready to come to the cabaret. When they reached her apartment she told Harry how much she enjoyed the afternoon. She reached over and kissed him on the cheek again. At the same time she put her hand on his other cheek, in a small caress. She rushed out to her door, waved and said I'll see you in a little while.

Harry couldn't help thinking in his mind what a sweet girl she was, so soft and gentle. She seemed like a young unspoiled girl, but she was truly a lady, the way she performed, how she spoke, and her demeanor. She could be presentable in any gathering.

The following Month, a telegram came for Nadia from her home. It was from one of her brothers. It read that her mother was quite ill, and could she come home for a while. Her mother missed her and wished that she could come. She showed the telegram to Harry and to Mustafa.

Both of them said:

"By all means, she should leave immediately." Mustafa, said:

"I'll will go now to the travel office and make arrangements for you on the first flight to Lebanon, or is it better that you go to Damascus?"

"No," she said, the transportation to my village is better from Beirut. I will send a telegram to my brother and perhaps he can meet me there."

Mustafa scheduled her on a flight the next day. It was lucky that that was one of the days they flew to Beirut. Harry told her that he would take her to the airport.

"Oh! You two are so kind; I am going to miss you terribly."

They told her that they would miss her as well, and that she had to promise that she would come back when her mother was better; Oh I will, I will.

Mustafa told her, "*Enshalla* – God willing - she will be fine soon."

At the airport Nadia told Harry again how wonderful she thought it was working for them and what nice gentlemen he and Mustafa were. She said that she would be back just as soon as she could. With that she reached up and kissed Harry on the mouth, just a small kiss, and gave him a big hug then turned and ran to the plane. Harry knew then that he was really going to miss her.

Mustafa and Harry looked around for someone to replace Nadia in the shows, but finding a singer to take the place of Nadia would be very very difficult. When it came time for the shows, Harry had to explain to the customers that Nadia was called away on an emergency, and was sorry for her absence. But he always said that she would be back soon, he hoped. Invariably the people applauded when he said she would be back.

Mustafa found a Spanish singer and dancer who did flamenco. They had a wonderful guitarist in the orchestra who could play just about anything, and with a little rehearsing, one would think that he was originally a flamenco guitarist. It was a good act and filled in much better than trying to find another singer like Nadia.

After almost two weeks went by, Nadia sent a telegram to the cabaret, saying that her mother was quite ill and was not expected to live very long but the doctors couldn't say how long. She was going to have to stay with her mother, but would keep them informed.

It was bad news for both Harry and Mustafa but nothing could be done. They just hoped that her mother wouldn't suffer or that perhaps she would get better.

Harry received letters from his mothers on a regular basis, but from Yvonne, the letters began to take longer. In fact Harry's letters to her were rather sparse as well. He had a hard time thinking of things to write about. He told her about meeting Tarik and their workouts, and about the new Flamenco singer in the show but he never mentioned anything about Nadia; for some reason even he was a little puzzled about. He had never actually considered making love to Nadia, yet he seemed to be missing her almost as much as he missed Yvonne. He waited anxiously for her next letter

His mothers notified him that they were coming for another visit and wanted to know if it was a good time to come. Harry got so excited; he shot them a telegram that said only "When is it NOT a good time to come, just tell me when you will arrive? Love. STOP."

Kathleen and Jeanne got a big kick out of his telegram and made arrangements to leave right away. They figured that he needed them. To comfort him, and to love him as they knew he needed to be loved.

Their arrival was terribly exciting for Harry. He was so happy to see his mothers and for them to be together again. He was beginning to feel almost like a prisoner in Algeria. If it wasn't for his new relation with Tarik, their weekly work-outs, and an occasional luncheon or dinner together, he really would have felt alone. Oh, he would occasionally go to visit with Mustafa and his family; they were almost like his own personal family. He always felt at home with them and he enjoyed being with the children. They called him Uncle Harry. He loved them and sometimes wondered if he would ever have any children of his own.

Kathleen and Jeanne seemed to be suspended in time, with their beauty. They hardly looked a day older. They took long rides to out-of-the-way places, toured the shops around town, especially anything that looked antique. They would often spend hours in some of the shops.

They didn't go to the Fez every night, but quite often. It was the nicest on the weekends, when there were a lot of people. They enjoyed sitting at the bar and talking to the patrons, especially some of the men. They found many of the Arab men to be quite handsome, and interesting. They enjoyed talking to anyone however. They were extroverts, both of them, although Kathleen probably was more so than Jeanne who seemed to have a little quieter personality. Harry would occasionally introduce them to some of the patrons who were their regulars and good customers.

Often the evening would wind up as a party with several of the guests gathering together at one of the big tables. And, on a couple of occasions they left the club with some handsome men they met and didn't come home until the next day and Harry worried a lot about them. Together however, he figured they could take care of themselves, he hoped. He also knew that most all of the people that came into their cabaret were of pretty good character, and most were rather familiar faces.

It was great having his mothers there. Mustafa seemed to enjoy them as much as Harry. He would often have his wife come to the club when he knew that they would be there. Mustafa wasn't a jealous person and he didn't stick to the old custom of keeping the wife at home and not being seen.

They would go on picnics together with the kids. Mustafa would have the cook make up a couple of picnic baskets, bottles of fine wine and fresh lemonade for the children. They would have a grand time. They also liked to go to the beach.

Finally Harry asked his mothers if they had seen Yvonne. They told him that they had not for some time. She hadn't come to the chateau, and they hadn't run across her in the village either.

"Hasn't she written you lately?" Jeanne asked.

"Yes I receive a letter now and then, but there isn't much that she or I have to write about. My activities are about the same day in and day out, except for my new friend Tarik, and I guess hers are the same. You hate to keep saying the same things over and over again all the time. I wish she could come and visit me again or perhaps for good. I don't know what is going to happen with our relationship. It doesn't look as though she is interested in getting married, to me or anyone else for that matter."

Harry changed the subject, and told his mothers about Tarik.

"I must take you over to meet Tarik."

He told them all about him and how they would work out once a week. How it made him feel good to get the exercise and do some sparing.

The next day He took them to meet Tarik. Of course, Tarik knew of Harry's mothers and much of the story of their life together, but he never imagined that they were such beautiful ladies. He was overwhelmed, but very gracious. Kathleen and Jeanne were also gracious to him. They liked him right off, just as Harry did. The next day was their day for the gym and the ladies were all excited to go and watch.

They stayed in Algiers with Harry for three weeks.

"That's a long time Mon Cheri," Kathleen said, kissing Harry a peck when he groaned about them wanting to leave.

"Can you come back for Christmas and New Year this year?"

"We'll see they said. Perhaps we could convince some of our friends to come over here with us.

"What a great idea!" Harry said. "Please start working on it right away, and convince them to come. What a time we could have."

"We'll see. We also have to see what is going to happen with this mad dog Hitler."

It was only the end of June. They still had months to plan for Christmas. Harry asked Mustafa:

"Where does the time go?" Mustafa just shrugged his shoulders and rolled his eyes.

"Do you realize it's only a few months and this will be our second Christmas here?"

"So it is, so it is."

"I hope Nadia can come back before then." Harry said,. "Me too."

Kathleen and Jeanne told Harry before they left, that they noticed that they had seen several Germans as they were wondering around and a couple of them in the cabaret one of the nights they were there.

"Haven't you noticed them around? And do they look like they're new to Algiers or do you think they have been here long?"

"Since you brought it up, I have noticed more obvious Germans lately than I did last year. I wonder if that has anything to do with what is going on in Germany. Maybe they came here to get away from the new Nazi Party." "Perhaps, but you never know what they are up to," Kathleen said. "Better keep your eyes open, and watch your back."

Well that's good advice at anytime, isn't it? Harry asked.

"*Vraiment!*" said Jeanne.

"I am concerned about this situation with Hitler and Mussolini. I think there will be another war, it seems inevitable. So what should I do? I am an American, but also loyal to France. I owe France a great debt for the life the country has afforded me. I must think of what I should do."

"Perhaps you should wait until we see what is going to happen, before you make up your mind." Jeanne said.

"Yes, of course I will, but I feel I must do something; offer my services somehow."

Kathleen said: "I have a friend, a general in the in the military. Let me contact him when I get back and see what he says. I'll tell him about your background and your languages. I'll tell him what you're doing now, as well as where you are in the world."

"That's a very good idea. Let me know as soon as you can find out anything."

"Bien sur, Cheri" She said.

"Would anyone think that we could have a war again with Germany after only a few peaceful years?" They were all silent, pondering on the enormity of the situation.

CHAPTER XXIX

WWII

Harry Enlists

Kathleen did know a man in the Military. She knew him from years ago when he was a young captain in the army. He was a lieutenant general now, and a very close friend of Kathleen's. He saw her at least once a month since the end of the war until she moved to Nice. A "steady" she would call him, only this steady was special. She hadn't seen him but once since she moved to Nice. He came to see her the year after Robert's death. He told her that he missed her terribly. She had been kind enough to tell him when she had made up her mind to move, and what prompted it all.

She had written to him, as well as a few others that she had had a long association with, but this General was different than the rest. If he had been available, she probably would have made an effort to marry him, but he had a wife and children ever since she knew him.

His wife was wounded in the war when the Germans were bombing Paris. She was hit with shrapnel that left her paralyzed from the waist down; he had already sired two children with her. They were grown now, but his wife was still living. He loved her but their sex life was nil. Still, he would never think about leaving her. When she called him she told him that she had something she would like to talk to him about. He stopped her and said, never mind discussing it over the phone, that he wanted come to Nice and see her and they could talk about it there.

She was elated and said:

"I'll be looking forward to your arrival. Shall I arrange to pick you up at the air port?"

"No, I'll be arriving on a military plane and I'll have a driver bring me to your place, if that's OK with you?"

"That will be excellent, how soon?" He paused just a moment checking his calendar, and then said,:"Day after tomorrow. I won't be able to stay long though, is that OK?"

"As long as you can, she replied. I can imagine that you are very busy these days."

"That's putting it mildly," he said before hanging up.

She told Jeanne about his pending arrival. They discussed some about what she should try to arrange for Harry, then they decided that they should just let the general offer something he thought would be appropriate for Harry's capabilities.

On his arrival at the chateau he dismissed his driver telling him that he wouldn't be needed again. He was a fairly big man about Harry's size, but she noticed that he had developed a little paunch, and his hair was nearly all gray now, but he looked healthy and virile. He told Kathleen how much he wanted to see her and that he was delighted that she called when she did because it was just time that he could spare to get down to see her. He kissed her and held her tight for a moment, then asked her what it was that she wanted to talk to him about?

"Oh no you don't! No serious talking until you prove to me that you are the man I have known for all these many years."

He said nothing but reached down, picked her up and headed for the bedroom.

"I'll show you what kind of a man I am right now, my lovely."

She hugged him around the neck and hung on until he laid her down on the bed. They undressed one another as if they were young lovers exploring one another for the first time, kissing warmly between each piece of clothing.

Over the years, each one learned how the other liked their loving. He was as virile as ever, and she was accommodating and warm as ever. Their union was extremely satisfying for both of them.

It was lunchtime after they finally relaxed and bathed. He put on some casual clothes he brought with him. She told the cook to make lunch and she asked him would he mind if Jeanne had lunch with them while they talked about the subject that brought him there. "Just to set the record straight, I was getting ready to call you to arrange to come to see you anyhow, even if you hadn't called me."

She kissed him, and said, "Any time, my love."

Richard, the General's name, knew Jeanne. He had met her many times over the years and he was aware that she knew the whole story about him and Kathleen, so he said:

"Of course not, I'd love to see Jeanne, please call her."

During a light lunch of delicious Mediterranean fish, spiced small potatoes, carrots julienne, salad with olive oil, lemon squeeze and crumbled brie cheese with some fine Chianti wine of their own supply, they discussed the issue of what Harry should do for the war effort, when, not if it comes. They all agreed that it was unavoidable.

Richard knew Harry, not particularly in a personal way, but he did know that he had been the contender for the crown of Europe, a fine boxer whom he always admired. He said that the fact that he held an American passport presented no problem. There were many Americans who fought in the first war with the French and the British as well. Do you think we could get him to come and be an instructor and teach "Self-defence?"

"Say! That's a great idea," Jeanne and Kathleen both speaking in unison. Jeanne said that he is probably in as good a shape now as he was when he was fighting.

"We would have to give him a few instructions of our special training technique, but it wouldn't take much to make him a pro at it. We would love to have him, and he would be a special inspiration for the troops, with his reputation and, as you say, being in top condition".

"I'm sure he would be delighted. We can talk to him tomorrow and see when he can arrange his affairs," Said Kathleen.

"That's a good idea, but he needn't hurry. Let me talk to him when you get him on the phone, and I can tell him just how to contact me when he gets to Paris. I don't know at the moment where he might be stationed, but we will try to get him to a place not too far away from home, "*c'est bien!?*"

"*C'est bien!*" they replied. It was July 1st.

The two ladies and Richard had a night on the town. They made nearly every club that had entertainment. They did keep a rather low profile however, but only because Richard didn't want to get into answering questions about the pending war, which he was sure was on everyone's mind. They didn't get back to the chateau until the wee hours of the morning, but Kathleen and Richard didn't waste any time continuing to catch-up on their lost time.

Harry was excited when Richard told him what he wanted him to do. Talking to Richard, Harry said:

"I appreciate the opportunity to do something worthy for the cause, and if I can train our men to be able to save their lives in mortal combat, it will be a great gratification to me." "Then it is settled" Richard said, "I will expect a call from you when you can prepare yourself to report for duty. Take your time and arrange your business well. You may not be able to get back to it for some time."

Harry told him: "I can imagine. This is a grave situation. That's why I am so appreciative to be able to contribute my talents to the cause. Richard turned the phone back over to Kathleen and Jeanne and they spoke for a few more minutes about the prospects of either one or both of them coming to Algeria to help Mustafa, if and when they might be needed.

"You know that we will be available at any time to help. Please tell Mustafa not to hesitate to let us know."

Harry just said: "I know. I'll tell him. Love you."

Richard left that same morning.

Harry and Mustafa got together the next afternoon and discussed the situation. As Harry expected, Mustafa was totally cooperative. He told Harry that whatever he had to do and as long as it took, it wasn't important. He would take care of the business, just as if he was there. The only thing he was concerned about was that Harry would come back when it was over.

"We will be partners no matter what *mon ami*." Harry held out his hand to Mustafa and said: *"Toujours!"*

So it was over. Nothing else had to be done as far as business was concerned. Mustafa insisted that Harry's profit in the business would be put in the bank for him in his absence, just as if he was there. When Harry protested, Mustafa stood up, held up his hand, and said *"fini!,"*, no more to say you are my partner and if you're here or there, no matter.

Harry went to see Tarik. He told him what had happened and what he was going to do. Tarik said he thought it was great, what a great opportunity to do something good. He said that he was seriously thinking of contacting the Foreign Legion and perhaps joining up, but now he thought he would see if he might arrange something along the same lines as what Harry was going to do. Harry told him that whatever it was he decided, he wished him luck and hoped that he would see him on his return.

"Yes, I hope so too, *Mon ami*." They shook hands and embraced. Harry left with a heavy heart. He wished he could take Tarik with him.

Mustafa arranged a special night for Harry's send off. He invited Tarik and several of the old customers, who had become friends. His wife was there and he decorated the room with flags and as many photos as he could find of the French military, some even of the First World War.

A banner that said: "*Bon Voyage Harry.*" It was a little sad, but mostly a fun night. Every one wished Harry good luck and hoped to see him back soon.

He left in two days, but not before he went to spend some time with Mustafa's children. After all, he was Uncle Harry, and he loved them. They were growing up, very fast it seemed. He wondered if he would recognize them when he returned.

Of course there was another big party his mothers arranged for him. They had made tentative plans with their friends, to keep the nights open because they didn't know exactly when Harry would come, but all turned out well, and everyone came, as they expected.

Many of the younger people had already left the area to the army or other service areas. Yvonne came too. Harry told his mothers on the phone when he would be arriving and to please call her. He wanted to see her before he left.

It was just like old times between them, as if they hadn't been apart. But, that is the way Yvonne was. Harry thought that no matter how long he would be away, it would be the same, no matter what went on in between. A little strange, but who could complain? This beautiful woman loved him, and he loved her, even though marriage was not in the picture. They had a wonderful time.

Harry called Richard at the number he gave him on Friday July 14th. The number was at his office and a secretary answered. He told her he called to talk to the General and told her what his name was. Richard came to the phone right away. Harry told him:

"I'm ready to travel, just tell me where."

Richard laughed and said fine. He gave him the directions of where to go to and asked when he would arrive. Harry allowed a day more than it took to get to Paris and Richard's office, so he would be sure to make it on time.

He said good-by to his mothers and all the people at the ranch. Only the older men and the women were left to do the work. It wasn't always difficult work. Generally, women could do everything as well as the men. If any heavy work had to be done, the older men could probably do it or they could hire some help from outside.

Harry wished them god's speed and told them to be careful at all times.

On July 20th Harry arrived at Richards's office. It was Thursday and Richard was a very busy man. There was so much going on with Italy and Germany it was hard to keep up with all the movements. In May, Italy and Germany signed a full military alliance. In March, just two months before, Germany invaded Czechoslovakia and Italy seized Albania in April.

France and Britain had been in a policy of appeasement, which did nothing to forestall aggressions by Germany. Everyone was on alert and preparations were being taken very seriously and rapidly to prepare for the conflict with Germany.

Richard was, nevertheless, calm and much a gentleman. He cordially received Harry in his office and offered a coffee. The two of them had a nice conversation that touched on Richard's friendship with Kathleen, but only the length of time that he had known her. Of course Harry knew of their friendship and of his wife's paralysis. Always non-judgmental as Harry was, he listened and they had a nice conversation. Richard said that he was going to enlist Harry as a sergeant. He knew that he would need to have a rank since he would be training men who were also sergeants and higher. He told Harry where to report and who to report to, but not today. He wanted him to report on Monday, but on this Saturday he wanted Harry to join him for dinner at a good restaurant he was fond of. He just wanted to spend a little time with him and talk some. Harry accepted with grace and they arranged to meet at the restaurant at 8 PM.

It happened to be the same restaurant where Harry first took Yvette, near the Arch de Triomphe, on Champs Elysee. It was strange to find that the same waiter who waited on him and Yvette was still there and happened to wait on them now. When he came to the table, he looked shocked and became so excited when he saw Harry. He could hardly speak rationally.

"It's you, Monsieur Harry, It's you! It's been so long."

He apologized to Richard and said that he was sorry, but it was such a surprise to see this gentleman after such a long time. But he was speaking in Italian, the language that Harry had spoken to him before. Harry stopped him and said in French, that he must speak in French, since the gentleman didn't speak Italian. He begged for pardon again and, regaining a little composure. He said how wonderful it was to see Harry again and that he hoped that he was in good health. The waiter was fairly old by this time and Richard didn't mind the attention given to Harry.

When ordering drinks, Richard ordered a bottle of wine. He asked Harry if he liked red wine. Harry said that he didn't drink a lot but he did like red wine more than white,

"Good", said Richard. "I always drink red with everything."

Harry was amused. This was a very kindly gentleman who desperately wanted to enjoy, and try to get the most out of life.

During dinner he told Harry that he would go into training for a short time to learn their special training for combat survival, hand to hand combat. We're not going to try to teach these men how to box, only to defend, and to kill when necessary.

Harry winced a little, but said: "I understand." They had a pleasant evening.

As Richard instructed, Harry reported for duty on Monday, July 24th. He completed a one-month instructor training course and started training men on his own on September 1, 1939, the day World War II started with the official declaration of war by England and France, three days after the invasion of Poland by Germany.

After what amounted to a stale-mate behind the Maginot Line; all winter, the Germans started advancing on the allies, and on June 22nd, 1940 France signed an Armistice with Germany, followed by an armistice with Italy, shortly after.

From London De Gaulle Proclaimed the "Free French," the French Resistance, which gave Germany such a hard time. During this period Richard arranged for Harry to be sent to London to serve under the orders of De Gaulle as interpreter and interrogator. Richard sent a letter along with his orders to be presented to the commanding officer under De Gaulle with the explanation that Harry was a linguist fluent in 10 languages and experience in resistance movements in the First World War.

He was received with welcome and became a prime translator and interrogator until 1943, when the French established a provisional government in Algiers. Harry who had been promoted to lieutenant asked his commanding officer to transfer him to Algiers and told him why. One other reason was that Harry, all this time had been studying Arabic. He was nearly fluent in the language, both reading and writing. The commander thought he could surely be as useful there as in London, perhaps more so, and gave him an immediate transfer.

After the Americans - with the help of the French and British - pushed the Germans out of North Africa Harry was anxious to be relived from duty, feeling that he had done his part. He waited until May 7th, 1945 when the Germans surrendered. Harry immediately asked to be relieved from duty, and be discharged. His resignation was accepted and he was ultimately sent his discharge papers.

Mail had been very sparse and it usually took long periods to receive or send mail, but he did correspond with his mothers and occasionally with Mustafa from London. Of course, he was able to see Mustafa often when he was moved to Algiers. He was even able to help out when off duty, but he was worried all the time about his mothers. He knew they were strong and clever, with all their experience, but they were getting up in age now. Kathleen was 62 and it wasn't so easy to carry on, as before. They made it through however, and when Harry was finally able to go back to Nice and see them again, he could also see the age slipping up on them. They had a reunion like never before. They were all so grateful to be together again, and alive, nothing else mattered.

They told Harry about how they had turned the chateau into a convalescent home for wounded soldiers. The army sent them there for rehabilitation. Kathleen had Richard arrange it through the Red Cross.

"We wanted to do something useful. We had soldiers everywhere. As some of them became well enough to get around, they would go and work in the Vineyards, for exercise as well as to show their appreciation for the care we gave them. After a while they stopped sending troops but we had them since 1944 when France was liberated.

We did make some arrangements to hang on to our finances when the armistice was signed. We thought we would have Germans coming and taking over everything."

They told Harry, first one and then the other, about how they took all their money and jewels out of the bank and safe deposit boxes. They chiselled loose some of the stones in the walls of the chateau, then they cut off the back of the stone, placed some of the treasures in place of the broken stone then replaced the stone. They mixed the mortar with colors so they matched the aged colors of the original mortar until it was undetectable. It took six different places to get everything stashed away.

"We didn't ware any of our jewellery all during the war. We just had to figure out a way to remember where we hid everything."

Harry asked: "Well, tell me how you did that, it must have been very difficult?"

"It wasn't easy. Jeanne said. "We didn't want anyone to be able to find something we wrote it on, so we wrote the location of each stone. Then we took out the stone that was the easiest to remember; the one at the top of the stairs just before the landing. We put the paper in there with the other things, and then sealed it. We figured we could take a chance on remembering where that one was."

Harry broke out laughing.

"How long did it take you to do all of this?"

"Four weeks, working every day, all day," said Jeanne. Harry laughed again.

"What a magnificent piece of work. I never would have imagined that you would, or could do such a thing."

"The hardest part was getting the stone loose. We used everything we could find. We had to be careful not to mark the outside of the stones. Finally we found some of those thin blades used to cut iron with. I don't know how many we used, and we dug and dug and dug. We used heavy gloves and wrapped a rag around the blade so as not to tear out hands up. When we got fairly deep into the side of the stones we could use a long sharp steel object, like a screw driver, a chisel I think they are called. We didn't have to be too careful then".

"Now do we have to go through it all again to get them out?" Harry asked. "No! No!" they both said. "We will have someone else to do it now."

Harry laughed again. They all laughed. They opened a bottle of champagne. They also told Harry that they had the wine cellar closed off and boarded up, until after the liberation. They had just recently opened it up. They had hoped that there were some American soldiers around to celebrate with, but there were none.

Harry and his mothers set about to find people to help with the farm. Some of the old people were still there, but now most of the young people were gone. Only the older help were left. They had done a good job of keeping things from going to pot, but they weren't able to do much of any heavy work. There was no way of knowing if any of the younger ones would come back, or even if they were alive.

After some time, things were in pretty good shape. Some of the vine died or had been destroyed, but most of them only needed care and nursing back to producing health. Kathleen and Jeanne had kept the vine's predominately cut back to preserve their strength and health.

"You know I must get back to Algiers soon. Mustafa has been caring for our business all this time, and now I must go and do my share. When do you think you will be able to come and spend some time with me?" He asked his mothers.

"The only thing we can say now is that we will as soon as we can. It is important that you go as soon as possible, we know that. We will be all right now that everything is in order. We want to make sure that the help is as trustworthy, as the others were. Fortunately our old foreman and the wine maker came back, so even though they are older now they can still take care of things. We must make sure of the others. Things aren't the same as they were before the war. People are desperate; there are too many poor now and no jobs. We must help as many as we can."

Harry said: "That's a wonderful way to look at it, but regardless, you must be careful. Benevolent as you are. There may be people who will want to take advantage of you or even rob you. You know how desperate people can get; they do bad things they wouldn't do otherwise. We must find a trustworthy person, a man of strength and stature to be here with you when you are tending to people." Harry was worried.

He made a call to Mustafa. He asked him if he would try to find out what happened to Tarik and where he might be now.

Mustafa said: "He is here. He has been here several times looking for you. He was just recently discharged from the Legion"

"How fantastic! Now Mustafa, listen to me closely, I need Tarik to come here to Nice. I want him to come and stay with my mothers for some time, until we are sure that they will be safe here alone as they were before, probably several months. Please ask him if he is willing to do this favor for me. I will pay him as well as any job he could find. As soon as he can come here, I can come there and take over my proper duties."

Mustafa, said:

"What proper duties? There is no hurry for you to worry about doing your proper duties."

"My old friend" Harry said, "No one would want a better friend than you, but you have done enough. It is time I do my share. You must promise me that you will take a long vacation when I am able to be there for you."

"*Oui! oui*, but for now, I don't want you to worry about it." "How are my children Mustafa?" Harry asked.

"They are hoping to see you again soon. They talk about you all the time. They think you were the one who won the war". They both laughed.

"And I guess you don't tell them any different?"

"I don't say anything." Mustafa told him.

"Please find Tarik as soon as you can and give him money for air travel and some extra, whatever he needs, and tell him I need him."

While he waited for Tarik he tried to contact Yvonne. She had been on his mind all the time. His mothers said that they had not seen her at all during the war. Harry tried the phone at the office. It was disconnected. She had left her apartment. The phone at the home didn't answer. He decided to go to the home to see if he could find anyone there.

There was a caretaker he found who told him that Yvonne and her father left nearly two years ago. Yvonne's father made arrangements for the caretaker to stay there until they returned. He received money each month sent from Bournemouth England. So that's where they are. I wonder why, he asked himself. His mothers said that at least you could assume that she was alive and well.

Tarik arrived in only eight days. He was so happy to see Harry. And he was also happy to see Kathleen and Jeanne. He remembered them well and they him.

Harry told him:

"I can't tell you how much I appreciate your coming to help me with this problem of watching after my mothers. You know how it is now, with so many displaced people, poor and desperate. You never know how safe you can be, especially elderly ladies. Oh, they are still beautiful, but nevertheless elderly and vulnerable."

"My friend, stop your worries, I will look after them as if they were my own," he said.

Harry grabbed him and hugged him.

"Thank you Tarik, thank you. You will want for nothing, I will deposit money in the bank for you each month, but you won't need any money, everything will be provided for you. If you need anything you only have to say so. If you want your money you only have to go the bank and ask for it."

"*Mon Cher Ami*, I am not concerned about money. I am concerned about protecting your mothers, my dear friends.

"Some howl knew I could count on you." Harry told him as he faced him and they pledged their honor with their eyes.

Harry made his mother's promise that they would come to Algiers as soon as they thought everything was in good shape. They promised. Then they said:

"Now you go and take care of your business."

Harry made reservations to Algiers and left three days later. He went to Mustafa's home, and stayed until he could find accommodations again at the Aletti Hotel. With everything going on in Algiers, most hotels and other apartments were full up.

The children, who were quite grown up now, were excited having Harry there with them, and he enjoyed them. They wanted to know everything he did in the war. They kept asking since he first returned. He tried to make light of it, but they insisted on knowing the particulars. He told them about interrogating prisoners, and using most of the languages that he knew. They were surprised that he could speak to them in Arabic. They liked to make him use it. They, of course, spoke both French and Arabic.

It seemed like old times being back with Mustafa at the cabaret. It dawned on Harry that Mustafa had not yet told him how it was when the Germans were here. "Did you have any trouble with them?"

Mustafa recounted those days. He closed his eyes for a moment, his voice taking on an ominous kind of sound.

"Both the Germans and Italians, not so many Italians, were everywhere. They came into the club and were very demanding. They expected us to wait on them hand and foot. Never mind! We catered to them. We treated them like each one was a little king. But the more they demanded and the more we catered. the more they paid" He laughed, shrugged his shoulders and held out his hands. "What else could we do, we were just happy to be able to stay in business. It is good that they all like to drink a lot!" He laughed again and Harry was very pleased.

"You will never know how wonderful it was when the British, and then the Americans kicked them out. After that, we were giving out free food and drinks to those great heroes for two hours each day in the afternoons. We were very happy."

"I know it must have been difficult, but you did very well. I am extremely proud of you. Thank God it's over and we're still here to talk about it."

Then he said:

"Did I tell I tell you that my mothers will be coming soon?"

"*Allah!* He said, clapping his hands together, they are much fun and he added, they bring good business too."

Harry laughed. He knew that Mustafa really did enjoy having his mothers there. He asked him if he had heard from Nadia. Mustafa said that they had received one letter some time after Harry left. She said that her mother had died. Then of course, with the war there were no more letters.

"We have her address, don't we?"

"Yes it is on the envelope she sent. I'll get it. I saved it for you, just in case."

"Just in case what?

With a raised eyebrow Mustafa said:

"I had a hunch that you would want to contact her as soon as you returned. I guess I was right."

Harry looked a little embarrassed. "Does it show that much?"

They both laughed.

"Let's try to get her back here as soon as we can. That's what we need to brighten up this place now." Mustafa said.

"*D' accord!*" Harry shouted it out. "I'll send her a telegram tonight."

CHAPTER XXX

Nadia Returns to Love

They waited for three days to get a reply from Nadia. She finally sent word to say that she had been hoping to hear from them and that she would be ready to come whenever they so desired.

Harry sent another telegram by return wire saying that they wanted her to come as soon as it was possible and if she needed money for travel or anything else he would send money to her right away.

They didn't hear anything else for four days. They were beginning to get worried. Then on the fifth day she arrived at the airport. She called the club but there was no one there except the cook and a couple of other workers. He answered the phone and told her that only he and a couple of cleaning people were there and he didn't know where Mr Harry was but Mr. Mustafa was at home.

He asked her where she was. When she told him that she was at the airport he said that he would call Mr. Mustafa's home right away and tell him.

Mustafa was at home and he went straight to the airport He found Nadia sitting on her suitcases out in front of the airport lounge. He brought her to his home. He told Nadia that they would surprise Harry. When Harry arrived at his hotel he found a message from Mustafa asking him to please come to his house. He just said that he wanted to discuss some business.

When he walked in the door at Mustafa's, Nadia ran to him, stood on her tip-toes and threw her arms around him and kissed him on both cheeks saying, surprise! She said she was so happy to see him alive. She looked at him quite seriously, with a compassionate expression,

"I was afraid that you got dead in the war."

Harry was surprised and delighted to see her and kissed her back. He laughed at the way she said, "Got dead in the war."

"Do I look dead?" He held her at arm's length.

"No! *Al Humdulillah*," – thank God - she said, saying it with a big smile on her face.

Harry, still holding her and shaking his head, replied in Arabic, *"Allahu Akbar,"* God spared me.

Then, still speaking in Arabic, told her that she looked as beautiful as ever. She was stunned that Harry was speaking to her in Arabic.

"You speak Arabic now?" Speaking to him now in Arabic.

Harry told her that he had studied it when he was in London during the War. He said that he didn't use it in London, but it helped to provide him with a good excuse to get back to Algiers.

He asked her about her mother. He and Mustafa knew that she had died, but he said, "I hope she didn't suffer, and she passed on gently?"

"Yes, *Al Humdulillah,* I took care of her for over a year, but finally she became so weak her heart could not beat any more."

It was a little humorous the way she said it, but they understood perfectly what she meant.

"I'm sorry Nadia." Mustafa also said he was sorry.

"Yes, it was very sad to me. I'm happy that I could be there with her."

Then he asked her if she was ready to go back to work? Her expression changed, she smiled, her face lit up again and she said:

"OH! Yes, I can hardly wait."

Harry started working with Nadia again, but he still stayed a little distant, not being able to decide just how close was safe for all things concerned. He still couldn't get over his long-standing policy of not getting involved with anyone working for him. It made it quite difficult, because he was incessantly drawn to her.

A few weeks later, in September, his mothers notified him that they were coming. Everyone was excited. Harry had found another apartment big enough for all of them, so nothing needed to be done in that regard.

Mustafa said:

"You know it's only three months until Christmas. I hope they can stay until the New Year, at least."

"Well, we will see how it goes. I don't know yet how they arranged to have the farm cared for."

When they arrived, Harry expected to see Tarik, but he wasn't with them, so he asked about him. They said that he was the kindest man. He enjoyed being at the chateau and offered to stay on and take care of everything. He told us to stay as long as we like and not to worry about anything. Harry was a little concerned. He couldn't help but wonder why he would want to stay in Nice.

When his mothers told him how Tarik had engrossed himself in the operation of the farm, and all the things he had done in starting to bring it back to what it was before the war, Harry began to see that perhaps he had found a home for himself; maybe a family that he could belong to as well. He hoped so.

Harry wrote Tarik a long letter. In it he related what his mothers had told him how he had taken over the operation of the ranch. Harry said he didn't realize that he knew anything about vineyards.

He told him:

"I guess the knowing how, is in the doing! And I guess you are just one of those who can." He told him how much he appreciated having him there and that he could stay as long as he cared to. "I consider you a part of the family."

That same month Harry notified the bank to increase the amount deposited into Tank's account each month.

Christmas and New Years came and went. His mothers stayed and it was a real celebration for the end of the war and the beginning of a new life, as Kathleen called it in her toast for the New Year.

They returned to Nice soon after. Things became rather normal after that. Business wasn't all that great for some time. People didn't have a lot of money to spend, but gradually it got better.

By the middle of May 1946, and after Mustafa took his family to Egypt for a well earned vacation, Harry began thinking of something he wanted to do for a long time.

He missed touring and doing shows, on the road. One afternoon, he and Mustafa sat down in the cabaret and he told him what he had in mind. He had it worked out, that after they signed up the acts, they would need for Mustafa to go out like he used to and book the shows, and sign contracts in different cities and countries. Harry would stay behind to run the Fez until he returned, then Harry would take the troupe on the road, while Mustafa continued to run the Fez.

Mustafa had to think about it, but not for long. He got excited thinking about getting away and seeing new and different places. He calculated that he wouldn't have to be gone long, certainly not more than a couple of months. Harry said to try to book him for most of the year, except for Christmas and New Year. He wanted to be here to help out and to be together. He would make sure that his mothers came again.

"So you want to be on the road for about eight months?"

"Yes, something like that." But I want to be back here in plenty of time so I can help you get ready for Christmas."

Mustafa was a top professional at this business. He seemed to be able to make contacts where one would never figure possible.

Mustafa booked Harry and his troupe in several different cities and two countries up to November 15th, 1946. He took them to Ireland, Scotland and stopped in Portugal on the way back.

After a very successful tour and on their return, Harry told Mustafa that they all enjoyed the places he had booked for them and they had a great run. He said that he would like to go in the other direction for a change, like into the Arabic speaking word, since he now spoke Arabic. He knew that people appreciated foreigners speaking their native language.

The holidays seemed to be even more fun for Harry. He was very relaxed, having great satisfaction from the tour. He kept his artists on half salary for the vacation over the holidays. He told them that they would be taking off again soon after and to look for his contacting them. Some of his people were so far from their native home that they decided to stay in Algiers.

Harry invited them to their celebration at the club. Ultimately, during the New Year celebration, with the cabaret full-of people, these entertainers got up with Harry and Nadia and put on a show people would not soon forget.

Once while Mustafa was still travelling and before he returned from booking them on their 1946 tour, Harry was preparing to take Nadia home, as he usually did. It was no trouble and better than calling a taxi every night. It was a good excuse also to be alone with her. He had had time to decide how far with her he wanted to go.

Before they turned out the lights and left the cabaret, Harry took her hand, turned her to him and said:

"There is something I have wanted to tell you for long time. Inquisitive but silent, looked up at him with her soft black eyes that made Harry melt.

"Nam?" She said softly in Arabic, yes?

"You remember when you left here to go to your mother?" "You kissed me," and he held her hands a little tighter.

"Yes, I would do it again."

She said it softly in a tone that seemed like she was embarrassed to get the words out, and she didn't look in his eyes when she said it.

He gently put his hand on her chin, raised her head to him and he said: "I never forgot it."

"I love you," she said, looking into his eyes.

Her words caught him off balance. They came so unexpectedly. He never thought to hear such words coming from this sweet and timid, young, beautiful woman. Finally he took her face in both hands and gently pressed his lips to hers. He kissed her, only now it wasn't just a peck. God! How she could kiss.

Harry remembered the room over the bar and asked her if she would like to go where it was more comfortable.

She said:

"I would go anywhere with you"

He took her by the hand and they climbed the stairs with her leading. When they entered the room over the bar, she was surprised to see such a lovely place. In all the time she had had been there working for them he had never seen it. Mustafa and Harry never had a reason to go there. They had left it just as Hussein had it.

It was very comfortable enchanting. She went directly to the bed and sat on the end of it. Harry sat on the floor in front of her. Her head was nearly level with his. He put his hands on each side of her hips as if to hug her and told her:

"I have had a devil of a time deciding if I should tell you how I feel about you. I missed you so much when you were away, and when I was away in the army I thought about you all the time. It's difficult for me, because I have always been reluctant to ever get involved with anyone working for me. You are different. I can't help myself any longer."

She spoke to him in Arabic now. She told him how she would dream of him at her home in the mountains, and imagine that he was making love to her. Her voice and the words she used thrilled him.

Then in French again, she said:

"It will never make any difference. I have loved you since the first time you played the *Dumbek* for me. It wasn't the *Dumbek* but the fact that you were willing to do so. I couldn't help myself either."

She leaned down a little and he leaned over and kissed her. Harry picked her up and laid her gently on the bed and lied down beside her.

He couldn't help thinking about the difference between Yvonne and this lovely submissive, demure, woman. Yvonne might be a little more beautiful, but in every other shape and form they were equal except, this sweet thing he was making love to was something very different than he had ever encountered. He was almost confused as to what to do next. The dimly lighted room made it easy to see her beauty, but it wasn't so bright that it spoiled the setting.

He was on the verge of asking her if she would mind if he undressed her, then he thought better of it and just gently began removing her blouse. She was very cooperative, submissive. She had lovely breasts that pointed straight up to the ceiling. It had been so long for Harry he was ready to jump out of his skin. He caressed her and kissed her full breasts. Her skin felt so soft. She put her hand on his cheek. She kissed him and said:

"OH, Harry I have waited for you for so long."

The way she always said his name, "Har-ree" was like music to his ears. They stayed there the night.

Harry never understood why or how he felt so content, so satisfied and relaxed as he took her home to her apartment. They didn't want to part. They sat for a few minutes, not doing much of anything but looking at each other. She reached over and kissed him and said as he was leaving:

"I'll see you tomorrow, OK?"

"Yes, see you tomorrow." watching her as she went to her apartment, moving as smoothly as a ballet dancer.

Mustafa took off soon after New Year's and started booking the troupe throughout the Middle East. They had enjoyed Egypt so much several years ago; he decided to start in some of the towns there. He booked them into some places they had stopped at before and some new. They did some one- and two-week shows in large cities, but mostly one night stands. In some places they did weekends with two nights. They always had to have time to travel but they didn't carry a lot of equipment with them such as scenery and stage props like they did before, since all their bookings were in theaters or playhouses, hotels and such. They really didn't need much in the way of stage settings that made travelling much easier.

CHAPTER XXXI

Iran

From Egypt they went into Syria, and then flew over to Teheran, Iran. That was another strange and interesting country and city. Some great riches came from Iran and most of them passed through here. The people of Syria were a little solemn; they seemed to enjoy the shows but were much less aroused than they usually found audiences to be.

The Reza Shah Pahlavi had been forced to abdicate his throne in 1941 by invading British and Russian forces because of his rapprochement with the Germans. The parliament of Iran wanted Mohammed Reza Shah, his son, to be a puppet king, but he refused. He said that he would be the ruling, reigning king or nothing. So, when Bill and Harry were in Iran, there was no king, only the rule of the parliament. The status quo remained until much later.

Between shows Harry and most of the troupe would visit the bazaar. This was a place like no other. It was miles long. Harry mostly liked to shop around in the Carpet Bazaar there were thousands of the famous, gorgeous carpets.

Aside from being one of the most interesting places Harry had seen, it was quite primitive. The sewers ran in gutters in the streets, which created an unpleasant odor. Otherwise, street cleaners kept the cobble stone streets quite clean. They cleaned the streets with brooms made from small tree branches (twigs) bundled and tied together, but they gathered up all the dung from the horse drawn carriages to make *"Chapattis."* The dung is first mixed with straw and mud, patted out into pancakes, dried in the sun and used to make fire for heating houses or cooking. It was a burgeoning business.

They did three weeks in three different places they then headed for Abadan. They made the trip to Abadan by an old railroad that was built by the Germans in 1925. The engines were coal-fired and the tracks took them through 26 long and short tunnels. They crossed some beautiful areas but there was a lot of desert along the way as well. The desert itself was interesting but also quite beautiful. However, when they went through the tunnels, the smoke from the coal-fired engines filled the cars and tended to make everything black, especially if the windows weren't closed. Not knowing exactly when a tunnel was coming up, it was usually too late to get them closed in time. With no air conditioning and being quite hot, the windows were always open.

Once along the desert area, they noticed up on a high hill, some men on horseback and camels that were carrying guns. Someone in the crowd on the train said that they were bandits who prey on travellers, robbing them and sometimes killing; very dangerous men.

They did several shows in Abadan then headed on back toward Teheran by bus, stopping in a couple of small towns to do one night stands on their way to Isfahan. There was no railroad between Abadan and Isfahan; there weren't hardly any roads, not paved anyhow.

It was about the middle of August. The weather was agreeable, and Isfahan was an interesting place like Teheran with their bazaar's that stretched from here to there. They were cities within cities. Some people lived there their whole lives, never leaving their homes in the bazaar. These bazaars are called "The Place of a Thousand Odors." One could distinguish everything from animal dung to spices and perfumes. The leather market was delightful. One could find some of the finest leather, but the odor wasn't so nice. Most of the leather was cured by animal urine. One could buy or sell almost anything: Persian carpets, animals from rabbits to camels, and copper pots, but probably the most interesting place to see were the places where they made the famous "Isfahan Silver." Starting from globs of silver, they could turn out, by hand the most exquisite silver pieces one could hope to have in their collection. The etching was all done by hand. Workers sitting on their haunches all day, using small, special tools accomplished the most intricate designs in both small and some very large pieces.

Another place of interest and beauty was the wood workers shops, where they made the inlaid boxes used for such things as holding cigarettes, or jewelry. The tables they made had the same tiny pieces of different colored wood and either bone or ivory cut to just the right sizes and placed with pointed tweezers that made the most beautiful designs and pictures. The workmanship and the pieces they turned out were gorgeous; they are sought out all over the world.

When Harry, Nadia, and the troupe arrived in Isfahan they went straight to the hotel Ferdosi, as was arranged for them. After cleaning up from the trip, which was really a necessity because of the hardpan dirt roads and Harry then went to the theater to check it out.

He made it a custom to do this to make sure there were no problems that had to be ironed out before their performances. He found the theater to be adequate except that the dressing room was very small. He told his people that they should make themselves ready for the stage at the hotel before going and just throw something over their clothes so they wouldn't be too conspicuous on their way over to the theater.

Phillip was the owner of the Ferdosi Hotel. He was a Greek who moved to Isfahan Iran and bought the hotel.

He got tickets for himself, his wife and Bill and they went to the show together.

He was a very nice, gentleman. His wife was there with him and mingled with the residents of the Hotel, she had a pleasant personality.

Phillip liked Bill a lot. One evening in the dining room of the hotel h is wife was having dinner by herself and sitting fairly close to where Bill was also having dinner.

A man sat down at her table and started making advances toward her. She rejected him and he became abusive. Bill was watching this activity and decided to do something about it.

He got up and grabbed the man by his coat collar and drug him out the front door. As they were going down the steps of the Hotel another man, obviously a friend of this man, engaged Bill and a fight ensued.

Bill decked both of them and about that time an officer – a military man, the military did the policing in the town –arrested all three of them and took them to the jail. They were thrown into a kind of a holding room. Shortly the chief – a colonel – called for Bill.

The chief was a large man dressed in a clean and well pressed uniform. He had a big mustache, well trimmed but otherwise was clean shaven. He had a pleasant voice and asked Bill what happened so Bill recounted the exact details of the scuffle.

The Chief happened to be a good friend of Phillip and was pleased to hear the story but especially when Bill spoke to him in Farsi. Bill had to use some gesticulations but he got through it OK.

The Chief ordered his orderly to keep the two men in jail and took Bill back to the Hotel where they both had some of the good Russian Vodka with Phillip.

When Harry's show was coming to Isfahan Phillip knew all about it. The manager of the show house was also a Greek and a good friend of Phillip's. He had told Phillip that the owner of the show was an American and Phillip was sure that Bill would want to go and see the show and meet the owner.

There weren't many automobiles in the town of Isfahan in 1947, but most of the ones that were, were taxis. The producer of the show was able to organize enough taxis to get all of the people to the theater for the three nights. They needed to have three nights because of the size of the theater. The tickets were sold out for all three nights far in advance. Had they not been able to get the taxis, they would have had to go by *durushki,* which is a horse drawn carriage, but otherwise, a very nice way to travel; not in costume however.

Harry had a crew of entertainers of eight different nationalities. All of them were exceptionally good at their respective talents. There were jugglers, acrobats of two nationalities who also tumbled, a knife thrower who was Turkish with a lovely assistant who was Greek, a magician like the one they had on his North African tour, but not quite as mysterious, bicycle riders who did some incredible stunts. Then there was Nadia and of course Harry.

The shows were terrific and a great success, especially so in a small city like Isfahan. Harry was the master of ceremonies. In Isfahan however, it did little good to announce anything. There were only about five people in the town at that time who spoke English or French. With Nadia however, he played the Doumbek and did a dance number.

Harry wore tails that made him look taller on the stage than he actually was, even though he was nearly six feet tall. The audience loved him, but they loved all the acts, and applauded violently for each one. They probably loved Nadia best of all. Her songs were just what they loved to hear, and it didn't hurt that she was very beautiful.

When the show was over, Phillip, his wife and Bill made their way backstage. Bill was excited to meet Harry and Nadia. Even more pleased when he found them both to be warm and personable. Harry was extremely surprised to see another American here.

They went directly back to the hotel where Phillip had arranged for them all to have dinner. They were delighted with the wonderful Greek food. It was the best to be found anywhere. The food was not only delicious but also healthy. Harry found it to be as good as any he had ever eaten.

Harry and Bill struck up a close friendship right off. First, Harry wanted to know all about Bill and what he was doing in Isfahan? Bill however, was much more interested in knowing all about Harry.

He told Bill just a little about how he travelled around parts of the world with his shows, not mentioning anything about the fabulous life he had experienced and how he survived before. The more Bill heard the more interested he became, and as time went on he virtually made Harry tell him his life story.

When Bill told him how disappointed he was with the delays he had been experiencing with the people he had been associated with there, and not being able to produce any revenue for himself over the several months he had been there, Harry was sympathetic and supportive. He asked Bill why he just didn't leave them. He explained to Harry that about the only way he would be able to get away from these people was to go to work for someone else. And because of such a small community it was very difficult. But, he was broke and couldn't afford to just quit them. He was dependent on these people for his very subsistence; rather a prisoner of sorts.

Bill had already told Harry of his background as an entertainer, so right away Harry said: "Why don't you come and work with me?"

"What?" Bill said.

He was so surprised at Harry's offer, he was at a loss for words, couldn't think of what to say. He was of course, delighted at the thought of getting back on the stage, but after the initial surprise he told Harry:

"My God that's a very kind offer. I appreciate your asking, but I don't see how I could. I don't have anything to wear on stage; I don't even have any tap shoes."

Harry took a step backward and looked Bill over a little and said:

"You know, you look like you're about my size. What size shoes do you wear?"

Bill told him size ten."

"Well what do you know, so do I. Come on with me and we'll see what we can do.

CHAPTER XXXII

Harry & Bill

Bill's life took a big change right away. As it worked out, everything that Harry wore fit Bill to a "T." The only thing that didn't fit Bill was Harry's hat. It was too small.

Harry said that he had to go back to Teheran to do a couple more shows. He was to take the troupe back to Abadan after that.

"I'll want you to stay here for now and work on your routines and get ready to do your first show in Abadan when you meet me there two weeks from now."

Harry paid Phillip for Bill's hotel room for the two weeks, gave Bill some spending money, and told him where to meet him in Abadan.

When the day came to leave for Abadan to meet Harry and the troupe, Bill went to the Anglo-Iranian Oil Company office and tried to purchase a seat in one of their trucks going to Qom. There was little public transportation in Iran, and in Isfahan there was only one bus a month that went from Isfahan to Qom; touted as the most religious city in Iran. The main mosque there has a gold-clad dome that can be seen from the desert from miles away. The train that runs from Teheran to Abadan passes through Qom.

The man at the Oil Company's office told Bill that they weren't allowed to transport passengers. He also told him however, that if he would go to a certain street leading out of town the next morning before six o'clock in the morning, he could probably get a ride on one of the big oil trucks. So one minute he couldn't, and the next minute he could. It just depended on what you asked for.

The driver of the truck was a happy-go-lucky type and was more than anxious to pick Bill up, for money of course. The truck was a huge German-built, seating five people across.

The driver put Bill on his left side and three other Iranians that he picked upon his right. They travelled all day and all night to about 4:30 the next morning, stopping now and then to relieve themselves. Bill wondered how the driver kept from falling asleep. He talked to him all night to be sure he didn't.

They finally came to an oasis in the desert where there was a small shack, probably 8 meters wide and 14 meters long, (about 26 ft. by 47 ft.) made of what looked like lumber sawed by hand from logs, and looked quite old. Outside was what looked like a big wine barrel, with a wooden lid lying loose on its top. The driver and Bill looked into it and saw that it had what the Iranians call *maast*, clabbered goat milk that is quite delicious. The driver and Bill were led to a platform covered with an old Persian carpet, and sat down on it in preparation to eat breakfast.

The driver ordered some *noon* (flat bread) and some beans, with a little meat. Beans were a common dish served at breakfast. Bill ordered a dish called *ob-goosh*, which is soup with lamb meat, corn and often some other vegetables, along with some *noon*. On finishing the soup with about three or four spoons left, Bill noticed about 5 flies in the bottom of the bowel. The driver saw them also, but made no comment. Bill called over the waiter and told him to take the soup away and bring him *"shast tokmamore, khali gearme, in ob"* (six boiled eggs). He was still hungry.

The truck pulled into Qom in the early afternoon and the truck driver very courteously dropped Bill off at the train station.

Bill spent the afternoon and the night in Qom in a huge room that served as the train station waiting room and slept on the floor like the rest of the Iranians, waiting for the morning train. He noticed that even though they were all strangers, how polite and considerate they were of one another.

He met Harry in Abadan, showed him the routines he had prepared and Harry was delighted. He hadn't realized how professional Bill was. The shows in Abadan went great. Harry put the troupe up in a rather primitive hotel, but it was clean at least and fairly comfortable. Harry and Bill stayed in a room that actually was a penthouse, but it was just a big room on top of an old hotel on the Khorramshahr side of the Shat al Arab River, across from Abadan. He left Nadia doubled up with the women in the other hotel.

Bill and Harry took great pleasure in watching the activity on the river at the port landing. They saw huge dhow's, with their lateen sails folded up being towed out to the Persian Gulf by men rowing in small boats. They were mostly Arabic natives of Iraq chanting in their native Arabic while they rowed.

"God give me strength to do this work," they chanted in rhythm. Harry translated the chant into English for Bill.

They watched the backbreaking work by other natives carrying heavy sacks of dates, flour, cement and anything else that came in on the barges and other dhows. Each porter would go down one plank from the quay, go across the barge and step up to where two other men on higher platforms would place one of the heavy sacks on his shoulders. He would then proceed to go up the other plank and deposit his load on shore. This went on all day, nearly every day.

They had long talks. Harry told Bill what a wonderful companion Nadia was, and how long it took for him to accept the fact that he loved her. Not that he didn't think she was beautiful, fun to be with, entertaining, warm and passionate, but he had been in love with another young woman named Yvonne for some time, and it was hard to give up the thought that one day he might marry her. In a way he had hoped he would, up to the last minute. He told Bill the whole history of his love life from the beginning. As far as Nadia was concerned, making up his mind was hard to do. But he said:

"I have never regretted marrying Nadia."

He had asked Nadia if she would marry him when they returned to Algeria from Europe. She said yes, of course as much as to say, why you have to ask. They both laughed about it. They had planned to go on to Nice for the wedding, but as it worked out, his mothers came to Algiers. They were married there with many of their friends, and some of their friends from Nice who also came. Even Tarik came along just for a few days. Nadia was able to get one of her brothers to come from Lebanon. He and Harry became close friends.

Harry waited so long to get married; it seemed as if he was thrilled just telling Bill about it. The way he talked about her, and when he said, "I have never regretted marrying Nadia," it was evident that he truly loved Nadia, and was very happy with their life, and why not?

Women in Iran, during the time of the Pahlavi rule were quite emancipated. The Shah tried to get them to stop covering themselves and become an integral, conspicuous part of the community. He built schools for them, and gave them their freedom to work and come and go as they pleased. None-the-less, Harry kept Nadia at a little distance in public, never knowing how some individuals might react, it being fairly obvious that Nadia was an Arab and he was not.

Harry was an avid chess player, and tried to teach Bill, who had never been introduced to the game. He enjoyed the exercise even though Bill didn't do very well. They used to play while watching the activity on the river from the rooftop, at these times Harry would reminisce and tell Bill all that he could remember about the stories of his life.

Harry didn't have any other contracts to go to after Abadan. Iran interested him in a way that other places didn't. He could see great opportunities here. In fact when he first arrived in the country he had notified Mustafa not to make any further contracts, and to cancel any that were still on the books.

He told Bill: "I'm going to send Nadia home and you and I are going to look this country over and see what's cooking."

He explained to Nadia what he had in mind and told her that he would be back in Algiers before too much longer, perhaps to bring her back depending on what he found here. He told her he would miss her terribly but moving around looking at possible business opportunities wouldn't be comfortable for her. She said that she wouldn't mind, but he insisted. She said she understood, and although she hated to leave him she felt that it would be best. That way Harry wouldn't have to be worried about her.

Harry flew to Teheran with the troupe and Nadia to see that they all got on the plane to wherever they were going, and sent Nadia back to Algiers to Mustafa. He left Bill there and asked him to wait for him and he would return shortly. Then they would hire a car and a driver to take them wherever they decided to go.

When Harry returned, they set out northbound for Ahwaz, then on to Isfahan. In Ahwaz where Bill had witnessed the shooting from the bordello roof some time ago, he took Harry to the nightclub that he had been in when the curfew caught him out. It was quite a nice place, not elaborate by any means but clean and well run. They sold all kinds of drinks, had musicians playing some relaxing and some dancing music. They served fairly good food and tidbits at the bar. They also had a near duplicate of the down stairs up on the roof. The roof was sheltered but not enclosed. As long as it wasn't terribly windy it was pleasant to be where there was fresh air.

Both floors were usually busy. They took turns upstairs and downstairs, watching what was going on.

"I'm going to buy this place," Harry said to Bill

Bill had been pessimistic, thinking that a foreigner, let alone a European would be able to purchase and own such a business. They found out, oddly enough, that it was perfectly legal. He negotiated with the owners and they decided on a price. Harry told them to continue to keep the place and run it as they always had and keep the profits until he could return and take it over. The owners agreed, and why not, it was a pretty good deal for them.

Then Bill and Harry took off for Isfahan. Travel was not as pleasant as it could have been had the roads been better. Yes, there were roads, but mostly hardpan, sandy and plain dirt. The early mixtures of asphalt didn't work well because the heat of the summer months made them practically melt. Still, it wasn't too bad. The scenery, the strangeness of the country and the people and the absence of violence, made life delightful.

Back at the Ferdosi hotel where they first met, they were happy to see Phillip again. Isfahan was, in its own way, a rather exciting place. Big parties were often held, and many times they were in the old palace of Alexander the Great, which was named **"Chahelsetoon,"** meaning forty pillars. It was named so since there were twenty huge, hand hewn pillars that held up the massive veranda over the portico entrance to the palace. The other twenty pillars were the reflection in the large rectangular pool, just in front of the portico steps.

Some very well dressed, handsome people could be found at these parties, officers of the army in their dress uniforms. Some of them from the Calvary dressed in highly polished boots. The ladies wore the latest fashions and nearly all of them were beautiful. Delicious food and fine wine was also served. The Sturgeon Caviar from the Caspian Sea was the best there is and always enjoyed by everyone.

People in Isfahan seemed content, happy, smiling and it was very pleasant to take a *"gardesh"* –stroll- in the evening on *Chaharbagh*. *Chaharbagh* was a divided street with trees bordering each side of the road division At one time this lane had been a small river which flowed down from a nearby mountain, but the river had been diverted, and its pathway filled in. It was only a hard dirt pathway, but it was wide. Eight or ten people could walk abreast if they wanted to. It was an enjoyable custom for people to take a stroll in the evening, greet each other, and swap news of various daily events. The Mosque ***Chaharbagh*** was very old. The building was made of the typical mud bricks and the paint was obviously of calcimine or something very similar.

The double doors at the entrance of the mosque were about 12 feet high and each one was about 6 feet wide. It was made of solid wood but clad with designed, hand-tooled silver. It was an awesome sight.

Harry liked to walk there in the evenings, taking stock of the people, their manners and mannerisms. One evening as the two of them were walking, Harry motioned to Bill to take a look at a piece of property across from the Mosque. It had a gentle rise to it and was quite a large plot.

"That would be a great place for a nightclub". Bill almost laughed. He was thinking about the mosque being just across the street.

It was a lovely spot in a nice area. There were big beautiful trees dotted all over the property and it was quite centrally located. Bill controlled himself and "then said:

"If it were possible to get an OK from the Imam at the mosque here, I think I could design a beautiful club for you."

"Well Bill, you better get to it, because I am serious, and I'll wager that the Imam will agree."

That same night Bill started working on the design. Together they decided what they wanted in the design. They wanted a club where there could be dancing, entertainment, food and bar, but that it should all be so that the patrons didn't feel like they were on display.

"I have an idea", "Bill said, "and the lay of that land, sloping as it does will make it easy to do exactly what you want."

There was a family that they met who was also staying at the Ferdosi. They were from Czechoslovakia. The man and his wife and two small girls seemed to be enjoying their life there in Isfahan. They had escaped the war in Europe and planned to make a life for themselves there in Iran. The husband was an architect and when Harry asked him, he agreed to draw out all the plans once Harry and Bill had decided on the design.

Bill worked feverishly day and night. It was something he loved to do anyhow. He wasn't a very good artist, but with a ruler and a square he could make his designs look like what he wanted.

As it took shape, they began to think about how they were going to equip it. In the kitchen for example, they would need pots and pans, not just for cooking but also for holding food, such as a steam table. Furniture wasn't a problem. Wood from the Elburz

Mountains, was plentiful and some of the most beautiful in the world, as well as most any kind.

They didn't know anything about galvanized metal in Isfahan in 1947. Copper is often used on the bottom of steam pans for efficient distribution of the heat, so it had to be that copper to be used for the entire steam table. Also the pans and lids were made of copper. It was no problem at all for the artisans in the metal market. When it was done, it looked like a jewel.

The design was finished and Harry told Bill, since he spoke Farsi and knew all about the proposed club and how they intended to operate it, to go to the Imam and ask for his blessing. Bill laughed and said he would try, but hoped that the Imam didn't throw him out on his ear.

Entering the Mosque, through those beautiful doors, Bill noticed a room off to the left of the entrance. There was a young person standing there, actually it was a classroom and he was one of the teachers, so he went to ask him if he could see the Imam.

"Yes, of course," he said, "the Imam welcomes anyone. Follow me."

So Bill proceeded to the Imams quarters. The young man left him at the door unannounced, which seemed strange. He entered the room and the Imam was sitting on an old ornate chair. It wasn't exactly fancy but it was massive and evidently hand carved but beautifully done. The Imam was quite elderly, white bearded, wearing a plain white robe, and his typical turban. He was spry in his talk and in his eyes and very polite. He offered Bill tea, which he graciously accepted since refusing would not be polite.

The Imam wanted to know something about Bill. Obviously he was *franji* - western. He asked him how long he had been in the country and mentioned that it was good that he was learning Farsi. After giving him a rough idea as to what he was doing in Iran, the Imam asked Bill what it was he came to see him about. Bill told him in the best Farsi he could muster, that he and his employer wanted to build a nightclub across the street on that beautiful piece of land and they wanted to know if he had any objections.

"What kind of business is a nightclub?" he asked.

Bill told him exactly that they would build a beautiful building, and that they would serve food, have entertainment, dancing, and that they would serve liquor. That it would be professionally run more or less on a European style but operated in good taste.

It was a little difficult to get it all out because he was still laboring with his Farsi. The Imam could see that Bill was having trouble with the language and helped him along with a smile. He seemed to be enjoying it. He complimented him on trying to learn the language at all, and thought he was doing well. He said that he had no objection to building a nice place for people to enjoy themselves. He hoped that they wouldn't drink too much though.

He didn't get it in writing, but Bill thought he could trust the Imam to stick by his word. They chatted a while longer and Bill left. Harry was ecstatic with the news. "Now we can go right ahead." He said.

Bill made a rendering of what he thought the place should look like as bad an artist as he was. According to the architect however, it was good enough. Starting with the entrance that was elevated some from the street and had a winding walkway leading to it, one entered into an oval shaped entryway which was nearly covered with an Isfahan Blue carpet. It was large enough for two massive wooden benches, shaped for the curvature of the room, to be placed for people to sit on who might have to wait to be ushered into the dining room. There was also a cloakroom off to the side.

The entry doors continuing straight ahead, led into the main dining room. Before passing into this part of the club however, a step up to the right led to the bar area. As one entered they saw a rather long, curved bar extending to the left all the way over to the far wall. There were no tables, just the bar, which could seat 16 people. There was a wall about shoulder high that separated the main dining hall from the bar. It extended over to another alcove on the far end. Over that half wall there hung a beaded drape, filling the void and it just touched the top of the wall. The drape helped to keep the noise and light of the bar from entering and disturbing the diners. When entertainment was being shown on the floor, the bartender would turn out the lights in the bar and the people could see through the beaded drapes as if they weren't there.

The dance floor was made of the hard wood of the mountains; they were wide planks and were of colors of light, nearly white swirling into nearly black. It made beautiful flooring in the center of the dining room and was oval shaped. At the far end was the stage and bandstand. Elevated high-backed booths on both sides of the room lined the floor, which were set back, enough for a walkway for waiters. Behind those booths was another elevated terrace walk area, with booths situated so they, as well as all people in the room, could see the bandstand and the floor. There was a lot of privacy in the room. There were candles on the tables and the room was dimly lit, with beautiful chandeliers hanging from the ceiling. Huge pots of foliage were strategically placed around the room to give additional privacy. And the room was carpeted with dark colored, maroon carpet. With the artistry of the local craftsmen the kitchen proved no problem.

Some European food would be offered, but mostly the menu was for the traditional Iranian food, which was, by itself wonderful, they just dressed it up with their preparation and service.

The architect had the plans finished in two weeks after some changes in the roof structure, which Harry wanted. Phillip knew of a building contractor who came to the hotel often. He knew that he had built many fine buildings in Isfahan. The man was from Iraq, but he had lived and been to school in Lebanon. Harry who now spoke Arabic got along well with this builder and they worked out a contract right away. It was surprising how fast they got started. Of course, there was plenty of help, not all experienced but they were willing workers. Abu Mussen, the contractor had his own experienced men of the building trades, but local laborers were easy to come by.

The entire earthwork was done by hand. With so many men working, it didn't take long to get all the levelling done and the foundation ready. The building was mostly of stone and mortar, which took shape fast. Harry, Bill, and the architect took some of the plans to the woodworkers and cabinetmakers and had all the doors, the bar and all the other woodwork done while the building was taking shape. Bill had to explain to the metal smiths what this big copper pan was to be used for. Once they knew, they had a steam table any chef would be proud to own.

In one month they were working on the interior. In two months, all the finishing touches were being made. When all the furniture was in and all the carpet was down, the bar was stocked and the lights turned on, it looked more beautiful than anyone had imagined it would. They were ready to open.

All this time, Harry and Bill became like brothers. Harry asked Bill if he would be willing to be a full partner in the nightclub in Ahwaz, go there and take over. Bill said he would have to give it some deep thinking.

Bill's father died when he was just finishing boot camp in the Marines in 1943. His mother now was much alone, and wrote him every week, not even waiting for him to answer. In her letters, she begged in a way that was not begging for him to come home. She missed him terribly and needed him. Bill, on the other hand, had been travelling now for almost one year. As much as he enjoyed Harry's friendship, he was getting a little weary of being away from home for so long. In fact he was a little worried and missed his mother almost as much as she missed him. He didn't think he wanted to get started in a long-term project at this stage of the game, so he had a serious talk with Harry about it. Compassionate, as always, Harry was quick to understand. He asked Bill when he wanted to leave.

"After the club is opened and not before; I have to see it in operation, I feel like it's my project and I want to know that it works."

"Good!" Harry said, "That will give us both great satisfactions. But Bill, don't feel bad about not staying on, I miss my mothers terribly also and I think about them all the time. I may not stay here too long myself. I want to see this thing through. When I get it going good, I may just sell it along with the one in Ahwaz and go home. I am anxious to make a life for Nadia. I want you to know also, that if you ever need anything, or you want to come to me, all you have to do is send me a letter, call, telegram, or whatever.

Bill was very touched by his kindness and sincerity. Of course, he knew well by this time what kind of a man Harry was and that he didn't say things unless he meant it.

He also said that whenever he did decide to leave Iran, he would clear up his business in Algiers as well and retire to the chateau in Nice. He wanted to spend the rest of his time with his mothers and try to repay them in some way for the care they had given him all his life.

"They will need me later and I want to be there for them. It will be great with Nadia by my side."

"That's just like you Harry, you're always thinking of others. I wish we could stick together for always, but I guess we travel in different circles."

"Let me give you an idea that may work out for you and for me; suppose I go to Ahwaz, take over the club there, see if I can get it going and in good shape, sell it for you then I can come back here and be on my way home. What do you think of that?"

Harry didn't even have to think about it.

"If you are not going to stay here and be a partner with me I think that is a wonderful idea, I would want to sell Ahwaz anyhow. I can't very well run both places by myself."

He said that he would make plans for a driver -a taxi - to take Bill to Ahwaz and said that he could make up his own mind as to whom he sold it to and for how much. He knew that Bill knew how much he paid for it so he had that to go by and hopefully there would be a profit.

The next afternoon a taxi driver with an old American car - an old Chevrolet - old yes, but in pretty good shape, came and picked bill up and he was on his way, Bill wondered how they kept this car running but it did run and they had no trouble on the way. The taxi was more like a shuttle; it carried other passengers as well as Bill. It turned out to be a rather pleasant trip and Bill learned a lot more Farsi on the way.

The club in Ahwaz was being run, as agreed by the previous owners. They kept it in the same shape as when Harry bought it. He couldn't tell for sure if they were disappointed or happy that he was there to take over the club but there was no problem in doing so.

Actually, Bill made a deal with them to continue on and manage the place for a while until he could get to know the market and all the suppliers. That part worked out fine then after one month he decided that he was familiar enough with the buying to handle it on his own. He ran the club for another two months and then let it be known that it was for sale.

It was another month before he had a serious offer. In the meantime the business was quite good and made good money. With the business being good and profitable, it brought almost a fifty percent profit in the sale.

Ultimately, Bill found another taxi and headed back to Isfahan.

Harry was not only delighted to see Bill again but the news of the sale was very well taken. He gave Harry all of the profits the club made plus the profit from the sale.

In turn, Harry gave him half of the total sum he brought back. Bill argued with that it was too much.

"You're too generous Harry".

"My friend you deserve it and I know you can use it as well."

While Bill was away, Harry sent for Nadia to return to Isfahan. Actually he had to go to Teheran to meet her and bring her back by hired car, since neither the train nor airplanes came to Isfahan and the bus trip was very bad. When Bill met her on his return she told him that the trip was a very pleasant one and she was so happy to be back with Harry.

So now it was time for Bill to say goodbye to Harry and Iran. He had mixed feelings about leaving. He wanted to get home but he enjoyed being there working with Harry.

"I do hope to see you again someday Harry. I want you to know how much I appreciate all you have done for me. I don't know how I would have gotten out of here if you hadn't come along. You can be sure I will always remember you and these times we have had together."

Two weeks later the nightclub was open and running like a charm, an immediate success, Bill was on a plane bound for Paris. He arrived at Orly airport on the first day of January 1948. Neither Bill nor Harry had ever thought to exchange addresses, oddly enough.

In the ensuing months before he returned home, Bill was never able to write to Harry in Isfahan and he didn't know how to contact him in Nice. Sadly, they never heard from one another for a very long time.

Shortly after arriving in Paris Bill went to work dancing in a Spanish nightclub called "Me Jaka" on Rue Faubourg Montmartre, not too far from where Harry lived when he was growing up there. While he was there he made it a point to visit some of the places Harry mentioned when telling him about the story of his life.

Anxious to get home, he didn't stay working in Paris very long but his departure came nearly as an accident. Fortunately there were two merchant seamen who came into the club one day. Talking to them, at the Bar Bill mentioned that he was about to make arrangements for a flight home.

"Why do that when you can go to Le Harve and catch a ship as a work away?" said one of the men. "It not only wouldn't cost you anything but you would get paid as well."

The men explained that a captain in a foreign port could hire anyone, as long as they had a valid passport.

Bill loved the sea and thought that was a great idea and proceeded to go to Le Harve the next week. He was only there for one day and was chosen to work on a tanker, which at that time was the second largest tanker in the world. The only drawback was that it took three months to get back to the USA.

The ship made two trips to the Persian Gulf to take on oil. They delivered the first load to Rotterdam, made another trip through the Suez Canal for the second load then came back again through the Canal and on to New Jersey, USA.

When he finally arrived back in California Bill and his mother were very excited to see one another. It was good to be home. After getting settled again he decided to partner with his cousin in a commercial fishing business. He began to pine for the good times he remembered having with Harry and Nadia in Iran.

Not knowing his address in Nice he just couldn't write to him. It stayed on his mind for many years but eventually he learned about a fellow who was going to Nice for a business trip and Monte Carlo for a vacation. He told this fellow about Harry and_described for him the Chateau there in Nice that Harry had told him about and asked - begged - him to make a concerted effort to look up Harry, at least to find his address and bring it back with him.

Bill was just overwhelmed with joy when the fellow came back with a note from Harry; in the note he wrote,

"Dear Bill,

I am here in Nice with my lovely Nadia, my mothers and my sweet little daughter Natasha. Now what do you think of that?

I know how concerned you are about the club in Isfahan. It was very successful, so much so that I sold it for an exceptional price. Nadia and I went to Algiers first and I reluctantly divested myself form all my ownership of the Fez. I say reluctantly because of having to depart from my old and dear friend Mustafa. I will however, see him and his family on an occasion, which will please us a lot.

All is well here and we think of you often and hope that one day you too will be able to come and visit us. My mothers are still well, thank god and we are all very, very happy. No more shows to do now but I must say that I miss it somewhat. Still, we do have parties, and they are something that all enjoy, especially us. It is these parties where we do a little entertaining sometimes when we can't get out of it, ha, ha."

He went on to ask Bill about his mother and if he had any intentions of travelling to France.

The letter was signed: "With great affection, Harry and Nadia."

Needles to say Bill was so delighted. He wrote back right away and told them about his trip to Paris, working on the tanker and everything. It took three pages but it was good to be in touch again.

So Harry did what he said he was going to do: retire to the Chateau De Vile Cabernet in Nice, take care of his mothers and enjoy the love he has for his lovely Nadia, his children and his wine cellar. He said in another letter that Tarik was still with him and had become a part of the family. To stay in good health, they still work out and spar with one another occasionally- **carefully.**

It is the year 20009 and now we are many years along since then. The letters stopped long ago but Bill still thinks of him and Nadia and wishes that he could have seen them again and met their children.

If Harry is still alive, for sure he is still there with Nadia by his side with more wonderful memories than anyone could dream of.

William I. McGehee

EPILOGUE

This story of Harry is a true story of the man depicted here. His name and the name of others are changed for privacy.

Liberty has been taken with some of the personal episodes however, Bill in the story, new Harry so intimately, he believed that all the events happened as they were described.

Harry was truly the kind of man depicted here: good, honest, and compassionate.

At parties and other gatherings Bill experienced, many times hearing Harry speaking the eleven different languages he knew fluently.

The author hopes that his life can be an inspiration for others.